Keepers of Light

Also in this trilogy by Louise Cooper

Keepers of Light

Louise Cooper

**Hodder
Children's
Books**

a Division of Hodder Headline plc

Copyright © 1998 Louise Cooper
Map Copyright © 1996 Clive Sandall

First published in Great Britain in 1998
by Hodder Children's Books

The right of Louise Cooper to be identified as the Author of the
Work has been asserted by her in accordance with
the Copyright, Designs and Patents Act 1988.

10 9 8 7 6 5 4 3 2 1

A Catalogue record for this book is
available from the British Library

ISBN 0340 66734 6

Typeset by Palimpsest Book Production Limited
Polmont, Stirlingshire

Printed and bound in Great Britain by
Clays Ltd, St Ives plc

Hodder Children's Books
A Division of Hodder Headline plc
338 Euston Road
London NW1 3BH

To keep and complete the theme (of course!) . . .
this is for scatty cat-slaves, Penny and Kim,
together with Merlin, Alice, Duncan, Ambrose,
Smoky, Nelson, Misty and all the regulars – and in
fond memory of Lucky, the 'honorary cat'.

Prologue

In a world far beyond our Earth, though not beyond our imagination, a great and ancient castle of black stone stands on a pinnacle of rock at the edge of the wild northern coast. The castle is home to the Circle, a company of sorcerers whose duty is to keep the balance – and the peace – between the gods of Order and Chaos and their human worshippers.

For the Circle adepts, magic and the supernatural are part of everyday life. They hone and develop their psychic powers, explore the astral planes, and work with elementals and other creatures of the supernatural realms. Their leader, known as the High Initiate, is one of the three rulers of the world, and to train as an adept under his benevolent eye is a great honour and privilege.

It had always been Shar Tillmer's dearest ambition to become a Circle adept, and to follow in the footsteps of her dead parents. She had thought that her dream would never be fulfilled – until she made a terrifying discovery that led her to the castle, to a deadly plot, and to a breathtaking revelation about her own supernatural powers . . . a revelation in which the gods themselves took a hand.

The story of Shar's awakening – and her final conquering of the evil that threatened to destroy her – has been told in *Daughter of Storms* and *The Dark Caller*. Now, her life as a Circle initiate seems set to run smoothly, and there is no more reason for sadness, or for fear.

But changes are taking place at the castle – changes in which Shar and her close friends Hestor and Kitto unwittingly had a hand. And though the danger is gone, another kind of threat still lies in wait for someone with powers as strange and special as Shar's. A threat not from outside, but from within herself.

The most deadly threat of all . . .

1

'It's my feet that really feel it,' Hestor Ennas said. 'Doesn't seem to matter how thick my boot soles are, the cold still strikes right through them.'

Shar Tillmer, hurrying at his side across the castle courtyard, flicked him a pitying grin. 'You should have worn wooden soles,' she said, 'and a decent, heavy coat like mine, instead of that velvet thing you're so fond of.'

'What, and go round looking like a Wester Reach sailor? No, thanks!'

Shar pulled a face at him. 'You're getting vain, that's your trouble! Anyway, the thaw's coming. Someone said at breakfast that the mountain road is passable right up to the West High Land Sisterhood cot, so the snow must melt here soon.'

'About time, too,' Hestor grumbled. 'Winter seems to last longer and longer every year. And I'm getting sick of salted meat. I'll give thanks to the gods when the first tithe-wagons get through.'

They were approaching the great black arch of the

castle gates now. The gates stood wide open, and other groups of people were converging on them, hurrying to join the crowd gathering outside. As she and Hestor emerged, Shar drew in a sharp, quick breath, as she always did when she saw the dramatic vista beyond the walls. This was the northernmost tip of the world, a finger of mountainous land known as the Star Pensinsula, that jutted from the jagged coastline into the vastness of the sea. The castle itself stood on a huge rock stack, towering above the tide and separated from the mainland by a dizzying natural stone bridge. The view of ocean and cliffs and islands and mountains, with the castle's four titanic black spires rising against the sky, was awe-inspiring. Which was fitting enough, for this was the home of the Circle; the highly trained sorcerers who served the gods of Order and Chaos. Shar and Hestor had both reached the second of the Circle's seven ranks and were training for the third. The work, as Hestor had recently put it, was hard enough to make him wish sometimes that he'd become a fisherman instead. But this morning, for once, there would be no studies. This morning a momentous experiment was taking place. If it was successful, it would bring about the greatest change to everyone's lives for nearly two hundred years.

Shar's pulse quickened excitedly as she saw the crowd outisde the gates. The High Initiate, Neryon Voss, was already there, with several members of the

Council of Adepts including Hestor's mother, Pellis, who had recently been elected to the Council's ranks. The wind had scoured most of the snow from the top of the stack, so that the grass beneath showed through, and the adepts were gathered round a particular patch – a rectangle much lusher and greener than the rest. One man stood in the middle of the rectangle, and Neryon was hanging something on a looped thong around his neck.

'We're just in time,' Shar said to Hestor, then grinned. 'How does it feel to be the person who effectively started all this?'

Hestor raised his eyebrows. 'No one would think I did, for all the credit I get! I thought I might at least be allowed to join in the experiment, instead of only watching. But both Neryon and Mother said I'm too young and inexperienced.'

'It *is* frustrating, isn't it? I'd have loved to be involved, too.' Shar stood on tiptoe, trying but failing to look over the heads of the people in front of them. 'We'll be lucky if we can even *see* anything. Maybe we should have gone with Kitto after all.'

Kitto was the third of the trio of friends, but he wasn't a Circle initiate and had no desire ever to be one. As he put it, learning to read and write was hard enough without trying to cope with Circle studies as well; and besides, sorcery scared him. He hadn't come with them but instead was in the castle's great dining hall, where another and much larger gathering was waiting. If this morning's trial was successful the people in the hall would see the result of it, and Kitto had tried to persuade Shar and Hestor to go with him. Shar had been tempted, but Hestor said no. If the experiment was taking place because of him (and despite the lack of recognition, no one could deny that it was), then nothing would persuade him to miss the very first moments.

Of course, it hadn't actually been his doing. Someone else had the credit for that, and though it had happened months ago, Hestor could still bring himself out in a cold sweat merely by thinking about it. Shar had been in terrible danger, but she was far away in Southern Chaun Province, and only Hestor had known the peril she was in. He had had no hope of reaching her in time – even a messenger-bird wouldn't have been fast enough – and in desperation he had called on the gods to help him. The gods had answered. Tarod, brother to Yandros, the highest lord of Chaos, had arrived minutes later, and had whisked Hestor instantaneously from the castle, using a magical device that, unbeknown to the Circle, had been right here under their very noses. The Maze, Tarod had called it. It lay just outside the castle gates, marked by this peculiarly lush patch of grass. The Maze was a gateway, and anyone who knew how to use it could, in theory, transport themselves in moments to any other location in the world. It had lain dormant for centuries, because the Circle had forgotten that it existed.

It seemed incredible that something so valuable could have been so thoroughly lost. There was no mention of it in any of the history chronicles or in the Circle's books of magical lore and practices, and the High Initiate had been stunned when he learned of it. He had hoped that Tarod of Chaos would explain how it had become neglected and, more importantly, how to use it – but Tarod had disappointed him. The Circle had forgotten a great number of things over the centuries, the Chaos lord said, and it wasn't up to the gods to remind them. They *could* learn to use the Maze again, for there was enough information in the castle library to enable them to selves the puzzle, if they could work out where to look. But they wouldn't receive any help, for that would be breaking the pledge of non-interference that the powers of both Chaos and Order had made two hundred years ago. Everyone knew that the gods – and the Chaos lords in particular – weren't averse to bending the rules when it suited them. But not even the High Initiate dared point that out to Tarod. If the Circle wanted to rediscover the Maze's secrets, they must do it without help.

So the search began, and eventually the first clues were found in the library's darkest, dustiest corners.

Painstakingly the adepts had pieced the mystery together, until at last the picture started to make sense. They believed they had found the Maze's secret. And now, they were about to find out if they were right.

There was a growing feeling of eagerness among the crowd, and Hestor and Shar managed to sidle their way far enough forward to gain a good view. Neryon had stepped clear of the greener patch, and the adept who stood in the middle closed his eyes. He was cupping the pendant the High Initiate had given him in one hand, and Hestor whispered, 'That must be the amulet.' He craned his neck. 'I wish they had let us have a close look at it!'

'So do I.' The amulet, Shar gathered, was the means of opening the Maze. The adepts had made it, following instructions found in an incredibly old and crumbling parchment, and the theory was that it formed a kind of key that unlocked the Maze's powers. Neither she nor Hestor had been allowed to examine it, and all she could see now was what looked like a small, tapering spiral of metal that gleamed dully in the daylight. Shar was consumed with curiosity and frustration. She would have given a great deal to be in the adept's shoes. But then, so would Hestor and probably every other initiate in the Circle.

Hestor whispered again. 'He's concentrating. Visualising the place where he wants to arrive.'

He suppressed a giggle. 'Hope he doesn't materialise in the middle of the fireplace!'

'Sh!' Shar nudged him. There was tense silence now, but for the sounds of the wind and the sea. The adept rocked slightly on his feet, steadied himself. Then he gripped the amulet with a sudden surge of mental energy.

There was a faint shimmer in the air above the grass rectangle. The adept's figure seemed to swim, making Shar blink in confusion. Then came a sound, not quite a crackling and not quite a hiss, but with something of both.

And the adept vanished.

Hestor hissed an oath under his breath. 'It's worked! They've *done* it!'

'Sh,' Shar warned again. No one else was moving or speaking; they all stood tensely staring at the spot where the man had disappeared. The air was still shimmering, distorting the view of the mainland beyond – and suddenly Shar glimpsed something in the shimmer. It came and went so quickly that she couldn't identify it, but she knew, *knew*, that whatever it was, it should not have been there. Something was wrong—

She grasped Hestor's arm, gripping it so hard that he winced. But before he could protest or pull away, there came another crackle-hissing sound, and the adept reappeared.

Or almost. For several seconds, bizarrely, he looked like a ghost, colourless and with the mountains clearly visible through him. He swayed on his feet, reaching out towards Neryon and trying to say something, though his voice couldn't be heard. Then abruptly everything snapped into focus; the distortion in the air stopped, and the adept's figure became solid. Everyone heard his gasp and the oath he uttered as he reeled dizzily out of the Maze. Neryon and Pellis hastened forward to steady him.

'Wilden, are you all right?' the High Initiate asked anxiously.

'Unh . . . yes. Yes, I'm fine; just a bit giddy . . .' Wilden's face was pale; he swallowed, as if he was trying to fight down nausea.

'What happened?' Pellis asked. 'Did you reach the hall?'

'Yes, and no.' He swallowed again, drew a deep breath, and the colour began to return to his cheeks. 'I was there. I saw it clearly, saw the crowd waiting, and I could feel the floor under my feet. But I couldn't break out of the Maze. It was as if something was holding me back. People were calling out but I couldn't hear them, and I don't think they could hear me, either.' He took another deep breath. 'But I *got* there, Neryon! We've a long way to go yet, but the Maze works!'

The crowd started to gather round him, talking loudly and eagerly. Hestor turned to Shar and said,

'We'll never be able to push our way through this press and hear what Wilden's saying.'

Shar didn't answer. She was staring at the bright grass patch, and there was a frown on her face.

'Shar?' Hestor prompted. 'Wake up!' He snapped his fingers in front of her, and she shook her head as though coming out of a dream.

'What?' she said, then: 'Oh . . . sorry. I was thinking about something else.'

'Something half a world away, by the look of you.' Then, belatedly remembering, he rubbed his arm. 'Why did you suddenly grab me just then?'

Shar found she couldn't answer. What she had seen had been so faint, so fleeting, she couldn't be sure what it was, or even if she had seen anything at all. Even the memory of it was fading now, leaving only a vague sense of unease somewhere at the back of her mind. She had probably imagined the whole thing.

'Sorry,' she said again, and backed up the apology with a sheepish smile. 'I got a bit carried away for a moment, that's all.'

Hestor hesitated, wondering if that was the entire truth. Knowing her as he did, he suspected that she might be hiding something, or at least making light of it. But she only smiled at him again, and after a second or two he shrugged and pushed the suspicion away.

'Come on,' he said, taking hold of her hand. 'Let's look for Kitto, and find out what happened in the hall.'

'It was eerie.' Kitto pushed his black hair out of his eyes and pointed to a spot by one of the dining hall's tall windows. 'He appeared right there, and he looked so *real*.'

'He *was* real,' Shar pointed out. 'Not a ghost or an illusion. He actually travelled through the Maze, from the stack to this room.'

'But he said that he couldn't quite break through,' Hestor added. 'People were calling to him, but he couldn't hear.'

'That's right,' said Kitto. 'He was calling out, too; I could see his mouth moving. But there wasn't any sound at all. Then he sort of flickered, and vanished again.' He frowned and added ominously, 'It scared me, and I don't mind admitting it. There was something *unnatural* about it.'

Hestor laughed. 'It's no more unnatural than the floor we're standing on. It's a part of the castle; something that was built into it from the beginning, like the Marble Hall.'

'Well, the Marble Hall's more than weird enough for me,' Kitto said firmly. 'I don't like it.'

'Then you're the only person in the castle who doesn't!'

'I'm not,' Kitto contradicted him. 'Quite a lot of people are saying that it ought to be left alone.'

'Oh, if you mean the servants—'

'I mean people in the Circle!' Kitto retorted,

annoyed by Hestor's condescending tone. 'If you listened a bit more carefully, you'd know. Some very senior adepts aren't at all happy about the Maze. Gant Birn Sangen for one; he says that it must have been abandoned for a good reason, and the High Initiate shouldn't allow it to be tampered with.'

Hestor snorted. 'Adept Gant? He's so conservative he's almost extinct! If he had his way, we'd all be living in caves because buildings are new-fangled and dangerous!'

'Plenty of others agree with him,' Kitto persisted.

'Old fools group together, don't they? Anyway, the High Initiate won't listen to them. This is the most exciting discovery since – since—' Hestor waved his hands, unable to think of an example, '—for *years*. And if the gods sanction it, Gant and his cronies can't argue.'

'But do the gods sanction it?' Kitto asked.

'Of course! If they didn't, Lord Tarod would have told Neryon to leave it alone.' Hestor made a sweeping gesture that took in the whole of the vast hall. 'The gods created this castle, so the Maze must be their creation, too, and they must have intended mortals to use it.'

Kitto, though, still wasn't convinced – and he had been attending to his history lessons. 'Maybe,' he said. 'But what kind of mortals? The first people who lived in this castle weren't sorcerers like the Circle are. They were far more powerful. They probably weren't even truly human.'

'Oh, rubbish! Our ancestors defeated them, so they can't have been that special! If they could use the Maze, so can we. And we will.'

'If it can be made to work . . .' Shar said.

The two boys had been so engrossed in their argument that they had forgotten she was there. Now they looked at her, at the thoughtful expression on her face as she stared at the spot where Adept Wilden had almost materialised.

'What are you thinking, Shar?' Hestor asked.

She shook her head. 'Nothing in particular. I've just got a feeling that . . . well, that they were doing something wrong this morning, and that was why the experiment wasn't completely successful.'

'Oh?' Hestor looked interested. 'Doing what wrong?'

'I've no idea, and I wouldn't even know where to start guessing. But *something*.'

'Well, if you can solve the mystery before the senior adepts do, they'll probably make you Margravine of West High Land!' Hestor grinned at her. Kitto, though, was starting to look distinctly uneasy, and suddenly he said, 'Shar – don't do anything silly, will you?'

'What?' She frowned at him.

'Just . . . don't *do* anything. On your own, I mean. Leave it to the High Initiate.'

'If anyone's being silly, Kitto, it's you, not me,' Shar said a little sharply. She swung away from him, stared at the wall for a few moments more, then added, 'There's no point standing here gaping; nothing else is going to happen. They'll start serving the noon meal soon. I'm going to put this coat away and play with Amber before I eat.'

Amber was Shar's cat; at least, as much as anyone could be said to own one of the many cats that lived in the castle. At this moment Amber was probably asleep on her bed, and several others with him. Cats were drawn to Shar like iron to a magnet; two, in fact, had followed her across the courtyard and into the hall, and were now sitting washing their paws on a nearby table. Kitto sighed, glad that the awkward moment hadn't flared into anything worse, yet still far from reassured.

'I'd better go, too,' he said. 'Lessons this afternoon. Geography. I'm supposed to have drawn a map, and I can't draw to save my life. I *hate* geography.'

The three of them left the hall together. As they headed towards the main staircase, Hestor watched Shar sidelong. There was a speculative look in her eyes, and he wondered if Kitto's warning might have had the opposite effect to the one intended. An idea was brewing in her mind, he was sure of it. And once Shar got hold of an idea, she wasn't easily put off.

He wouldn't press her about it, Hestor thought. He

would wait and see what developed. But if Shar was thinking along the lines that he suspected, he was determined about one thing. Whatever plan she was hatching, he wanted to be part of it, and she wasn't going to keep him out this time.

Shar and Hestor would both have given a great deal to overhear the private talk that Adept Wilden had with the High Initiate when the first excitement had died down a little. Wilden knew about the unprogressive faction that wanted the experiment stopped, and thought it best that what he had to say should be for Neryon's ears alone.

It wasn't exactly a problem, he said, as the two of them sat in Neryon's study; more of a peculiarity that he couldn't explain. At the moment when he had shifted from the stack to the dining hall, he had seen both locations at the same time, one superimposed on the other. It had been confusing and dizzying, but he had expected it and was prepared – until a third location had suddenly merged in with the other two.

'I've no idea what or where it was,' Wilden said. 'Certainly I didn't try to visualise it – in fact it wasn't any place that I've ever seen. It just appeared, out of nowhere.'

'Try to describe it,' Neryon said.

Wilden did try, but found himself defeated. The trouble was, he said, there was really nothing *to* describe. Just an impression of movement – possibly clouds in a sky, or fast-running water – and something that might or might not have been a cliff face or a rocky outcrop. And, briefly, he had heard a sound like either singing or laughter; he couldn't tell which. Then abruptly the images vanished as he went through the Maze, and instead he saw only the dining hall. The rest, he added, Neryon already knew.

The High Initiate was intrigued, but not unduly worried. They had a lot more to learn about the Maze; today was only the beginning of their explorations. Still, he was glad that Wilden had told him – and told him privately, rather than revealing this part of the story to the whole Circle Council. If Gant Birn Sangen and his allies knew about it, it would be fuel for their arguments, and Neryon did not want that kind of complication.

He thanked Wilden and asked him to say nothing to anyone else. He himself would alert a few trusted people, and they would keep a careful watch on further experiments. For the time being, there was no need to do anything more.

2

By the time she went to bed at the end of a studying day, Shar was usually flaggingly exhausted. Tonight was no exception, for she had spent all afternoon and most of the evening practising visualisation exercises with her tutor; but as she sat in bed brushing out her auburn hair she knew instinctively that she wasn't going to be able to sleep.

Amber, the ginger cat, was curled up beside her, making a noise halfway between a purr and a snore. Shar looked enviously at him, then sighed. She was *over*tired, that was the trouble, and until and unless she could get rid of the thoughts whirling around in her mind, she was doomed to stay awake.

Third-rank training was very demanding. Shar was dealing now with far greater forces than the simple, low elementals that had always been her friends, so she had to learn to develop and control her special powers very carefully. Because of those special powers, everyone expected her to be the best, and thus to work harder than any other junior initiate in the Circle. And sometimes she found herself resenting it.

It wasn't the work itself that irked her. It was the fact that although being 'special' made extra demands on her, it didn't bring any extra rewards to compensate. The fame and attention she had had a few months ago had faded, and now she was treated just like any ordinary person. To begin with, Shar had been relieved, for she had not truly enjoyed being the focus of so much interest. But after a while she had, perversely, begun to miss it. Life seemed to have become dull and boring. And when something exciting did happen, like the experiments with the Maze, she was considered too young and inexperienced to take part.

It was the same for Hestor, of course – worse really, because without him the Circle wouldn't have known about the Maze in the first place. But unlike herself, Hestor wasn't expected to work twice as hard, or achieve twice as much, as anyone else. To Shar's way of thinking, it was all very unfair.

Which brought her back to what had happened this morning. Shar hadn't forgotten the momentary flashes of disquiet that had assailed her, firstly outside on the stack and later in the dining hall. Something wrong. Something the adepts should have done but didn't, or that should not have been there but was . . . She had not had time to think much about it during the rest of the busy day, but now her mind latched on to it with new interest. What *had* she glimpsed in the moment that Adept Wilden disappeared? She couldn't shake off the thought that it was somehow significant – so much so, in fact, that several times today she had been on the verge of telling her tutor about it and asking his advice. But something had held her back. She didn't want to tell anyone; not even Hestor. For reasons that she didn't care to go into too deeply, she wanted to keep her thoughts to herself.

At least, until she had done some private investigation.

She wished she could get a closer look at the amulet that had been used to open the Maze. More to the point, she wished she knew how it had been made. The formula had been found among the ancient papers in the library, but those papers were now safely under lock and key in the High Initiate's study, and she wouldn't be allowed to look at them. Even if she could see them, she probably wouldn't understand half of what they contained; she simply wasn't knowledgeable enough.

And yet . . .

Shar put her hairbrush down and lay back, staring at the ceiling. She knew perfectly well why she wanted to examine the amulet. In fact, it went much further than that. She wanted to try it for herself – for she was certain that where the senior adepts had only partly succeeded, *she* had the ability to do more. She believed she could open the Maze and travel through it. All she needed was a little bit of nerve . . . and the amulet.

It was then that the real idea came to her, and it was so mutinous, yet so obvious, that she sat bolt upright again, disturbing Amber who *wowl*ed a grumpy protest. Then, as his telepathic mind caught an inkling of her thoughts, the cat suddenly opened his eyes very wide and stared at her.

'Go back to sleep,' Shar said to him, trying to reinforce the words with a mental command. Amber took no notice; only continued to stare. He knew what was brewing in her mind, and he was extremely interested. Shar tried to tell herself that she mustn't let him influence her; cats were notoriously disobedient and she should not take her lead from him. But truthfully, Amber's mischievous curiosity had nothing to do with it. The idea had struck her, and taken root. And she thought she knew how to achieve what she wanted.

The sky was cloudy, hiding the two moons so that she could not tell what the hour was. Instinctively it felt late, which was all to the good, for she didn't want to be disturbed by anyone. To be sure that all was quiet, Shar slipped out of bed and went to the door, opening it and peering into the passage beyond. Three cats were sitting outside. They stood up when they saw her, raising their tails eagerly, but they made no sound. *They* knew that she wanted privacy, Shar thought, and they would warn her if anyone approached. She smiled, feeling a little shiver of excitement ripple through her. In their own mysterious way the cats were giving her their approval, and it was all the encouragement she wanted.

She projected a grateful image to the creatures and closed the door again. Now: what would she need? Something warmer to wear, for a start; with the fire burning down to embers the room was turning cold. She pulled on a long woollen robe, tied it with a sash, then went to fetch her work box. Every initiate had such a box, to hold their magical paraphernalia; as yet Shar's contained only a few items, but they would be enough for her purposes tonight. Air and earth: that meant a yellow candle, crystal, sand and the incense in the white bag. Better not risk chalking symbols on the floor, in case someone should notice them in the morning.

She gathered the items she wanted and moved her small table to the middle of the room. When the yellow candle was burning she extinguished the one at her bedside, then lit incense in a crucible. She still wasn't used to working in such a formal way, with tools and rituals and prescribed routines. In the old days – in fact since she was very small – she had communicated with her elemental friends as simply and naturally as with any human, and there had been no need for all these trappings. But since her third-rank training had begun, that had had to change. She was dealing with more powerful beings now, and her tutors never ceased to remind her of it. 'Caution, caution, caution,' they said. 'The higher elementals can be dangerous, so don't take risks and never cut corners.' Privately Shar thought that all these restrictions were unnecessary. She obeyed them, of course, when the tutors were watching; but tonight, with no one looking over her shoulder, there was no need for time-wasting safeguards. The creatures she intended to summon were her friends and she could easily control them.

With the sharp-scented smoke of the incense tingling in her nostrils, she stood before the table, closed her eyes and began to summon the creatures of earth and air. In one hand she clasped a piece of clear rock crystal; in the other she held a small heap of sand, letting the grains trickle slowly through her fingers and fall to the table, where they formed a strange, curling pattern.

'*Friends of earth and friends of air,*' she whispered. '*Come to me, come to Shar. I call you from the sky and from the land, from the wind and from the stone. Hear me, and answer. Hear me, and answer!*'

The candle flame guttered and a sudden draught blew through the room. Shar's pulse quickened. The draught was warm, and that was a good sign. The last of the sand-grains fell and the crystal in her other hand moved, sending a hot pulse and then a cold one through her fingers. Focusing her will more powerfully, Shar repeated the call, emphasising it with a mental surge of welcoming affection. The air stirred again, more strongly this time; a tingling sensation ran down her arms and spine, and abruptly she sensed other presences in the room with her.

Her eyes opened. A shape danced and swayed in mid-air before her; it was pale and ghost-like, constantly changing its form, but she glimpsed huge, shimmering eyes and fragile wings beating in a blur of movement. On the floor something else curled and shifted like dark, heavy mist. A faint, thin noise, like the ringing of a tiny glass bell, sounded in her ears, and she felt rather than heard a deeper tone like a rumbling hum. The two sounds merged with Amber's steady purring, and Shar felt a glow of satisfaction. These were greater and stronger beings than the low elementals with which she had worked all her life, and the fact that they came to her call as readily as their small brothers and sisters delighted her. With a thought for her tutors, she greeted the elementals in the formal way of the Circle, then told them what she wished them to do. *Find for me. Show me. Bring to me. Let no one know.* They understood, and she felt them give assent. The draught came again, ruffling her hair and Amber's fur; for an instant the floor beneath her feet seemed to shift slightly. Then the presences were gone.

Shar let out a gusty breath and sat down on her bed. She felt quite shaky; the summoning must have taken more energy than she had realised. Well, she could have a few minutes' rest now, until the elementals returned from their mission. She held out a hand to Amber, who stood up and padded across the counterpane towards her. Then, as he made to rub against her fingers, the cat stopped. His body tensed, his head turned, and his whiskers stiffened as he hissed a warning.

Shar looked up quickly, and saw what Amber's sharper senses had already detected. There was a new-comer in the room. It hovered above the hearth, and for a moment she thought it was a flickering reflection from the fire. But the fire was almost out; there could *be* no reflection. This was something else.

She got to her feet. Instinct almost made her call out, 'Who's there? What are you?' but Circle training stopped her in time. Besides, the shimmering shape was familiar. And the air had turned *hot*.

A fire elemental had materialised. Not one of the tiny, sparkling beings that often came to her call but a much larger creature, radiating heat as though an oven door had suddenly been opened.

She hadn't summoned her friends of fire . . . Fear

stirred in her, and automatically Shar took up a ritual posture: feet apart, shoulders back, hands spread palms-outward at her sides. There was a smell of singeing in the room now, as if the elemental's essence was starting to make itself felt on the rugs and curtains.

'Be still!' she said, and reinforced the words with a stern psychic command. The flickering stopped; the being hung motionless over the fireplace, as though waiting for her to speak again. Shar swallowed.

'Peace, friend of fire,' she said, determinedly, refusing to let her voice tremble. 'I did not call your kind, and I need nothing from you now.' She traced a sign of command in the air. 'Go back to your own world.'

For a moment she thought the elemental would not obey her. Its colour deepened from yellow-orange to an ominously sultry red, and it swelled briefly, emitting a surge of heat that made sweat break out on Shar's face and body. She heard a sound like flames crackling, another like the hiss of water vapourising – but then the sound and the heat snapped away, and the fire-being vanished.

This time, Shar's expelled breath was a gasp of shock and thankfulness. She stumbled back and sagged on to the bed, feeling as if all the vitality had been sucked out of her bones. What had *happened*? She hadn't given a thought to the fire plane; yet one of its creatures had broken through the barrier between dimensions and appeared, uninvited, before her. How had it happened? And, more importantly, why?

Her racing pulse was slowing down, and the prickle of sweat faded. She looked at Amber, and was surprised to see that he had settled back on the bed, paws curled and eyes closed, completely untroubled. Tentatively she tried to project a question to him. But there was no answer. Amber only opened his eyes for a moment, blinked contentedly at her, then went back to his doze. As far as he was concerned there was nothing to be afraid of, and Shar felt herself relaxing. Probably the fire elemental had been urged by curiosity, and there was nothing more sinister to it than that. After all, she was working with more powerful forces now, so perhaps this kind of thing was only to be expected. Any of her tutors would doubtless have said, 'What did I tell you?' and added yet another lecture about caution.

Shar gave a snorting laugh, then swallowed it back and composed herself more soberly. Very well; she had learned a lesson tonight. But there was no harm done. She would just remember to take greater care next time.

She was calming down, though her nerves were still jangling a little, when there was a soft sound at her window. Shar went to draw back the curtain, and was in time to see the iron catch lifting, apparently of its own accord, and the window swinging open. With a *hush*ing sound a gust of wind blew in, and with it came something else. Something small but solid. Shar could just glimpse what looked like a frail, ghostly claw holding the object, then the claw disappeared and the object fell to the floor with a metallic thud.

She picked it up, and her eyes lit with delight. It was a pendant, in the shape of a tapering spiral, made from several different metals and some other substances that she did not recognise. The elementals had succeeded – they had found the amulet that opened the Maze, and they had brought it to her!

Her hand clenched tightly round the amulet and determinedly she thrust down a surge of guilt that told her this was theft. She was only borrowing the amulet for an hour or two. The elementals would return it when she had finished, and no one would be any the wiser. It wasn't *truly* stealing.

Her conscience started to disagree again, but before the internal argument could go any further Shar reached for her clothes and hastily dressed. Amber had woken up again and, alert now, followed her as she slipped out of the room. The elementals wanted to come too, but she commanded them to wait in the room until she returned. If any senior adepts were awake, they might sense the creatures' presence as they followed her, and that would be disastrous. Confident that they would obey her, Shar hurried away along the passage with Amber trotting at her heels.

Within a few minutes she reached the deserted courtyard. No lamps shone in any of the castle windows, and without moonlight the courtyard was pitch dark; but Shar knew the layout well enough to find her way. Feet slithering on half-melted snow, and taking care to avoid the frozen central fountain, she hastened to the great black arch. The gates were closed, but there was a small postern door in one of them that was never locked, and she stepped through it to emerge on the top of the stack.

The wind had dropped and there was a smell of the coming thaw in the air, but it was still cold enough to make Shar shiver as she peered about, looking for the telltale patch of brighter grass that marked the Maze. When she found it, her courage suddenly ebbed. It was one thing to stand among a watching crowd while someone else made this experiment; but it was quite another to be out here alone in the night, facing the prospect of trying the same experiment for herself and with no one to help her if anything went wrong.

Oh, nonsense! Shar told herself sternly. *Stop being a coward!* She hadn't gone to all this trouble for nothing. Besides, Amber was here, and if anything did go wrong – which it wouldn't – he'd alert Hestor or Kitto.

The method of travelling through the Maze was

no secret, and in theory it was easy. You visualised, as clearly as possible, the place that you wanted to reach, and when the picture was complete, you focused your concentration on the amulet and willed the way to open. No ritual, no preparation; it was as devastatingly simple as that. Shar stepped into the green rectangle, took several deep, steady breaths to compose herself, then closed her eyes and formed a mental image of her own bedroom. At first she was too keyed-up to concentrate properly, but after a minute or so the picture became stronger and clearer, until she almost felt that she was there. Good; *good*. Now the amulet itself . . . Her fingers tightened possessively around it, gripping until the spiral pattern dug into her palms. *Just will it to happen—*

The ground shifted sideways beneath her feet, and a dizzy rush of light-headedness hit her. Shar's mouth opened in shock, but if she made any sound at all, it didn't reach her ears. A wall of whirling colours rushed towards her, over her and away, and something black, shot through with silver, twisted past her face at breathtaking speed. There was a distant shriek of laughter, abruptly cut off; then a momentary image of the entire castle as though she was looking down on it from a vast height. She glimpsed the black walls, the towering spires – *and something else; a mass of movement, surging against the gates like the sea or an invading army—*

The air above the green rectangle shuddered violently and a tongue of fire blazed briefly at its heart before it settled to quietness again.

Shar stumbled against something solid that barked her shins. She yelped, lost her balance – and sprawled ungracefully, face-first, on to her own bed.

Slowly, giddily, she raised herself on her elbows and blinked at the scene before her. She had done it . . . she truly had! The amulet was digging so hard into her palm now that it hurt, and she let it go, wincing at the sting of the indentations it had made in her flesh. She started to stand up – then without warning an enormous wash of nausea churned in her stomach.

'Oh, gods—' Shar just managed to get to her washstand in time, and was giddily sick into the bowl that stood beside her water-jug ready for the morning. The elementals, who had waited obediently, closed in on her, shrilling and rumbling their concern, but she willed them back and, when the bout was over, sagged on to the bed once more, wiping her mouth and trying to control her spinning senses.

It was a reaction, she told herself, nothing more. Perfectly understandable. Hestor had said the same thing had nearly happened to him when Lord Tarod took him through the Maze. She hadn't known what to expect, that was all. She felt better now. And she had succeeded. *That* was what mattered, and the sickness was a small price to pay.

It took her a few minutes to recover, by which time Amber was back from the courtyard and mewing at the door. Shar let him in, then turned her attention to the elementals. She ritually thanked them for all they had done, then charged them to return the amulet to its rightful place before departing to their own worlds. As they disappeared, taking the spiral pendant with them, the last of Shar's energy drained away. She was *exhausted*; so much so that she could easily have lain down on the floor and gone to sleep on the spot.

Mustering a last effort she climbed into bed, still fully dressed and only just remembering to kick off her outdoor shoes. Amber stretched out at full length beside her, and within minutes they were both sound asleep.

Outside in the corridor a strange, hot light flickered, like the reflection from a fire. It danced along the wall, reached Shar's door, hovered. Beyond the castle walls, near the bright rectangle of grass, an answering flicker showed momentarily in the cold night air. Then both lights dimmed, faded, and were gone, leaving only a faint, sulphurous scent in their wake.

3

Frustratingly, early tutorials the next day meant that it was noon before Shar was able to see Hestor alone. They met in the dining hall, and she all but dragged him to a quiet table where, in a hasty whisper, she told him what had happened the previous night.

Hestor was astounded and excited in equal measure. Most importantly, he wanted to see the thing for himself. If Shar's elemental friends could borrow the amulet once, he urged, they could surely do it a second time, and the experiment could be repeated tonight. His eagerness squashed the qualms of conscience that Shar had been having, and fired her with new enthusiasm.

'All right,' she said. 'Tonight, then. We'll meet in my room after second moonrise. This time, I'll see if I can transport myself *back* to the Maze as well.'

'What about Kitto?' Hestor asked. 'Should we include him?'

Shar had been considering that and said, 'Yes, I think we should. I know he's afraid, but if we can show him that the Maze isn't dangerous, and that it truly can work, that's all to the good. Besides, if I'm going to try to travel through in both directions, it would be useful to have a witness at both places.' She didn't voice the third and far less worthy reason why she wanted Kitto to be present; the blunt fact that she wanted to show off. It was an understandable weakness, she told herself, and forgivable.

Hestor nodded. 'We'll talk to Kitto this evening, then, and persuade him to join us.' He looked around the dining hall, his eyes avid. 'Gods, I'm so impatient to see this! I don't know how I'm going to get through this afternoon's classes.'

Shar agreed. To concentrate on the humdrum formality of lessons seemed pointless when there was something so exciting in the wind. To experiment with the Maze had real meaning; it was an achievement, it was *action*. She needed it, to lift her out of the dull routine into which her life had slumped.

She put a hand over Hestor's and pressed reassuringly. 'Don't worry. The time will pass soon enough – and it'll be worth the wait!'

As the second moon started to climb above the castle walls, the three of them – together with Amber and two other cats – gathered in Shar's room. Shar and Hestor were keyed-up almost to feverishness, but Kitto was sombrely quiet. He had been very reluctant to join in, and it had taken the others a lot of time and energy to persuade him. Now, he sat on Shar's bed, shoulders hunched as he concentrated hard on stroking Amber, as though he didn't want to acknowledge what was going on around him.

Shar was getting ready to summon the air and earth elementals. This time, remembering the fire-creature that had appeared so unexpectedly, she took more care with her preparations, and when the summoning began she used the proper ritual words of the Circle. As before, a warm draught wafted through the room, and Hestor exhaled softly as the elementals appeared. He had always admired Shar's affinity with the creatures, and envied the ease with which she could call them to her. When they departed on their mission he waited, tension growing in him, until, again, there was a whispering at the window. Shar opened it; the amulet fell into her hands, and Hestor gazed at it in awe.

'It's *incredible*.' Somehow, he hadn't quite believed that the 'borrowing' – like Shar, he refused to call it theft – had been so simple; in fact he had doubted that it would or could be done at all. Now though, he had the proof.

He reached out to touch the amulet, but a little to his surprise Shar's hand closed tightly over it. He frowned at her, and she said quickly, as if to cover herself, 'It's probably better if we don't touch it more than we have to.'

Kitto made a snorting noise. 'Better if we don't touch it at all!'

Hestor looked daggers at him, then shrugged. 'As you like.' He was annoyed; the amulet wasn't Shar's property, and he had wanted to examine it to see how it was made. Rather than spoil the moment by sparking an argument, however, he let the matter drop. There would be time enough for a closer look later.

'Well,' he said, forcing the traces of resentment away and looking at Kitto less ferociously. 'One of us stays here, I suppose, while the other goes out with Shar to the stack. Which would you prefer, Kitto?'

Kitto eyed the elementals. He did not want to be left alone with them, even for a few moments; the night outside might be cold, but it was a good deal safer. 'I'll go with Shar,' he said.

'All right; then I'll stay here.' Hestor glanced in Shar's direction. 'Do I need to do anything?'

She shook her head. 'No. Just wait, and watch.'

Shar was aware of Hestor looking down at them as they crossed the courtyard. She turned once and waved to him, but the candle in her room had been put out lest anyone should see it and be suspicious, and in the dark she couldn't tell whether he waved back. Kitto lagged behind as they reached the gates and she opened the postern. His hands were shoved deep in his pockets, and the moonlight showed his face pale and nervous.

'Come on, Kitto,' Shar said reassuringly. 'I promise you, there really is nothing to be afraid of.'

Kitto opened his mouth to say that he'd believe that when it was proved to him and not before, but thought better of it. It was his own fault for allowing them to talk him into this. He should have stood firm – said no and meant no. But then Shar and Hestor had always been good at cajoling him into things he didn't want to do.

The only problem was, it usually led to trouble.

He sighed a small, resigned sigh that Shar couldn't hear, and followed her out on to the stack.

It seemed to Hestor that he had been waiting for too long. Trying to think logically, he told himself that he was being impatient; time always crawled in situations like this, and it was possible that only a few minutes had passed since Shar and Kitto disappeared through the gate. But instinct told him that wasn't true. They *must* have been gone for a good while now, and he was beginning to feel distinctly uneasy.

How long had the first experiment with Adept Wilden taken? It had all seemed to happen very quickly; over almost before it had begun. Shar should have appeared in the room by now – unless something was wrong.

Hestor stood up and started to pace the room. Perhaps Shar had not been able to open the Maze a second time, and was still out on the stack? It would be typical of her to keep trying, stubbornly refusing to give up; left to her own devices she would likely as not stay there until dawn. Hestor smiled faintly . . . then the smile vanished as a new thought struck him. Shar believed that the elementals had covered their tracks when they took the amulet – but could she be certain? What if the creatures had left some trace of their presence; enough to alert the High Initiate? Alarm grew in Hestor as his imagination churned over the awful implications. If Neryon suspected that someone had been tampering, he might well have set up a trap to catch the culprit. It could explain why Shar was unable to open the Maze again.

Much more to the point, it could mean that they were all in imminent danger of being discovered.

Hestor felt sick as the horrible consequences of this came home to him. Neryon would be furious beyond any hope of reason; he would expel them both from the Circle, and that would be the end of their training! He had to warn Shar, and quickly!

Amber gave a querying chirrup as Hestor lunged for the door, but Hestor took no notice. He ran out, raced along the corridor and took a back stairway to the courtyard. As he headed for the gate he half-expected a senior adept to step suddenly out of the darkness into his path, but none did. If this *was* a trap, then it hadn't yet shown its teeth, and he reached the postern and scrambled through.

What he saw stopped him in his tracks. Kitto was there on the stack, a small, lonely and lost-looking figure, pacing in circles and flapping his arms against his sides in an effort to ward off the bitter cold. He was alone.

Hestor opened his mouth to call out, but before he could do so, Kitto saw him.

'Hestor!' He sounded very aggrieved. 'About time, too! What do you two think you're about, keeping me . . .' Suddenly the complaint tailed off and Kitto's voice sharpened. 'Where's Shar?'

Hestor stared back at him. 'I was just about to ask you the same thing.'

'You're telling me she hasn't appeared?'

'Not a trace. I've been waiting. There's been no sign of her at all.'

Kitto's face blanched. 'But she went into the Maze . . . I saw her vanish—'

Hestor's nausea of a few minutes ago was nothing to what he felt now. 'Oh, gods,' he said hollowly. 'What's happened to her?'

Kitto was staring at the brighter patch of grass that

marked the Maze's boundaries, as if he hoped it would give him an answer. It didn't.

'*I saw* her go,' he said softly. '*I did*. I was waiting for her to come back again. I thought the two of you were in her room and you'd forgotten about me. Then when you came out . . .' He shook his head helplessly.

Hestor, struggling against the onset of panic, tried to think rationally. 'How long has she been gone?' he demanded.

'I don't know,' said Kitto miserably. 'It seems like ages, but . . .'

'I know. All right; when she went, what *exactly* did you see?'

Racking his memory for details, Kitto replied, 'There was a sort of . . . shimmer in the air, like you described when Adept Wilden went through. Shar started to fade – that was how it looked, anyway – and for a moment I could see the outlines of the mountains through her.' He shivered. 'She said something, but I couldn't hear her voice, I just saw her mouth move. There was a kind of faint hiss, like water spitting on a fire, and then she was gone.'

'Nothing else happened?' urged Hestor. 'You're sure?'

'Certain. That was all.'

It didn't provide them with a single clue, Hestor thought. Shar could be anywhere; but the grimmest likelihood of all was that she was trapped inside the Maze, caught in limbo between one location and another, and unable to reach either. How and why that had happened was unimportant; all that mattered was finding a way to get her out. And he was realistic enough to know that he and Kitto couldn't hope to do that alone.

He said: 'We've got to get help.'

Kitto swallowed. 'You mean . . . tell the Circle?'

Hestor nodded. 'We'll count three more minutes.' It was a ridiculously slender chance, but it was still *just* possible that Shar would return of her own accord. 'If she isn't back by then, we'll alert the High Initiate.' *And take the consequences*, his mind added, though he didn't say that aloud.

They counted silently, neither speaking nor looking at each other. One minute. Two. Nothing happened. Then the three minutes were up, and with a leaden feeling in the pit of his stomach Hestor said, 'Come on. We can't put it off any longer.'

They turned and ran towards the castle gates.

If Shar had stopped to think about the alarm her change of plan would cause, she might not have done what she did. But she had not stopped to think. The rash idea had come so suddenly that it hadn't even occurred to her to consider Hestor and Kitto. In any case, she had meant the experiment to take only a minute or two. But when it had succeeded, all thoughts of haste had gone completely out of her head.

The idea had struck her as she stood in the Maze, clutching the amulet in her hand and focusing her willpower for the transference. The image of her bedroom was forming in her mind's eye when abruptly she thought how unambitious it was to transport herself such a short distance. In theory, the Maze could carry her to any destination, provided she could visualise it clearly enough, and it could bring her back just as easily. When Hestor had travelled with Lord Tarod of Chaos, they had crossed half the world in a single instant. Why, then, should *she* not try? Not quite the same distance, perhaps. But somewhere beyond the castle. Somewhere that she knew well.

It was pure impulse, but Shar made her decision there and then. Her expression gave nothing away to Kitto as, quickly, she blotted out the mental picture of her room and replaced it with another image. A bustling town, bisected by a great river that ran through it and on towards the north-western coast. A jumble of docks and warehouses, ships crowding the quays. And a big house behind a wall whose iron gates stood welcomingly open.

As the picture of the house grew sharp and clear, Shar felt a momentary twinge of discomfort. The place had more unpleasant memories than pleasant ones. Yet she *had* made some good friends there, and when the thaw came and courier riders could get through the mountain roads again – messenger-birds were too expensive for her allowance – she had planned to write to those friends and see how they fared. Now, she could find out without having to wait for spring.

She clutched the amulet, gathered her will, and directed a surge of mental energy at the Maze.

This time she was ready for the giddying lurch as the ground under her seemed to shift and twist. The world warped, turned upside-down, and again she was plunged into a rushing maelstrom of colours that snatched her up and whisked her away. Kitto, the castle and the stack all vanished, and she felt as if she was tumbling over and over through endless space. She thought she cried out, though as before there was no sound. Then came a jolt, a brief but awful sense of nothingness – and a painful return to reality as her feet grounded and she tottered forward and ran slap into a solid mass.

Shar opened her eyes and found herself standing in drizzling rain, with her nose and the palms of her hands against a rough stone wall. She stumbled back, blinking, and suddenly sound swelled and returned, in the form of the night noises of a busy dock. The slap of water, the creak of timbers, the rumble of carts as ships were loaded and made ready to catch the tide . . . Men were shouting orders; in the distance, from one of the sailors' taverns, came laughter and a burst of song.

Among the general cheerful hubbub Shar caught a few words: '. . . drunk, probably. Leave her to it. The Keepers will give her a bed for the night if need be, and a stern lecture into the bargain . . .'

She looked quickly over her shoulder and saw two men a short distance away, looking at her with a mixture of derision and amusement. They grinned and walked on, and Shar brushed the wet from her hair and clothes. What the men thought of her didn't matter, for they had told her what she needed to know. *The Keepers*. She had come to the right place. The experiment had worked!

Through the iron gate in the wall, there stood the house she remembered so well. Its windows were brightly and warmly illuminated, spilling light into the well-tended garden, and from inside, faintly, came the sound of chanting. Shar was surprised. The Keepers of Light, that eccentric but benign sect of people dedicated to the gods of Order, were very pious, but she hadn't expected to find them at their devotions at this hour. She would have to be careful. It wouldn't do for her to be seen, or word might reach the Circle, and the High Initiate would put two and two together and make a very definite four.

Hunching her shoulders against the rain she moved

cautiously towards the front door of the house. The chanting continued, rising and falling in a rhythm that she remembered from her own stay here the previous year. The Keepers had done their best to help when the Sixth-Plane entity had tried to trap her, and even if their efforts had almost led to disaster, Shar felt grateful affection towards them. They had been duped as surely as she had been, but that was hardly their fault. So this, in a way, was a nostalgic visit.

The front door was not locked. Shar eased it open and stepped into the deserted hall, where a lamp burned in its bracket on the wall. A scent of incense wafted from the direction of the square, white-painted room where the Keepers performed their rituals, and Shar moved to peer into the passage that led towards it. Her feet shuffled softly on the floor, and the sound made her realise that there was nothing incorporeal about her presence here; she was as real as anyone else in the house. The thought excited her, but it also stressed the need for caution. She wouldn't venture too near the shrine room. She would merely listen to the chanting for a few more minutes, then return through the Maze to the castle.

There was movement farther along the passage, and she drew back to a place from where she could look without being seen. A figure appeared, vague in the darkness, and approached the door of the shrine room. He opened it, and as he entered, the muted light from within illuminated him. He was an elderly, kind-looking man with neatly clipped white hair, dressed in the peculiar uniform of the Keepers of Light; a shirt and trousers of dark blue linen, with white lightning-flash patterns stitched on it. Shar recognised him immediately – he was Lias Alborn, the Keepers' leader, who had done so much to try to help her. She would have loved to show herself and greet him, but of course that was out of the question. Still, she had at least seen a familiar face.

The door closed behind Lias, and Shar stepped back into the passage. She tiptoed towards the shrine room, wanting to get just a little closer before turning back.

Footsteps sounded on the stairs that rose from the entrance hall behind her.

Shar turned quickly. The footsteps, light but firm, reached the foot of the stairs, and a candle flared, throwing a wavering human silhouette across the floor of the hall. Heart jolting under her ribs, Shar pressed herself against the wall where shadows were deepest, praying that the newcomer would pass by and not look in her direction.

But he did not pass by. Instead, to her horror, he turned into the passage. Shar sucked in breath and tried to squeeze herself into the wall. The candlelight danced, growing brighter; then the silhouette resolved into a solid figure.

He stopped in his tracks, and his expression was so astonished that under other circumstances it would have been funny. But Shar's own shock was as great. For she knew him. And he was the last person in the world she would have expected to find here.

Like Lias, he was wearing the zig-zag patterned clothing of the Keepers. His brown, curly hair had been cut short, so that it barely covered his ears, and a narrow band of gold fabric was tied round his brow. In one hand he carried his candle; in the other was a lute.

It was Reyni Trevire.

Reyni said, '*Shar?*' in a voice so stunned that he could barely force it out.

Shar's mouth worked but she couldn't utter a sound. There was no time to even *think* about what Reyni could possibly be doing here, why he was wearing the Keepers' uniform, what it all meant. The one thought that swamped her mind was the sheer awfulness of being discovered, and piling in over it came the instinct to flee. She didn't consider, didn't hesitate – the amulet was in her hand and she gripped it with all her strength, groping wildly for the mental picture of the stack, the castle, the Maze. If she had paused even for a moment, she might have realised that this was the surest way to betray her secret. But she did not pause. The picture came. She willed herself to *be* there.

The air around her distorted, flickered, and Shar vanished.

Reyni stood stupefied, gaping dazedly at the spot where she had been. A turmoil of possible explanations came to him but none of them made any sense. After a few paralysed moments he put the lute down and reached out, feeling the air, half-expecting to find Shar still there after all. His fingers touched the wall and nothing else. She was gone.

Reyni knew better than to wonder if he was dreaming. This was real. Shar had appeared; she had been here. *What was going on?*

He took a pace backwards. Then he snatched up the lute and ran towards the shrine room.

4

It was lucky for Shar that Hestor and Kitto had lost their nerve on the way to the High Initiate's chambers. When she lurched out of the Maze to find herself alone on the stack top, she realised that she must have been gone for longer than she had thought, and the rest was easy to guess. Alarmed, she fought back the dizzy, spinning nausea that the Maze had stirred in her head and stomach, and ran unsteadily back to the castle.

She ran into her friends in the entrance hall, dithering nervously as they tried to muster the courage to face Neryon Voss. Relief and anger were equally mingled as they bombarded her with questions, but Shar refused to tell them anything until they were back in the privacy of her room. The elementals were still there; Shar gave them the amulet, charged them to return it, then at last told Hestor and Kitto what had happened.

But not all of it. She didn't mention Reyni. Hestor would scold her for being so foolish as to let him see her, while Kitto would start worrying again. So Shar told them only that she had transported herself to the Keepers' mission house in Wester Reach, and that distance seemed to be no barrier to the ease with which she could travel through the Maze.

Hestor was very excited. This, he said, was a real breakthrough; and next time they borrowed the amulet he was determined to experience it for himself. Shar said vaguely yes, of course he must, and she would help him. But she didn't mean it. She was starting to formulate other plans; plans in which Hestor would be a nuisance at best and a liability at worst. She didn't want him involved, and the less he knew, the better it would be for them all.

Catching Kitto's eye Shar saw a hint of suspicion in his look. For a moment she wondered if he had some inkling of her thoughts; but then she pushed the feeling away. Kitto had a natural talent for picking up cats' telepathic images, but humans were a totally different matter. He couldn't have guessed anything. He couldn't know what was in her mind. He was suspicious simply because he was frightened, she told herself.

Saying that she was tired and wanted some sleep, Shar managed to persuade the boys to leave soon afterwards. She had no intention of sleeping, though. Instead she climbed into her bed and, with Amber curled beside her, settled herself to think.

Shar felt a sense of enormous triumph at the ease with which she had travelled to Wester Reach. She was far, far ahead of the senior adepts; they hadn't yet had any real success. To Shar, using the Maze seemed to be no more difficult than walking through a door. She smiled to herself. She really *was* special. She had talents and powers that the rest of the Circle couldn't match – and if they chose to ignore those powers, and treat her like any ordinary junior initiate, they could not expect her to do the same. They had no *right* to expect it.

A sudden surge of resentment rose in her mind. If her 'superiors', as they thought of themselves, had any sense, they would welcome her achievement and give her proper credit for it. She should be *leading* the Circle's experiments, rather than being ignored and excluded just because she was, as they saw it, too young and too inexperienced. Shar snorted softly. Inexperienced? She had probably had more real magical experience in the past year than most of the senior adepts would have in their entire lives! How many of *them* had faced a Sixth–Plane entity? Or fought against the evil of a man like her uncle, Thel Starnor, and proved themselves stronger? Shar was a Daughter of Storms. She was a Dark–Caller; born with power at her fingertips, and she could use it without the need for years of tedious study! Tonight's adventure had proved that, and if the Circle doubted her abilities, they would have to learn that they were wrong.

She reached out and stroked Amber. 'Reyni could tell them the truth, couldn't he?' she said softly to the cat. Not that Reyni would say anything to anyone; he was too good a friend, and anyway, he probably believed that her startling appearance at the mission house was a waking dream or hallucination. But the thought of Reyni brought something else to mind; a question that she hadn't yet had a chance to consider, and which deeply intrigued her. What had Reyni, of all people, been *doing* at the Keepers' mission, and dressed in their distinctive clothing? However affected he had been by the terrifying events of a few months ago, he had never seemed the kind of person to devote himself to a religious life. So why had he apparently joined the sect? Shar's curiosity was thoroughly aroused, and it seemed to her that the best way to solve the riddle was to make a second foray through the Maze to Wester Reach. She would be prepared next time; instead of losing her nerve she would speak to Reyni, swear him to secrecy and ask him what was afoot. Even if there was a perfectly mundane explanation, it would be good to see him again.

The prospect of renewing her friendship with Reyni spread a pleasant feeling through her mind. Better not to tell Hestor about her plan, though.

When Reyni had first entered their lives, Hestor had got quite the wrong idea about Shar's attitude and had been jealous; he was over it now, but there was no need to stir up the memory. Another night; another small task for the elementals. It should be easy enough.

Shar blew out her candle and settled down to sleep. Still thinking about Reyni, she started to make plans. She would have to make sure that she could find him alone when she went back; it wouldn't do to risk being seen by any of the Keepers who knew her; Jonakar or Amobrel, for example – and most importantly Lias. For all his kindness Lias was very conventional; if he suspected for one moment that she was there without the Circle's permission, he would feel duty-bound to tell the High Initiate. Lias believed that rules were meant for obeying, and as the Keepers' leader—

Like a stream of water suddenly drying up, Shar's train of thought trickled to a stop. *Lias*. A cold sensation started to crawl through her, beginning at the base of her spine and creeping horribly upwards. *Lias*. The Keepers' leader; the kindly old man who had tried so hard to help and protect her, who had always had her best interests at heart . . . and who had died in a savage sorcerous attack when he dared to challenge the entities of the Sixth Plane.

Shar stopped breathing and lay rigid, staring into the

dark as shock pulled her mind into sudden sharp focus. Lias Alborn was *dead*. He had been dead for months. Yet not two hours ago she had seen him – alive and well – at the mission house in Wester Reach. It wasn't possible, Shar told herself. She must have made a mistake; must have seen someone else who resembled him.

But she knew she hadn't. The man who had entered the shrine room *was* Lias. Alive. Not a ghost; ghosts didn't open doors. Not a hallucination.

What, then? *What?*

Picking up her confusion, Amber made a peculiar sound and came padding over the bedcover to sniff at her face. His mind projected fuzzy, perplexed images, but for once Shar ignored him. Mulling over one mystery, she had suddenly woken up to another, and one far darker than the mere puzzle of Reyni. She had known about Lias's death. But when she saw him it was as if the knowledge had been blanked from her mind and forgotten. Even when she returned, it hadn't occurred to her that anything strange had happened. But now she knew she wouldn't have a moment's peace of mind until she had got to the root of this. Either she had made a mistake, or something utterly bizarre was afoot. It was all the more vital now that she should see Reyni and talk to him as soon as possible.

Her shock was subsiding a little, and she began to

breathe again. Amber, reassured, lay down once more, put his chin on his outstretched paws and relaxed, and Shar raised her head and looked around, half-expecting to see a vision of Lias – or something even stranger – hovering in the room. There was nothing there; though the room and all its furnishings seemed to have turned to an eerie monochrome of black and silver, as though all the colour had been stolen away. Shar shut her eyes then opened them again, but the peculiar effect didn't change. She was overtired; must at least try to rest, or she would be fit for nothing in the morning and that could well arouse her tutors' suspicions.

She lay down again. She thought she might be able to sleep, but expected that her sleep would be shallow and filled with dreams.

There were dreams, and they weren't especially pleasant. But Shar slept on as a strange sound impinged on her room; a sound like water running, or frail, distant laughter. She didn't wake to see the room change, colour seeping slowly back into it as something very vague and ghostly evaporated like mist under the door and away.

Nor was she aware of the white cat that had been sitting outside in the corridor, and which raised its head as the drifting mist went by, gazing after it with an intelligence and awareness that was not that of any normal animal. The cat glanced once, briefly, at Shar's door, sensed that she slept on, then looked along the corridor again. The mist had vanished. Slowly, the cat rose to its feet. It stretched, yawned . . . and its small form faded and was gone.

The following afternoon, a messenger-bird arrived at the castle. It was one of the regular birds, carrying letters from Wester Reach; and senior adept Gant Birn Sangen was pleased to find that one of the letters was from his cousin Fosker.

Gant and Fosker had both been initiated into the Circle when they were young, but Fosker had left some years ago. He had always had a strong bias towards the gods of Order, and had never been happy with the idea of paying equal homage to Chaos, whose powers he distrusted. He would much rather have been born before the age of Equilibrium, when Order held sway over the world and anyone who worshipped Chaos was denounced as a heretic. Gant, who held similar views, had been disappointed when Fosker left, for Fosker had been a staunch ally against what Gant considered the Circle's 'wrong' way of thinking. But Fosker had found another cause to champion. He had joined a small but very pious cult dedicated to the lords of Order, and had become master of their mission in his home province of Shu. Then a few months ago, following the death of the cult's leader, he had been called from Shu to take charge of their headquarters in Wester Reach.

Fosker Sangen was the new head of the Keepers of Light.

Gant was sure that his cousin would be a worthy successor to Lias Alborn. He and Fosker wrote to each other regularly, so this latest letter wasn't unexpected. But when Gant opened it and began to read, he was surprised and alarmed. For Fosker had some very disturbing news.

Fosker knew all about Reyni Trevire's involvement with Shar the previous autumn, so when Reyni had come running to the shrine room to report his bizarre encounter in the corridor, Fosker was instantly alerted to trouble. He ordered a thorough search of the house; Shar, of course, was nowhere to be found, but they did discover telltale wet footprints near the spot where Reyni had seen her – footprints that stopped abruptly halfway along the passage.

The footprints gave Fosker a clue to the truth. He questioned Reyni very closely about the details of the incident, and what he learned added fuel to his suspicions. Shar *had* paid a visit – but not by any conventional means. She had come and, it seemed, gone, by using magical skills so great that they should have been far beyond the reach of a high adept, let alone a junior initiate. In theory such a thing was impossible. But it seemed Shar had done it.

Fosker didn't know about the Maze. Neryon Voss had decreed that, until the Circle had made more progress with their experiments, no one outside the castle was to be told any details. So, though he guessed what Shar had done, Fosker couldn't begin to imagine how she had done it. Gant, however, could.

He put the letter down and glared at it, feeling indignant but also, in a way, triumphant. This proved what he had been trying to make the High Initiate understand from the start. The Maze was an outlandish and potentially dangerous force, which should not be tampered with by anyone. If an untrained child like Shar could learn to use it – and she must have done so in secret, Neryon would never be so irresponsible as to give her permission – then great Aeoris alone knew what might happen in the long term. The greatest disasters, as Gant was fond of telling his pupils, began with the smallest of mistakes.

So, then; what to do about it? The most obvious course of action was to take this news straight to Neryon, but it occurred to Gant that that might not be such a wise idea. If confronted, Shar might deny everything, and Gant couldn't actually prove his accusation. He wasn't even certain yet that she *had* been meddling with the Maze. Gant was a stickler for facts, and he didn't want to be made to look a fool. So, before he made any decisions, he resolved to investigate a little further.

He waited until evening, when dusk had fallen, then locked the door of his room and prepared to perform a conjuration. With great care and many precautions he put his mind into a trance and called upon the beings of the fifth of the seven astral planes. This dimension was also known as the Plane of Oracles, and though the creatures that lived there were capricious and sometimes deceitful, they had great seeing powers and could answer almost any question with unfailing accuracy. Gant wanted to find out more about Shar's actions, and he was a skilled enough sorcerer to compel the Fifth-Plane beings to tell him the truth.

The ritual took longer than it should have done. The entities seemed particularly difficult tonight, and Gant had trouble controlling them. Several times it seemed to him that another force was trying to break in; now and then there were flickers of vivid colour in the black and silver images he saw, and that shouldn't have happened. But at last he forced the creatures to obey him, and what they told him was enough to confirm what he suspected.

He banished the Fifth-Plane elemental and brought his mind back to the physical world. He felt exhausted and his head ached fiercely (another thing that shouldn't have happened), but he was satisfied that he knew, now, what Shar had done. He wasn't altogether surprised. The girl had been trouble from the start;

she was too clever for her own good, and lately he had started to see signs of rebelliousness in her. She might have special talents, but she was a potential menace, not just to herself but to the entire Circle. Neryon said that she only needed training and they must be patient with her, but in Gant's opinion Neryon was too lenient. Shar needed to be *curbed*, as much for her own sake as for anyone else's. And if the High Initiate wouldn't see the sense of that, then perhaps this newest development might give Gant the chance to show him how wrong he was.

He cleared away the trappings of his ritual, then sat down at his desk by the window and took out paper, pen and ink. He felt a pang of unease at the idea of directly disobeying a Circle order, but told himself that it was for the good of all and therefore justified. This *had* to be done.

The pen began to scratch on the paper:

My dear Cousin Fosker,

   Your letter, and the news it carried, came as a surprise to me — but not, I fear, as a shock. There is something afoot here; I am not strictly permitted to tell you about it, but under the circumstances I believe that my conscience must outweigh all else. The matter concerns certain experiments that the Circle have recently begun to make. And it is my firm belief that there is a connection with the extraordinary

*appearance of Shar Tillmer at your mission house last
night . . .*

Shar had been in such a peculiar and distant mood
all day that by evening Hestor had given up. Sitting
alone in the dining hall, he told himself morosely that
if people chose to be temperamental and wouldn't
even try to control it, their friends could only try
so hard before they lost patience. When they met
for lunch Shar had been distracted, not listening to
anything he said, then when studies were over for the
day and he had asked her if she'd had any thoughts
about investigating the Maze again tonight, she all
but bit his head off. Well, all right, he thought; if
she wanted to be precious about her experiments and
keep them to herself, so be it. He wouldn't take any
more interest — and if Shar suddenly found herself in
trouble and needed help, he just might not be willing
to oblige!

Kitto, who had observed enough of Shar's state
and Hestor's reaction to get a good idea of the rest,
was worried. He said nothing to either of them —
in their present moods, that would only have made
him unpopular — but he remembered the events of
a few months ago. That near-catastrophe had started
in much the same way: Shar becoming restless and
secretive, Hestor responding with anger and jealousy . . . the pattern was disturbingly similar, and

Kitto didn't like it. This whole business with the Maze was bad enough, but by keeping her thoughts and activities to herself, Shar was inviting yet more trouble. And he didn't want even to think about what would happen if the High Initiate ever found out the truth.

Shar had gone to her room as soon as her lessons were over, and didn't reappear all evening. With a half-formed idea of at least trying to talk to Hestor, Kitto suggested a round or two of Handstaves when they left the dining hall, but Hestor shook his head.

'I'm too tired,' he said brusquely.

'Well, something less energetic, then. Quarters, maybe; or—'

Hestor interrupted. 'No. I don't want to play anything. I'm going to bed.'

He walked away, leaving Kitto feeling frustrated and faintly hurt. What were friends supposed to be for, if you couldn't talk to them? Hestor and Shar were as bad as each other in their different ways, he thought. Well, bad dreams to them both. If the choice was between a moping companion and a sulking one, he'd find something better to do on his own.

Finding something better to do, however, was not so easy, and after an hour of wandering around the castle at a loose end, Kitto was bored. There were plenty of options: he could have found someone else to play a game with; or there was usually music and singing in one of the small halls; he could even have gone to his room and practised his reading and writing (though that, however worthy, didn't appeal to him at any time). But nothing could snare his interest. He was worried, and it made him too restless to concentrate on anything.

When midnight had passed and almost everyone else was asleep, Kitto was still wandering aimlessly around the castle. He had wasted the whole evening, but it hardly seemed to matter; there didn't even seem any point in bothering to go to bed.

He was in the dining hall, which was deserted now and unlit but for the orange-crimson glow of the fire where the servants had banked it down for the night. It was warm near the hearth, and Kitto was sitting staring into the embers and idly trying to invent pictures in them, when at one corner of his vision he saw a shadow move at the far end of the hall.

He looked up, suddenly alert. The broad corridor beyond the doors was lit by a few torches that burned throughout the night, and he was in time to see the silhouette of someone passing by. There was nothing sinister in that, of course; people came and went as they pleased, at any hour. But it *was* unusual for anyone to be about this late. Kitto's curiosity stirred. Then he thought of Shar . . .

He was on his feet and moving stealthily down the hall almost before his consciousness could catch up with what his instinct was doing. What he would do if the silhouette *was* Shar, he didn't know; he hadn't thought that far. But he wanted, needed, to be sure.

He emerged into the corridor as the unidentified figure turned a corner. Kitto had one glimpse before it disappeared, and it seemed to him that the figure was too tall to be Shar. But torch-shadows were often misleading, so, on quiet and cautious feet, he followed.

At the junction with the next passage he saw that his quarry was heading towards the High Initiate's study. Kitto's skin crawled as he jumped to the awful conclusion that it *was* Shar and that she was going to steal the Maze amulet personally, physically, from Neryon's locked cupboard. She wouldn't be so stupid. Surely, she couldn't be?

The figure stopped outside the High Initiate's door. Here two smaller torches burned in their wall brackets, casting a stronger light, and as the figure's silhouette resolved into solid detail Kitto drew in a sharp, shocked breath. The person he had been following was not Shar. It was Gant Birn Sangen.

Kitto didn't know whether to feel relieved or angry; but either way he felt utterly foolish. To have mistaken that tall, sour stick of an adept for Shar just showed how far he had let worry and imagination carry him. No doubt Adept Gant had some late appointment with the High Initiate –

Council business, probably — and he would be none too pleased if he turned round and saw Kitto on his trail. There would be sharp words at best and awkward questions at worst, so Kitto started to draw back, meaning to duck out of sight around the corner.

He stopped as he realised that Gant had not knocked at Neryon's door, but instead was standing before it, and drawing a sigil in the air. He traced it too fast for Kitto to see what it was — and it probably would have meant nothing to him anyway — but when the sigil was completed, the air before Neryon's door began to glow faintly. Kitto eased back into the deeper shadows, feeling suddenly very uneasy. What was Gant *doing?* The glow was becoming stronger, and it was a strange colour, not quite purple and not quite blue, and with a hint of murky and none-too-pleasant green in its depths. Frowning, and trying to ignore the nervous twitchings in his stomach, Kitto watched as Gant took a pace away from the glow, then stopped and folded his arms as though waiting for something.

A sound broke the quiet. Or rather, two sounds: a high, sweet tone like distant chiming bells, and a deeper, faintly ominous rumbling. Kitto had heard those sounds once before, and when a draught of warm air suddenly came dancing down the passage, it confirmed his fears. Then he saw them. The creature of air looked like a bird's ghost, making every torch gutter and dip as it passed, while the earth elemental took the form of a heavy, sluggish mist that flowed along the floor like a slow flood.

Shar had sent her friends to fetch the amulet. And Gant was waiting for them.

Kitto stayed only long enough for his brain to register fully what his eyes were telling him. Then he started to back away, around the corner, praying that the elementals weren't aware of his presence. Two more paces, three, four, torn between urgency and the need to ensure he was out of Gant's earshot. He heard a chiming call from the air elemental. He heard Gant reply, sternly, commandingly.

Kitto's caution snapped, and he turned and raced with all the speed he could find towards the main stairs.

5

'Shar!' Kitto hissed her name and scratched harder on the door, too afraid to knock in case he should wake someone in a nearby room. '*Shar!* It's me, Kitto! Let me in!'

There was a shuffle of movement on the far side of the door, then the sound of a bolt being drawn back. The door opened a crack, and Shar looked out.

'What do you want?'

It was hardly a friendly greeting, but Kitto was too agitated to care about that. 'Let me in!' he said again. '*Quickly*, Shar! It's important!'

She hesitated, then abruptly pulled the door open. Kitto ran inside, snatched the door handle from her and shut it again, only just remembering not to slam it. He shoved the bolt home, then turned to face her, breathing hard.

'You sent the elementals to get the amulet again, didn't you?' he demanded.

Shar's face closed up and her eyes became hard.

'And if I did,' she replied, 'what business is it of yours?'

'It isn't my business. But someone else has made it his.'

She stared at him. 'Hestor?'

'No. Adept Gant.'

If he had been the kind to bear grudges, Kitto would have been pleased by the instant change in Shar's expression. From frigid hostility her face collapsed into a look of consternation. But it lasted only a moment before she got herself under control; then, like shutters closing over a window, the uninterested mask came back.

'Adept Gant,' she said. 'I see. How do you know?'

'Because I just *saw* him, outside the High Initiate's study. Casting a spell, or something – whatever it was, it looked like a trap. He was waiting for your elemental friends!'

Shar stood very still. 'And did they come?'

'Yes! That's what I'm trying to make you understand, Shar – Gant must know what you've been doing!'

Shar's eyes flared with sudden fury. 'Then someone told him. If you—'

'Great Yandros and Aeoris, what do you think I am?' Kitto hissed. 'If I make a promise, I keep it!'

That was probably true, Shar told herself. Anyway, even if either Hestor or Kitto *had* decided to betray her secret, Gant was the last person they would have tattled to.

'The simple fact is, you haven't been quite clever enough, have you?' Kitto went on. 'For all your special powers, you're not a fifth- or sixth-rank adept – you *don't* know everything they know, and you can't do everything they do. That's why—' He stopped. He had been about to plead with her, again, to leave the Maze well alone, but this wasn't the time or place to do it. For one thing, Shar wouldn't listen. For another, they had a much more urgent problem on their hands.

'Look,' he said, pushing his thoughts aside. 'However he did it, the fact is that Gant's found out about the amulet being taken, and when the elementals went to fetch it tonight, he was there to stop them. He's not an idiot, Shar. Even if he doesn't know who sent them yet, it won't take him long to solve the puzzle. He'll go straight to the High Initiate, and then—'

'No, he won't,' said Shar.

Kitto stopped in mid-sentence, astonished. 'What do you mean, "no, he won't?"'

'Exactly what I say. Whatever he might suspect, Gant can't prove that I was the one who borrowed the amulet. And you know what he's like: he does everything by the rules. Unless he *can* prove it, he won't dare go to the High Initiate.'

'The elementals might tell him who sent them,' Kitto persisted.

'Not willingly. And even if he forces them to tell . . .' Shar shrugged. 'Elementals play tricks; everyone knows that. Whatever they say, it won't be enough evidence for Gant to take to Neryon.'

Kitto sighed with a mixture of exasperation and confusion. He didn't understand how Shar could be so calm; he still feared that at any moment Gant could come storming into the room in a towering rage, ready to denounce her and have her thrown out of the Circle. Yet at the same time, reluctantly, he saw the logic of what she had said. Without absolute proof, Gant wouldn't dare accuse her of anything, because it would simply be his word against hers, and it was well known that he disliked and disapproved of her.

'You see?' Shar said, more gently. 'There's nothing to worry about.'

Something in Kitto boiled over. 'Oh, well, that's all right then, isn't it!' he said explosively, flinging both arms ceilingwards. 'Nothing to worry about! Only the fact that Gant Birn Sangen knows what you've been up to, and we've no idea what he's going to do about it, and you're getting yourself into what's probably going to turn into the worst mess since – since—'

His outburst tailed off and Shar said ominously, 'Since what?'

'Nothing.' Kitto's shoulders slumped in defeat. 'It doesn't matter. You're right; why should I worry about it? Why should I worry about anything?'

Shar didn't reply for a few moments. Then she moved away across the room.

'I'm tired, Kitto. I want to go to bed.' She hesitated, glancing at him over her shoulder. 'Thanks for warning me about Gant. Goodnight.'

Kitto stared at her. 'That's it? You haven't got anything clsc to say?'

'Should I have?'

'It doesn't even seem to bother you that Gant stopped you from taking the amulet tonight – or probably ever again!'

'No,' Shar said. 'It doesn't bother me very much.' She looked at him again, and there was a gleam in her eyes that Kitto could only interpret as sly. 'Besides, he didn't stop me tonight. The elementals weren't taking the amulet. They were putting it back.'

In truth, the fact that Adept Gant had discovered her secret was a blow to Shar's plans. Obviously, she couldn't have continued to 'borrow' the amulet indefinitely; but she had badly needed at least a few more chances to experiment. For something had happened tonight. Something very strange and, possibly, very far-reaching.

Instead of going out on to the stack, she had

attempted, tonight, to transport herself directly from her room to the Maze. It had worked; and so from there she had travelled again to Wester Reach. This time she had taken care not to be seen, resisting the temptation to find Reyni again – she wasn't ready for that yet – and staying for only a few minutes before returning to the castle. But in that few minutes she had made an unexpected discovery. And if the theory taking form in her mind was right, then the mystery of Lias Alborn's presence at the mission house was explained.

During her very first experiment, as the Maze had begun to open, Shar had momentarily felt as though she were soaring high above the castle, looking down on it from a huge distance, and in that moment she had also glimpsed what looked like a great horde besieging the black gates. She knew that the castle had been attacked only once in its history: many, many centuries ago, when an army led by the very first High Initiate and High Margrave drove out and destroyed the race of half-human sorcerers known as the Old Ones, and ended their long, cruel reign of terror. The image had vanished in an instant, and later she had dismissed it as some kind of hallucination. Now though, she wasn't so sure.

Then last night she had seen Lias Alborn, and tonight there had been two more anomalies. Firstly, as she clasped the amulet and willed herself to be taken to Wester Reach, the scene around her had shifted briefly from winter to high summer, and she had seen the castle festooned with banners and garlands as though for a Quarter-Day celebration. Secondly, when she entered the garden of the Keepers' mission house something had been wrong. To begin with, she couldn't work out what it was; but then she realised that the gates were different – not the familiar wrought iron but old and crumbling wood, in need of replacement. Then, when she looked again, they were back to normal.

So, then: four peculiar visions. Each one had lasted only a few seconds, but they all had one thing in common – they were visions of another age. From there, it had taken Shar only one logical step to arrive at a breathtaking theory.

The Circle knew that the Maze could transport people through physical space. But if Shar's deduction was right it seemed that it could also carry them through time. The implications were awesome. To be able to step into the past, to witness events as they actually happened instead of having to rely on incomplete or biased history records ... The Circle could rediscover so much ancient knowledge; knowledge, perhaps, of other devices even more powerful than the Maze, which had lain forgotten since ancient times. This had *incredible* possibilities.

And she, Shar Tillmer, was the only living mortal who knew about it.

Shar thought of Adept Gant, and wondered if he had learned anything from the elementals. It was hard to guess how much he could force them to tell him, but the fact that he hadn't yet come hammering at her door was a hopeful sign. She believed, as she had told Kitto, that without concrete proof Gant wouldn't go to the High Initiate; but on the other hand she also knew that if Gant had any evidence at all, he wouldn't let the matter rest. Even if he didn't confront her directly he would be watching her very closely from now on. She couldn't borrow the amulet again. It was too dangerous. She would have to find another way of using the Maze – and she thought she could do it. After all, who knew for certain that an amulet was necessary? Lord Tarod had never said so, and the old records didn't actually state it. Most magical implements were simply focuses for the mind's own power. So why should an adept not be able to travel through the Maze using only that power, without any trappings? If it was possible, Shar believed that she, more than anyone in the castle, was capable of doing it. It wouldn't be easy, but the only alternative was to give up her experiments altogether, and that was something she was not prepared to do.

If she had been older, she thought, it would have been different. With her natural abilities she would have been involved in the Maze experiments from the start, so she could have gone straight to the Council of Adepts with her discovery and enlisted their help. She laughed hollowly at the thought of what would happen if she did that now. The Council wouldn't even listen. She would be expelled from the Circle in disgrace. It was *ridiculous*.

Feeling ruffled now, and just a little self-pitying, Shar climbed into bed. Very well, she said to herself: if she was forced to be secretive, then she *would* be secretive. She wouldn't even tell Hestor what she was doing from now on; though she trusted him, there was always a chance that he would accidentally let something slip. She would work alone. It was safer, and better, that way.

She went to sleep with that thought in her mind. While in another part of the castle, Adept Gant Birn Sangen sat down to complete his letter to his cousin Fosker . . .

When Gant's letter was delivered to the mission house, Fosker Sangen read it through very carefully, then, leaving word that he did not want to be disturbed for a while, he went to the room where the Keepers made their daily devotions to the lords of Order.

The shrine was much as Shar would have remembered it; the white-painted walls, the benches, the incense brazier, the three votive lamps that were never extinguished. One thing, though, had changed – the huge painting of Aeoris, stern and serene, was no longer there. The painting had been destroyed when the Sixth-Plane entities had attacked and killed Lias Alborn, and in its place on the wall a golden plaque now hung, with the circle-and-lightning-flash symbol of Order inlaid in darker gold and diamonds. The plaque had been a gift from Neryon Voss, to thank the Keepers for all they had done to help Shar, and Fosker found it a very helpful focus for his meditations. Now, he sat down on one of the benches and began silently to pray to Aeoris for help and guidance. He stayed there, unmoving, for an hour. Then he sent for Reyni Trevire.

What he had to say alarmed the young musician. There was reason to believe, Fosker stated, that Shar Tillmer was faced with a new threat, and that it was connected with her appearance in the mission house two nights ago. It was perhaps inevitable (Fosker added sadly) that a girl born with Shar's extraordinary powers would suffer many difficulties in her life. There were always outside forces eager to use such a person for their own ends, as Reyni knew all too well. And her powers were also a danger in themselves.

'We ordinary mortals can't imagine how hard Shar's life must be,' Fosker told Reyni gravely. 'She is so young, so inexperienced; and yet she is forced to bear the burden of these Chaos-inspired abilities, whether she wishes to or not. The Circle expect great things of her, and I'm sure they have the best intentions. But I think they demand too much. Shar is hardly more than a child – how can she have the self-control, the self-discipline, to use her powers wisely?' He sighed. 'Jonakar and Amobrel hoped that she would turn to the gods of Order and allow the influence of our lord Aeoris to guide her future path. But Chaos had – and has – too strong a hold on her. And now,' he indicated Gant's letter, the gist of which he had read to Reyni, 'this has happened. The Circle are stirring up an ancient contrivance that should have been left in obscurity, and Shar has become involved. The Maze could be very dangerous indeed, and for all her natural talent, I fear Shar may not be strong enough to cope with the forces it will unleash.' A pause. 'She needs help, Reyni. She needs *our* help.'

Reyni's face had grown more and more tense as he listened, and now he sat forward, clasping his hands together as though crushing something between the palms. 'Fosker, you know how fond I am of Shar. If there's anything at *all* I can do—'

This was exactly what Fosker had hoped to hear, and he smiled. 'There is. You are Shar's friend; she trusts you, and she will listen to you far more readily than she would to me, or to my cousin Gant, or to anyone else who is aware of the Maze's dangers. I'm going to write back to Gant and suggest that, as soon as the roads are clear of snow, I visit the castle, assess the situation for myself and offer my services in helping to persuade Shar to a wiser way of thinking. And I would like you, Reyni, to come with me.'

When Reyni had left the room, Fosker sat for a few minutes before the shrine. He was very pleased with what he had achieved, and reflected that it had been a satisfying day for the Keepers when Reyni had asked to join the cult. At the time Fosker had been newly appointed as leader; he had known the story of Reyni's involvement with Shar, and had a shrewd idea of how the young musician had been affected by the ordeal of his adventures. It was little wonder, he thought, that someone who had been so calculatingly and cynically used by the lords of Chaos should now turn against them and wish, as Fosker saw it, to devote himself to the true gods. He had welcomed Reyni to the Keepers' ranks, and Reyni had proved to be as dedicated a follower as anyone could wish. Fosker had thought from the start that he would be an asset to them. But now it seemed he might prove to be more of an asset than anyone could have known.

He moved from the bench and knelt down before the shrine. Closing his eyes, he visualised Aeoris of Order; tall and ascetic with his white hair and golden, pupilless eyes; and he spoke aloud, though softly.

'Great Lord Aeoris, I offer humble thanks for your guidance, and I ask that you will look kindly on our endeavour. I pledge that I will do all within my power to kindle the light of Order in the heart of our sister Shar, and bring her to enlightened understanding and the way of the true gods.'

He bowed his head until his brow touched the floor, then rose to his feet, took three respectful paces backwards, and quietly left the room.

6

It was easy to put Hestor off the scent. In that sense Gant had done Shar a favour, for Hestor was appalled when he heard what Kitto had discovered, but believed Shar's declaration that she wouldn't risk any more experiments.

Despite her pretended bravado, Shar spent the next two days in a state of suppressed anxiety that Gant would, after all, act on what he had found out. She didn't dare try the new experiments she had planned, and was in dread of a summons from the senior adept or even from the High Initiate. But no summons came. She saw Gant only once, at a lecture that she couldn't find an excuse not to attend; but he didn't speak to her at all.

By the third day her confidence was coming back and with it her impatience. She couldn't wait any longer. Tonight, she would attempt to open the Maze again – without the amulet.

One of the junior initiates was celebrating her birth-anniversary, and a party had been arranged in the dining hall. A winter rheum was going round the castle, but everyone who wasn't too stricken with sneezing and snuffling was invited, and to cover her tracks Shar joined in the fun for a few hours. Then, as the festivities started to get raucous (the younger guests were bellowing out popular songs by this time, to the horror of anyone with an ear for music), she slipped away unnoticed and went to her room. Hestor and Kitto had both been drinking apple-brew and were caught up in the cheerful mêlée of a snake-dance down the length of the hall, so they wouldn't miss her and come searching. The party would go on until everyone dropped from exhaustion, while the older and staider castle inhabitants went to bed and tried to ignore the din. It was an ideal opportunity.

But within two hours, Shar's soaring hopes had crashed to the ground. For no matter what she did or how hard she strove, she could not make the Maze work.

She had begun by trying, as before, to transport herself from her room directly to the Maze's gateway out on the rock stack. She wasn't especially disappointed when the attempt failed; it was, perhaps, over-ambitious to expect to open the Maze from a distance when she had no amulet to help her. So, still in her party clothes to avert suspicion, she made her way outside, across the courtyard and through the postern gate. By the light of the moons, which turned the sea and the sharp frost to a silver panorama, she stepped into the bright grass rectangle and focused her will.

Nothing happened. At first, Shar flatly refused to accept it; inwardly railing, she persevered, using every mental trick her mind could conjure. But at last she was forced to admit defeat. She couldn't do it. Without an amulet, the Maze simply would not work.

Bitterly disappointed, and chilled to the marrow, Shar returned to the castle as the first moon started to sink below the horizon. The dining hall windows still blazed with light, and the noise of the party echoed across the courtyard, making her want to storm in and stamp and shout at all her friends for being so crass. She forced the desire down, and took a roundabout way back to her room. Two cats followed her but she shut her door in their faces, and when Amber greeted her affectionately she hardly acknowledged him. It wasn't *fair*. She was a Daughter of Storms, she was a Dark Caller; she was *special*. The Maze *should* have worked for her, and the fact that it had not felt like a personal insult.

Shar slumped down on her bed and stared miserably at the window. Her fire was almost out but she couldn't be bothered to rake up the embers and put on more fuel. Let her bones freeze. She didn't care.

She thought about Adept Gant. Had he set a

watcher to trap her elemental friends if they tried to take the amulet again? Hestor thought it was likely; much too likely to be worth the risk. But Shar was less sure. After all, two nights had passed without any attempt being made, so Gant had probably relaxed his guard. And tonight, with the party in full swing, he had something else to distract his grumbling attention. Yes, Shar acknowledged, it *was* a risk. But just this once, it was worth taking.

So again she called to the creatures of air and earth, and again she charged them to fetch the amulet to her. When they had gone, she sat down on her bed and tried to concentrate on a calming exercise, but she had barely begun when, unexpectedly, the elementals returned.

Shar knew immediately that something was wrong. The creatures were agitated; the air elemental darted wildly about the room, and its high, piercing whistles clashed with harsh rumblings from the earth being, like the sound of boulders being rolled down a hill. It took her some while to calm them enough to communicate sensibly, but when she finally did understand what had upset them, her fears were confirmed.

They could not bring her the amulet. Someone had set up a psychic field around it that the elementals were unable to penetrate; they had tried, but had been rebuffed. They were sorry, sorry, sorry; they did not want to disappoint their friend; they did not want to let her down; they would not have—

Shar silenced and soothed them, assuring them that they were not to blame. Briefly she wondered if the fire or water beings might do better, but that idea was a nonsense; they were no more powerful than their cousins. Very well, then. She would have to resort to something more drastic.

She dismissed the elementals, with more reassurances, then stood in the middle of the room, thinking hard. In the back of her mind she had formulated a plan for this circumstance. But though in theory it was a good plan, putting it into practice would take a great deal of nerve, for it meant making contact with creatures of a much higher order. She had never tried such a working before, and though she believed she could do it safely, the belief had yet to be proved.

Well, there's only one way to prove it, isn't there? Firmly, Shar visualised a cloak falling away from her shoulders; a cloak made up of her qualms and uncertainties. Nothing venture, nothing have, as the saying went. Water would be her best choice. Water elementals were the surest diviners of information, and they also tended to be gentler than the rest, which might be just as well.

She fetched her workbox. This time she would take all the proper precautions, including the drawing of a circle to protect herself. And Amber must be put out of the room. Like all cats he detested water, and he might easily disrupt the ritual at the wrong moment. So: chalk, her small silver chalice, a glass rod to use as a wand. Water in the chalice, of course; she must have a medium through which the creature she summoned could manifest. No incense, for incense needed fire to burn it and an elemental of this kind would not tolerate fire's presence. Shar rolled back her rugs; beginning at the western quarter of the room she carefully chalked a circle on the floor, then set everything ready on a table at its centre. Amber did not like it when she picked him up and put him outside, but Shar ignored his protests and closed the door firmly in his indignant face. All ready. Now, she must rally her courage.

Standing before the table, with the glass rod held in both hands, Shar closed her eyes and began to focus her mind. She had snuffed out all the candles and the darkness seemed to squeeze and crush in beyond the shutters of her eyelids; she could *feel* it, like a huge, muffling, almost threatening presence. *No. Not threatening. There's no threat. You can do this.*

She took several deep, steadying breaths, and her mind formed images of water: the sea; a river; rain; a vast, still lake. She tried to see the lake as blue, but against her will it kept turning to an ominous grey-green, which she had to fight to return it to the shade she wanted. The temperature in the room was dropping now, and there was a damp feeling in the air. That surprised her, for usually there were no outward signs until the proper summoning began. But no matter; if the elementals were to come easily, that was all to the good.

She started to sway. The movement was slight at first, but as the rhythm of it took hold, it became more and more exaggerated. *The roll of a gentle tide, the smooth flow of a stream, the undulating veils of soft, grey squalls blowing in from the sea* . . . Shar moved as though under water, slowly, fluidly; and silently she began to repeat the words that would call the water-being to her.

The cold was so intense now that it clamped down on her skin. She felt herself start to shiver and resolutely controlled the reaction. *Concentrate.* She could sense something coming, getting nearer and nearer, and her lips parted, mouthing the silent invocation. *Over and again; over and again; keep repeating, keep willing, again, again, again* . . .

It happened so fast that Shar was taken completely by surprise. There was a rush of noise – it was a warning, but too sudden for her to assimilate it in time – and then a stunningly violent physical shock, as though she had plunged with terrific force into ice-cold water. She staggered, arms flailing wildly in a bid to stay upright. Then the shock rolled over her and away, and, gasping, heart thundering, she regained her balance and opened her eyes.

She was soaking wet. Her clothes were saturated through to the smallest stitch, and water ran down her face and from the bedraggled ends of her hair, which was plastered to her skull. She looked, and felt, as if she had spent two hours in a drenching downpour, and her mouth opened and shut like a landed fish as she stared through water-blurred eyes at the sight confronting her.

The room was alive with rippling reflections. They danced across the walls, shimmered coldly on the floor and ceiling, and writhing within them were vague, sinuous shapes that eluded her gaze whenever she tried to look at them. Invisible currents stirred the air, pushing gently but irresistibly at her so that she swayed back and forth under their pressure.

At the edge of the circle she had drawn, a creature was staring down at her.

Later, Shar couldn't even begin to conjure the image of it to her mind again. It was huge; as high as the ceiling and as wide as the wall; and it gave the terrifying impression that what her eyes could see was only a paltry fragment of the whole. It had scales, and it had fins, and there were tendrils like seaweed flowing from it – but its shape was so alien that it defied any comparison with an earthly creature. Even in the bleak, unmapped northern ocean that lay beyond the Star Peninsula's horizon, nothing as strange as this could exist. And it was powerful. *Very* powerful.

As though it had read her mind, the elemental shifted, sending a new tide of ripples through the room, and the two shining circles that Shar could only presume were its eyes glowed with a cold, liquid light. She felt it touch her mind, probing, exploring, and with a fresh shock she realised that she had dropped her mental guard and was horribly vulnerable. The circle on the floor gave her some protection, but if the being should choose to attack her, she had no other defences ready.

Hastily, she snatched up the glass wand and raised it before her own face, visualising a blue light radiating out from it and blocking the elemental's probing. The sensation in her head faded, but the feeling of cold increased, and now it carried a tinge of impatience and anger.

Then, in her mind, a single word formed.

WHY?

It wasn't so much a question as a demand, and Shar shuddered inwardly. The elemental clearly resented having been called into the mortal world, and wanted to know the reason for the summons. She must take control, show no sign of weakness. This creature was nothing like her friends the lower beings. It was *dangerous*.

Licking her lips, which were very dry, strangely, considering that the rest of her was drenched through, Shar squared her shoulders and tilted her chin.

'I require knowledge,' she said, in a clear, authoritative voice. 'I have called you because you have the power to gain that knowledge for me, and I charge you to obey me submissively and without deception.' Yes, *yes*; she could see the blue light shining from her wand now. Her will was rallying, strengthening.

For a few moments the elemental did not respond. Then it writhed in the air, and Shar felt a cold, prickling sensation crawl over her skin.

She looked quickly down at herself. Water was oozing from her clothes again, dripping on to the floor, and also streaming from her hair and into her eyes. Beyond the circle, the rest of the room seemed to be filling up with water, as though a silent, deadly flood were flowing in under the door. Shar knew it was an illusion, but the sight was no less terrifying for that. The being was trying to intimidate her, and if she didn't resist, she would lose the battle of wills.

'No,' she said firmly, calmly. 'I am not afraid of you. I am a Daughter of Storms and a Caller of the Dark, and those gifts were granted to me by Yandros of Chaos. I am stronger than you are. And I will be obeyed!'

For the space of three heartbeats she thought the

elemental would not yield. It seemed to swell, inflating itself like the poisonous bloat-fish that lived in the clear seas around Summer Isle, and the illusory water heaved like a huge wave rising. On the brink of panic, Shar thrust all the mental energy she could summon into the glass wand and the protecting circle. Blue light flared – she could physically see it now – and the blue was tinged with red tongues of flame.

There was a savage hiss, like steam. The vision of the flooded room faded and vanished, and the elemental shrank back to its former size. Its alien eyes glared at Shar, and she heard its voice in her mind again.

WHAT?

She had won. Relief tied a knot in her stomach and she gulped a breath, tasting brine in the air. The water elemental pulsed and rippled, but its movements were submissive now, and anger had subsided into sulky resentment.

Shar smiled triumphantly, and spoke. 'I want you to discover for me how the amulet that opens the Maze is made. I want to know every detail, and how I might make one for myself.'

New ripples shimmered across the wall, and the elemental replied sullenly, *WHAT YOU ASK IS NOT EASY. THE AMULET IS PROTECTED NOW.*

'Then you must find another way to give me what

I want,' Shar told it. 'Seek out the papers that hold the secret. Show them to me when I sleep, and put the knowledge they give into my mind.' She paused, to add emphasis to her next words. 'This is my will, and you *must* obey.'

There was a soft sigh, like a tide-surge, and the elemental replied, *VERY WELL. THIS I CAN DO.*

Shar smiled again. 'Then I ask nothing more, and I give you leave to depart to your own world.' She spread her arms, adopting a ritual stance. 'Go, with my thanks – in the name of Yandros and in the name of Aeoris.'

The being's strange, deep eyes gazed back at her for a moment. Then it faded and was gone. The rippling reflections vanished from the walls, and the temperature in the room rose noticeably

Shar let out a vast sigh. Her nerves were still jangling, but overtaking that feeling was a sense of elation. She had summoned a far more powerful elemental than she had ever tried to call before, and controlled it. The working had had its hazards, as her sodden clothes testified, but she had won the first tussle and after that there had been no trouble. Now, it only remained to see if the creature could carry out its task.

She had started to shiver, not with reaction but with the plain, down-to-earth effects of wet and cold. Quickly she lit some candles, then pulled off her clothes and rubbed herself dry with a towel before putting on her warmest robe. A piqued howl outside the door told her that Amber was still there; she let him in and he prowled the room suspiciously, tail swishing, pausing every few moments to give her a reproachful look. Pictures came to her from his mind, but they didn't make much sense. Shar talked soothingly to him, gave him a titbit she had brought from the dining hall earlier, and by the time she had put away the chalice and wand, he had forgiven her enough to settle down on her bed and begin a thorough wash.

Shar hoped her excitement would not keep her awake. Water elementals worked through dreams; if she was to have the information she wanted, then she needed to sleep. Get warm, think of something calming and dull. Tomorrow's studies; that should do the trick.

Amber yawned, and it made Shar yawn too. She blew out the candles, lay down and closed her eyes.

The rain began soon after Shar had fallen asleep. It was unusual for the far north to have such a heavy deluge at this time of year, and it showed no signs of stopping. The first roar of thunder came an hour later and was loud enough to wake a number of the castle's inhabitants. Several went to their windows, thinking that this was no ordinary storm but a supernatural

Warp, yet there were no wheeling bands of colour in the sky, and no high, wailing shriek that always heralded a Warp's approach. With wry thoughts about yet another disturbance so close on the heels of the party in the great hall, people returned to their beds.

Shar did not wake – but she was not in her bed. Instead, she was sitting at the study-table near the fireplace in her room, with paper and stylus in front of her. Her eyes were closed, her breathing shallow and rapid, and she was writing on the paper at a speed that would have astounded her tutors. From the bed, Amber watched her puzzledly, but his occasional mewing queries brought no response.

Shar had no conscious knowledge of what she was doing. She was sound asleep. When at last her stylus wavered to a stop and slipped from her grasp, she rose, like someone in a trance, tidied the sheets of paper neatly, and walked calmly back to bed.

She did wake, finally, to the sound of the rain streaming on to stonework and gurgling in the castle's gutters. Heavy cloud made the room look gloomy and unwelcoming, and when she sat up Shar couldn't at first disentangle the real world from the tatters of half-remembered dreams.

Then dream and reality separated and became clearer, and her eyes widened as she looked at her study-table.

Papers . . . They hadn't been there last night. And

there was a stylus on the floor, lying where it had rolled off the table top.

Shar scrambled out of bed and ran across the room. Five sheets of paper had been filled with close, careful writing, in a script that wasn't her own. She looked at the first sheet, took in the gist of what it said, turned to the second with her pulse starting to race—

Yes! It was a formula, instructions, neatly and accurately set out, and complete in every detail. A magical formula. For the creation of an amulet.

Shar gripped the table edge to steady herself as dizzy excitement flooded her mind. She had what she wanted. It was *hers*. And nobody and nothing could stop her from using it.

She closed her eyes and let out a hissing breath that seemed to mingle with the noise of the rain.

'*Thank you*,' she whispered, thinking of the elemental. '*Oh, thank you!*'

7

'It's certainly unseasonal.' Neryon Voss looked out of his study window at the rain pelting down into the courtyard. 'In fact, I don't think I can remember ever seeing such a downpour at this time of year.'

Pellis Bradow Ennas, Hestor's mother, smiled wryly. 'Neither can I,' she said, 'and I'm a good few years older than you. Still, it'll help to melt the snow in the mountains. The passes will be open much earlier than usual.'

'Barring floods, landslips and anything else the elements decide to throw at them.' Neryon turned away from the window and flexed his shoulders, easing stiffness. 'If that *does* happen, I won't shed any tears. Open passes mean another kind of flood – all the early visitors who come to the castle petitioning for something, and think they're being clever by beating the rest to it. Which they're not, because the others have all had the same idea. Quite honestly, Pellis, that's something I could well do without. I've got more than enough to cope with as it is.'

Neryon was definitely not in a good mood this afternoon, Pellis thought. It wasn't surprising. The experiments with the Maze were taking up a lot of time and proving very frustrating; they had taken one step forward, with the first attempt to open it, but since then their efforts had achieved little. No one had yet succeeded in actually travelling through the gateway. They could see their destination, and be seen by others waiting there; but so far they had been unable to break the barrier and physically step into the new location. The castle's best minds were working on the problem – sorcerers, philosophers, historians, mathematicians; they were all devoting enormous energy to it – but they were baffled.

Neryon slapped a hand down on a sheaf of papers that lay on his desk. 'Look at these!' he added sourly. 'Letters announcing the arrival, as soon as the weather improves, of visitors from each and every province!'

'Well,' Pellis said gently, holding out some papers of her own, 'then perhaps I'd better just leave these for you to deal with later.'

'What? Oh, the Council meeting notes. Yes; put them on the desk, I'll get round to them. Have to, won't I? They include Adept Gant's latest complaints about the Maze, I suppose?'

'They do,' said Pellis dryly.

'Well, if our lack of progress continues, Gant will get his way in the end. That *galls* me. We call ourselves sorcerers, yet we can't even manage to—' Abruptly Neryon stopped and gave her a sheepish smile. 'I'm sorry; I shouldn't rant on. I'm as bad-tempered as a dog with toothache today, but there's no reason why anyone else should have to put up with my mood.' He sneezed suddenly. 'I think I'm going down with this rheum that's spreading round the castle. That's *just* what I need!'

'If it forces you to rest, it might be a blessing in disguise,' said Pellis. 'You work too hard.'

'Maybe. But there's thin chance of that improving in the near future,' Neryon rejoined. 'Some success with the Maze, Pellis. That's what would make a difference.' He sneezed again, then sighed. 'It would make all the difference in the world.'

The rain still hadn't stopped after two days. Shar was secretly a little thrilled by the thought that the elemental she had summoned had had this effect on the weather; the fact that she could control such a powerful creature proved – to her – that her magical skills were a force to be reckoned with. The only disappointment was that she dared not broadcast her success. Tempting though it was to at least tell Hestor, she had to keep her pledge of secrecy; anything else was simply too risky.

Besides, she had other preoccupations, and now they had taken on a new urgency. The elemental had given her the secret of the amulet, and after a day and night studying the information on her sleep-written pages, she was almost ready to attempt to create one of her own.

Almost: for one piece of the puzzle didn't quite fit into place. The making of an amulet involved sorcery. Shar had expected that and the ritual didn't look too difficult. But in the instructions for performing the rite was a cryptic reference to a 'gate' that did not seem to mean the Maze itself. The writings implied that this gate was somewhere in the castle, but did not say whereabouts. All Shar had to guide her was a brief and almost careless remark about a black circle, and the enigmatic statement that: 'the Speaking of the Way should not be performed, lest the gods should be displeased by such a trivial usage; for this purpose it is sufficient merely to enter the circle'.

Shar had no idea what the Speaking of the Way was, nor could she think of any black circles anywhere in the castle. Considering that the castle itself was built from black stone, it seemed highly unlikely that black would ever have been chosen to mark any special place within it. Yet the black circle must be here somewhere, and the casual reference suggested that it was well known to senior adepts. That was what Shar found so frustrating. If the senior adepts knew about the black circle, it should be the simplest thing in the world to find out by asking. But she couldn't ask. For one thing, they would probably say that the information was not to be given to junior initiates in case they should use it wrongly. But more importantly, her query would have an all-too-obvious connection with the Maze experiments. The seniors would draw the obvious conclusion, and that would be the end of her hopes.

She must therefore solve the conundrum of the black circle for herself, and the most obvious place to look for the answer was the castle's library, in its vaulted chamber below the west wing.

Over the next five days Shar spent every spare hour in the library. If the seniors were surprised to see her there, rummaging on shelves or sitting at a table and poring over some old book or manuscript, they didn't show it. One tutor made a passing comment that it was refreshing to see a junior applying herself so eagerly to her studies, but no one suspected anything untoward. There was no reason for suspicion, for Shar was searching mostly through volumes of the castle's history.

And they produced nothing of any use whatever.

Hestor and Kitto, who knew Shar much better than anyone else did, might have wondered what was afoot, but at present they were both too busy with their own concerns to pay much attention to hers. Hestor was having trouble with his studies. He was trying to learn a particularly difficult exercise in trance inducement, and so far the knack of it eluded him. The fact that Shar had mastered it at her first attempt rankled just a little, and until he could match her skill, it suited him not to see her too often. Kitto, meanwhile, was spending every waking hour – or so he grumbled – working. He was now, officially, an ostler, entrusted with the care of the castle's horses. If the thaw meant visitors, visitors meant extra horses, and horses must have stabling and feed. So, under the severe eye of the head groom, the ostlers were checking stores, cleaning disused stalls, getting everything ready for the expected rush. Kitto's days were an unbroken round of work, food and whatever sleep he could get, and he had no time to spare for himself, let alone for anyone else.

The first trickle of new arrivals began on the sixth day after the rain finally stopped. The first party consisted of dignitaries from Empty Province, while the second was a group of very senior Sisters. Faced with these notables to entertain, Neryon reluctantly decided that the Maze experiments must be abandoned until the Circle could ensure some uninterrupted peace and quiet, and ordered that the small lecture hall should be set aside and made ready for a private banquet.

And that, unexpectedly, led to the solving of Shar's puzzle.

Adept Farial Brynd Dorien had been due to give a

talk and demonstration to a group of junior initiates in the lecture hall. Adept Farial was one of the Circle's finest and most respected teachers, and her lessons were too important to cancel. So, with nowhere else available, her students found themselves filing down the narrow passage from the library that led to the Marble Hall.

The Marble Hall lay deep underground, and this was the only way to reach it. The gods had also created the Hall when the castle was built, and it was believed that it did not quite exist in the same space and time as the rest of the mortal world. Certainly its dimensions seemed too huge to be contained within the castle's foundations; though its true size was impossible to judge by eye, for it was filled with a soft but dense mist that hid its boundaries from view. According to one legend, the Hall could not be measured; anyone who tried would find themselves returning to the point where they'd started, and be none the wiser.

There was a sharp aura of excitement as Adept Farial opened the Hall's door. The students stepped through and the mist swirled to meet them; it shone with soft, pastel colours that cast shadows where shadows should not be. A stone forest of tall, pale pillars reached up towards the indiscernible ceiling, and the mosaic pattern of the floor seemed to move and change with a vitality of its own.

Whispering voices fell silent, and the only sound

was the faint shuffle of feet on the floor. They had all seen the Marble Hall before, at their rank initiation ceremonies, but to perform magical work here was strictly forbidden to all but the most experienced adepts. Shar and Hestor, though, had broken that rule more than once, and Shar felt a thrill of memory go through her as she gazed around. Hestor was not here today. She couldn't decide whether she was sorry or glad.

Adept Farial called the group around her. 'Because the lecture hall is needed for other purposes, the High Initiate has consented to allow this lesson to take place here,' she said. 'I don't need to tell you that this is a very rare privilege for lowly juniors', a smile caught at the edges of her mouth and there was a murmur of laughter, 'and it seems only sensible to make the most of it. So instead of my planned lecture on ritual technique, I'm going to teach you about the Marble Hall itself; its history, its powers and its properties. You won't be in a position to make use of the Hall for a good few years yet, but I see no reason why you shouldn't begin to learn about it now. If nothing else, it will help you to understand the traditions and principles of the Circle; and it will also help your knowledge of history, which from what I hear will be no bad thing!'

More laughter. Shar joined in, but she was only half-listening. She could hear – or rather feel, for it wasn't quite an audible noise — a slow, deep rhythm that seemed to be coming from below her feet. It was almost as if somewhere under the floor a very large animal was breathing. *In . . . out. In . . . out.* It sent a prickling chill through her, but when she glanced cautiously at her companions none of them seemed aware of it.

She mentally shook herself and tried to ignore it. Probably it was nothing more than her own pulse in her ears. Maybe she was catching the rheum. She had sneezed several times this morning.

Adept Farial was leading her class across the hall now. Ahead of them darker shapes loomed in the mist, and as they drew closer, the shapes resolved into seven towering statues. Each depicted two figures standing back to back, and another shiver, of excitement this time, went through Shar as she looked up at the stone faces of the central statue. Yandros of Chaos and Aeoris of Order; and beside them, the forms of their six fellow gods, each one paired with his counterpart. She could put names to two more of them now, and her gaze moved to the sharp-boned face and narrow, feline eyes of Tarod, Yandros's brother. But for Tarod, she would be dead and the Circle would know nothing about the Maze . . .

Adept Farial was continuing her talk. 'These statues of the gods were carved two hundred years ago, when Equilibrium was first established,' she told them.

'They replaced seven much older and cruder carvings, but no one knows for sure whether those ancient figures depicted the Lords of Order or the Lords of Chaos.'

Someone spoke up. 'Is it true, Adept, that before Equilibrium no one knew what the gods looked like?'

'Yes, it is,' said Farial. 'In those days, of course, only the lords of Order were worshipped, but still no one had ever seen Lord Aeoris or any of his brothers, for they hadn't taken any hand in human affairs for centuries. It was only when Chaos returned and Equilibrium began that our ancestors had any direct contact with the gods at all.'

One of the girl students sighed. 'I wonder who the first person was who actually *saw* all fourteen of the gods,' she said, half to herself. 'I think I should probably die if it happened to me.'

Farial turned to look at her. 'It was Keridil Toln, the High Initiate of the time,' she said. 'He guided and instructed the sculptors when they carved these figures.' She smiled. 'And he certainly didn't die of it; in fact he lived to a very great age.'

They continued along the row of statues, and after a few moments Farial went on.

'You've all learned about Keridil Toln in your history studies, of course, and about the tremendous changes that took place in his time. But there's one point of interest that your tutors probably haven't mentioned.' She stepped up to the plinth of the furthest statue, and pointed to something cut into its base.

'Most people don't notice these when they look at the statues; they are concentrating on the figures of the gods, and that's as it should be. However, I want you to see them. Gather round and look closely.'

Carved on the plinth was a symbol that Shar recognised immediately as the sign of the element of fire. As she crouched to see better, Farial indicated three more of the statues and said, 'Each brother of Lord Aeoris or Lord Yandros has a special affinity with an element or natural force. You'll see that Fire, Air, Water and Earth are represented on the bases of these four figures. But I wonder if any of you recognise the other two sigils?'

The four statues that Farial had pointed to did not include the figure of Tarod of Chaos, and suddenly, for no apparent reason, Shar's pulse started to quicken. Trying to seem casual she crossed to where Tarod's statue stood and looked at the symbol carved there.

'Do you recognise it?' Adept Farial asked.

Shar didn't; to the best of her knowledge she had never seen it before, and she shook her head.

Farial smiled. 'Few people would now; it's fallen into disuse since Keridil Toln's day. But when he was High Initiate, this sign was used to denote Time.'

Something inside Shar seemed to lock up, constricting her stomach, and her mind jumped back to her experiments with the Maze. She believed that it could be used to transcend time . . . and now she knew that time was the special domain of Tarod of Chaos. This was not a coincidence. It *couldn't* be!

She heard herself speak, though the words didn't come consciously. 'We learn to control elementals . . . does that mean we could control time, too?'

Farial laughed. 'If we could, then no one has ever discovered how! No, Shar; I don't believe that's possible. Anyway, we don't really *control* elementals, do we? We command and manipulate them, but that isn't quite the same thing. If time can be controlled at all, I think only the gods have that power.'

They spent a few more minutes by the statues, while Farial talked about elemental energies and how the Marble Hall could amplify them in sorcerous ritual. Shar pretended to listen, but her thoughts were spiralling in another direction as she mulled over this new discovery. Time, Lord Tarod, the Maze . . . it all tied together, she was certain of it. But how, and why?

At last Farial led her students away from the seven towering figures and towards another part of the Hall. Still distracted, Shar gazed down at the mosaic floor as she trailed at the rear of the group. The pattern of the mosaic was changing subtly, becoming smaller and more closely set, as if it were drawing in towards some central point. She noted the changes idly, not thinking anything of it, until, as her attention wandered back to the lecture, she heard what Farial was saying.

'. . . the Gate is reputed to stand at the exact centre of the Hall; though, as you know, legend has it that the Hall can't be measured and therefore its exact centre is impossible to judge.'

One word registered on Shar's mind. *Gate.* She stopped, staring at the senior adept, but before she could do or say anything, another student spoke up.

'Have *you* ever tried to measure the Hall, Adept?'

Farial's eyes glinted humorously. 'Yes.'

'What happened?'

'I failed, dismally. Which proves either that the legend is true, or that I'm a hopeless mathematician! However, that's by the by. As I was saying, this small and unremarkable-looking mark is the living heart of the Marble Hall, and thus of the castle itself. And it is far, far more than that – for this Gate, if opened, is the way to the realms of the gods themselves – the dimensions of Chaos and Order!'

There were murmurs, hisses of breath, even a soft whistle from someone in the group. But Shar did not hear them. Farial's words were reverberating in her mind. And her eyes were staring at the 'small and unremarkable-looking mark' to which the adept was pointing.

A mosaic circle. A *black* mosaic circle.

The constricting feeling came back then, with such force that it snatched the air from her lungs. She tried to breathe, couldn't; she put a hand to her throat but there was something else there and she couldn't swallow. Darkness surged before her eyes; the figures of her companions were fading, receding . . .

'Shar?' Farial saw what was happening and started towards her. 'Shar, whatever is it?'

Shar's face had turned dead-white. She tried to say that she was all right, but no sound came, and she *wasn't* all right; the Marble Hall was starting to turn and twist around her; her head was light and heavy at the same time, and she couldn't keep her balance.

Someone caught her under the elbows as she sagged like a sack of grain. Then Farial was there, kindly and efficient, feeling her brow, then the pulse behind her ears. Suddenly and violently Shar sneezed, and Farial's face blurred before her as her eyes started to water.

'Oh, dear,' said Farial. 'Another one for the infirmary, I think! Fenar, Kern, help me, please; that's it, support her shoulders . . . The rest of you wait by the door. We'll take her to Physician Eln, then we'll continue our lesson. Come along now, that's the way . . .'

Too dizzy to do anything but submit, Shar let herself be helped towards the door of the Marble Hall. She looked back once at the black circle, the

Gate. For a moment it seemed to her that there was something else there. A shadow, almost but not quite human-shaped, that wavered and flickered above the mosaic. It looked like . . . but no; it was gone, and all that remained was a dull aching in her head, and the sense of a rhythmic throbbing that pulsed through her in slow, deep, soundless waves.

8

It was nothing more serious than the rheum, Physician Eln said, but he excused Shar from her studies for a day or two and advised her to stay in bed until she felt better.

Shar was delighted to be excused from work – but she didn't take Eln's advice for long. When she woke the following morning, she was still sneezing and her nose and throat were sore. But her mind was clear, and she couldn't bear the thought of wasting a moment. So she ate breakfast in her room, took her prescribed herbal powder, then as soon as no one was around to see her, she dressed and went to the library.

She found what she wanted within minutes. It had been under her nose all the time; she had simply been looking in the wrong direction for it. A book containing nothing more than dry and dull lists of the rituals that should or should not be performed in the Marble Hall. Shar would never have thought to search here for her answers, but Adept Farial had given her the vital clue. Among the lists was a reference to the Gate — and to the Speaking of the Way.

The Speaking of the Way was, quite simply, the ritual that opened the Gate in the Marble Hall. Whether that Gate truly did connect to the realms of the gods, as Farial had said, Shar neither knew nor cared. All that mattered to her was that she had found the solution to the one obstacle that stood between her and an amulet of her own.

Out of sheer curiosity she went back to the shelves and looked for a text of the ritual itself, but it wasn't there. No doubt it was too powerful — or too dangerous — to be available for anyone to read. No matter; the instructions for making an amulet said, anyway, that it should not be performed. To stand in the circle was enough.

Shar left the library feeling keyed-up with antici-pation. Crossing the courtyard and going in at the main door, she met Hestor in the entrance hall.

'Shar!' He greeted her with a wry smile and held up a pile of study-papers. 'How are you feeling? I heard you'd caught the rheum.'

Shar returned the smile. 'It isn't serious. I'm a bit better today.'

'Oh — and I was just about to ask if I could spend some time with you, so I could catch it and get out of this work!' They fell into step together and he added, 'I seem to be immune to it, more's the pity. Half the senior adepts have gone down with it since the last Council meeting; even Neryon's got it now.'

'Really . . .' Shar registered this with sudden interest.

'And Mother wasn't feeling too good this morning, so I suspect she'll be next.'

Neryon *and* Pellis. This, Shar thought, was the best news she could have had. Or almost . . . 'I suppose Adept Gant's as fit as ever,' she said carelessly.

'Oh, yes.' Hestor grimaced. 'Nothing ever touches him; I think he just gives maladies one of his looks, and they're too frightened to go near him. Speaking of Gant, I've got a tutorial with him in a few minutes. Better go, or he'll have my hide for being late. See you later!'

Shar watched him hurry out of the double doors, then returned to her room, aware of a sharp feeling of exhilaration. If half the Council, including Neryon and Pellis, had fallen prey to the sickness, then Adept Gant and the rest of the seniors would be kept too busy attending to the increasing number of visitors to concern themselves with her. Also, she had Physician Eln's sanction to miss lessons for at least two days. It was the perfect opportunity, Shar thought. And she fully intended to make the most of it.

It wasn't as if she hadn't done it before, Shar told herself as she stood before the door of the Marble

Hall. Soon after she'd first come to the castle she had ventured here, without permission, in a bid to thwart her uncle's malevolent plans. But Hestor had been with her then; his presence had given her confidence. Now, alone and in the dead of night, the prospect of entering the Hall was far more daunting.

She reached out to the door, touched it. For a moment it resisted – then slowly and silently it swung open. Shar hesitated, half-afraid that once she entered the door might close and refuse to open again. But that was irrational. This wasn't a trap. The only danger lay in the twists and turns of her own imagination.

Or, more prosaically, in the possibility of being caught.

That thought spurred her on, and she stepped quickly over the threshold, letting the door ease back on its hinges. The mist came swirling to meet her, curving around her like the touch of gentle, spectral fingers; holding her breath and feeling like a swimmer under water, she forged into it, heading for where – if her memory was accurate – the black circle would be.

To her relief, she *had* remembered it rightly. Silence closed in eerily as she stood gazing down at the perfect dark ring, so incongruous in the pale mosaic of the rest of the floor. The thought that this might really be the gateway to the gods' own realms made her shiver, and she was suddenly glad that the seven statues were in another part of the Hall, invisible through the mist. She knew they were only stone, but the thought of the gods' carved faces watching her as she performed this working would have sapped her courage altogether.

She set down the satchel she was carrying, and began carefully to take out its contents and place them on the floor, well clear of the circle. Firstly, the papers she had written under the water elemental's influence. She had memorised the rite, every word and every action, but all the same it was reassuring to have the document here. Then her implements – a small crucible, a white cloth, and a piece of iron roughly the size and shape of her middle finger (easy to find; she had simply taken a scrap of a broken horseshoe from the forge beside the stables). It didn't seem possible that so much could be done with so little; but the formula stated clearly that this was all she would need.

Well, then: she was ready. Nerves were beginning to give way to excitement now, as Shar picked up the three articles. The crucible was to be placed in the black circle, near the edge, *so*. Then she must lay the white cloth over her right forearm, and take the piece of iron in her left hand, *so*. Standing at the edge of the circle, she closed her eyes, turned slowly, carefully, until her back was to the black mosaic, then steadied herself and took two smooth paces backwards.

Reflexively her eyelids started to flicker, and she

hastily squeezed them together again. The ritual was emphatic about that; she *must* keep her eyes closed, and could only trust that she was now standing on the black mosaic with the crucible to her left. Setting her feet a little apart, she prepared to begin. The rite was not to be spoken aloud, but must be repeated silently in her mind: she paused for a few seconds to clear her thoughts, then, slowly and carefully, began to project the words she had memorised.

'Lords of the day and lords of the night; lords of the dark and lords of the light; I, who am servitor and dominator both and in one, do call upon you to witness my task, and to hear and answer my petition . . .'

The phrasing was strange and old-fashioned, and Shar couldn't pretend that she understood all of it; but it didn't matter. Provided she made no mistake, it should work.

The broken horseshoe felt rough-edged and uncomfortable in her hand. It was also starting to feel unnaturally heavy – so heavy, in fact, that her arm was sagging. With an effort she raised it again, but the dragging weight was getting worse by the moment, and now it took a tremendous effort to hold the piece of iron steady. Whatever happened, she must not drop it! Shar clenched her teeth, only just remembering in time not to make a sound, and continued with the words of the rite.

Then, all around her, she started to feel heat. There

was a light rising behind her closed eyelids; not the gentle glow of the mists but something harsher, hellish red shot through with flashes of purple. A hissing crackle sounded in her ears, faint as yet but rapidly getting louder, interfering with her concentration. She was so *hot!*

She struggled on. *'Within me and without me are the boundaries that know no limitation; and as my will shall break all barriers, so do I command that my will be obeyed!'*

The iron was cutting into her hand. Slick wetness trickled between her clenched fingers – blood, her own blood – and the weight of the horseshoe piece was so enormous now; she would *have* to let it fall—

'I command, and I command!' Her mind screamed the next words of the ritual. *'Earth and fire, air and water, join and merge, and by my will effect the transmutation of dormancy into life and power and energy! In the names of Yandros and Aeoris; by the agencies of Chaos and of Order; I call you once and I call you twice and I call you three times! Awake to life! Awake!'*

A shrill, sweet note cut through the crackling – and the terrible weight in Shar's hand vanished. In the space of an instant the iron piece was suddenly so light that she could barely feel it; it was thistledown in her grasp, rising, floating, trying to escape from her hand and fly away up into the mist.

The ritual was working! Elation filled Shar; and now she was straining to hold her hand down as the piece of iron writhed with its own life-force. The blazing heat gave way to glorious cold, and the light glaring beyond her eyelids swirled blue and green and silver, as a great wind rushed over her and through her and past her, so exhilarating that she thought she would be snatched off her feet and whirled away with it. Somehow – she didn't know how – she held on to her reason, remembering the ritual, remembering what she must do. No more words now; her right arm moved convulsively and she swathed the white cloth over her left hand, wrapping the piece of iron (oh, and it had so *much* life now, so much energy!) in its folds. As the cloth covered it, the iron stopped trying to escape from her grip. Suddenly it was dormant again, just a thing, an object. But its shape had changed . . .

Then, the cloth caught fire. Or at least, that was how it seemed to Shar; scarlet light flared again beyond her eyelids, and she heard the sound of flames, smelled the stink of burning fabric. Hot, excruciating pain assailed her fingers, and she clamped her teeth together, telling herself desperately that it wasn't real, only the illusion of the magic. The instructions had warned her to expect this – but she hadn't thought it would hurt so much! *Hold on!* her willpower said, *hold on, it won't last, it can't last!*

The crucible – in the shock of the burning pain she had forgotten the crucible! With a quick, jerky movement Shar turned (don't drop the iron, whatever you do, don't drop it now!) and, calling on all the self-control she possessed, lowered it slowly, slowly to where the crucible should be – oh, please Yandros that she hadn't misjudged and couldn't find it!

She felt the rim of the crucible, and relief gave her renewed strength. Another fraction, get it absolutely right – and with a violent movement she let the iron and the burning cloth (which she knew wasn't really burning, but oh, how it *hurt!*) on to the dish.

There was an eruption of white-hot brilliance that sent her jolting back. The agony in her hand vanished, and a sound like a vast, metallic groan echoed through the Marble Hall. Shuddering, Shar froze motionless on the spot, her senses straining as she waited. If she had performed the ritual correctly, there should be one final sign before the amulet was complete.

The echoes of the groan faded away, and silence held for what seemed like a long, long time. Then, so softly that her ears could barely detect it, came a deep, soft sigh, followed by a gentle *click*.

It was over. For nearly a minute Shar didn't dare move, terrified that when she looked, she would find that she had failed. At last, though, she couldn't bear the suspense any longer. With a silent, fervent prayer, she opened her eyes.

The crucible was where she had placed it on the black mosaic. The white cloth, undamaged, lay in the dish, and something was wrapped in it. Heart lurching painfully, Shar dropped to a crouch and cautiously unfolded the fabric.

The horseshoe was a horseshoe no longer. It wasn't even a piece of iron now, but a fantastic blend of many different substances, some metallic, others that Shar couldn't recognise, all twisted and tempered into a delicate, tapering spiral. It shone faintly, reflecting the colours of the Marble Hall's mists, and when she reached out with a tentative hand (which, like the cloth, was unmarked), it was pleasantly warm to the touch.

Shar wanted to scream aloud with the joy of triumph, but instead she kept a sober hold on her excitement, reaching out again to pick up the amulet. It lay in her palm – joy surged again at the thought that it was hers, entirely *hers* – then she started to straighten up.

The floor under her feet seemed to lurch sideways. It was only a momentary giddiness, but enough to make her sway and blink. Then, as it passed and everything returned to normal, she froze, staring in shock.

There was someone else in the Hall! A figure, vague in the mist but unmistakable, was moving across the floor, coming towards her. Horrified, Shar thought wildly of hiding, but there was nowhere to conceal herself, and anyway if she moved now she would certainly be seen. It must be one of the senior adepts – she had gambled that none of them would come here at this hour, but now it seemed she had been wrong.

Then she had a second shock, as a faint, shimmering wall appeared around the black mosaic circle. It flickered and wavered like ghostly grey fire, distorting the scene beyond it, and particles of light streamed upwards through it, dancing and skimming on an invisible wind.

The circle, the Gate – something was happening to it! *What had she done?* Panicking, all thoughts of hiding forgotten, Shar opened her mouth to call to the adept for help.

There was no one there.

Shar clenched her teeth, trying to crush the panic down and think rationally. The particles of light in the ghost-flames around her were streaming faster now, and beyond them the mist seemed to be darkening, obscuring the Hall. Sick with fear at the thought of touching the ring of fire, yet equally afraid to stay where she was, Shar stretched out one hand, slowly, tentatively—

As she did so, a voice spoke clearly behind her.

'. . . *Hear me, o you princes. Hear me, you creators and contenders—*'

Shar whirled. At her back, outside the black circle and distorted by the shimmering flux, a woman was standing. Shar had a rapid impression of brown hair, a handsome if slightly heavy face, and intense grey eyes that were filled with anger and strain. She had never seen this person in her life before, and even as confusion spun in her head she realised that the woman was completely unaware of her.

The woman raised her hands in an unmistakably ritual movement. Her lips moved and, chillingly out of phase with the movements, Shar heard her words.

'I stand before you in this place and I walk towards you on this way. The way is long but the way is old, and the way is the way of power . . .

Even as she spoke, she was changing. As Shar stared, motionless and stunned, the brown hair became blonde, the grey eyes turned to blue, and there were hollow shadows around those eyes, like hideous bruises – and other bruises, too; real ones; on her face and neck and arms.

'With the feet that are my flesh I tread between dimensions, and I shall speak the way.'

She was so *thin* – and there was something in her hand; a wand; glowing—

'With the hand that is my flesh I reach out across the abyss, and I shall speak the way.'

There were two voices now, and the other was

a man's, whispering through the mist though Shar could see no one else.

'With the eyes that are the windows of my soul I look from world into world, and I shall speak the way.'

For no rational reason terror hit Shar then like a fist, and she cried out, *'No!'*

NONONONONO . . . The echoes rippled out-wards. And the woman was no longer there.

Then, from somewhere in the distance, quick footsteps sounded on the marble floor, and another voice called sharply, 'Tarod!'

'What?' Shar turned round so fast that she almost lost her balance. But her momentary hope and dread that she would see the Chaos lord stalking towards her collapsed. There *was* someone there, but it was not Yandros's brother. A man, tall and fair, wearing purple robes and a cloak made from gold thread . . . He was crossing the Hall at an angle to where she stood, and in one hand he held a heavy, dully gleaming sword. Faint sounds of a dirge-like chant drifted from an invisible distance; then came a cry of pain, abruptly cut off . . .

Shar's heart was banging so hard that it felt as if her ribs would break, and she clutched the newly made amulet until its edges cut into her hand. *What was happening to her*? This wasn't her world, the real world; it couldn't be! Strange voices, strange faces – there was another man in the mist; he looked like Neryon, but he was not Neryon . . . An old woman in the white robe of the Sisterhood hurried across the floor with a rapid *pit-pat* of feet. And there was Hestor, surely it was Hestor; but he looked younger, no more than twelve years old—

Then, as suddenly and as swiftly as they had appeared, all the confusion of people vanished. In their place, a group of men and women were gathered a short distance away. They stood in a circle, hands linked, and a different chant from the dirge Shar had heard earlier murmured through the Hall. Peculiar lights danced around them. And one man looked very familiar.

'Uncle Thel . . . ?' Shar's stunned hiss whispered flatly into the mist and was swallowed without an echo. It *was* her uncle, Thel Starnor. But Thel was dead.

Like Lias Alborn . . .

Slowly then the incredible truth dawned. She was seeing through Time itself – all those people were from the past; a past she had never known but which was unravelling before her like a forgotten tapestry. She could have been looking at men and women from centuries ago; from before the age of Equilibrium even began.

But this newest tableau was not from that ancient time; for with a certainty that brought sickness rising in her throat, Shar recognised two more of the chanting figures.

One was Lemor Carrick, who had been her uncle's accomplice in his plot to destroy the High Initiate. While the other . . .

He had died when Shar was only a baby, killed by Thel and the death made to look like an accident. A magical accident, when a ritual performed in the Marble Hall had gone horribly wrong. Shar did not remember him. But she had seen his picture.

She was about to witness the murder of her own father.

9

It was all unfolding with such horrible inevitability
that for several minutes Shar could only stand staring
in appalled silence from her vantage point in the black
circle. She could hear the adepts' chants, even make
out some of the words; and she saw that Thel and
Lemor had now moved to stand on either side of
her father. The rest of the group had no idea that
anything deadly was going to happen. But Shar knew.
And there was nothing in the world she could do to
prevent it.

Was there? The thought struck like an ice-dagger
in her vitals, and suddenly her paralysis was broken as
it slammed home. This was no longer history – it was
taking place here, now! Time had shifted out of phase,
and with its shifting the past could surely be altered!

She didn't stop to consider the foolishness, even
the danger, of what she was doing. A huge emotion
had welled up in her; fear and fury and a wild desire
to protect the father she had never known, and she
acted on it. Uttering a cry that contained all the

passion bursting to life in her, she launched herself at the ghostly fire-wall, clawing at it as though it were solid, and not caring if it burned and consumed her.

'*FATHER!*'

She flung herself through, out of the circle — and a blast of clear light exploded against her eyes. Shar's warning turned to a scream; she staggered backwards, covering her face, dropping the amulet as the brilliance blinded her—

And found herself on her knees on the hard, cold floor of the Marble Hall, with silence all around.

Her hands fell away from her face. Glaring colours danced before her eyes, the aftermath of the flash's effect, and for several seconds she couldn't see anything but their mad patterns. At last, though, they began to fade, and with dread in her heart she dared to look up.

The adepts were gone. There was only the swirling, pastel mist, calm and gentle and untroubled. When she looked over her shoulder she saw the mosaic circle behind her, with the white cloth and the crucible lying where she had left them. The spectral flames and the streaming lights had vanished. And she knew with a sure intuition that the rift in Time had vanished with them.

Shar made a choking sound and climbed to her feet. She had been so *close* — one more minute, just one, and she might have changed the tragedy of the past. Now, instead, she had been hurled back to the present and everything was as it had always been. Her father was dead. Thel Starnor had succeeded, and her chance was lost.

Then she saw the amulet. It was lying on the floor a few paces away, and a wild hope leaped. When she had dropped it – that, surely, had been the moment when the door to the past had closed!

Shar scrabbled across the mosaic and snatched up the amulet. Nothing happened. The scene before her did not change, and her hope turned to anguish.

'No!' She hissed the denial, her fingers tightening on the metallic spiral. Focusing every shred of concentration she willed the amulet to work, to lift back the curtain between present and past again. She could see the image in her mind, it was clear, it was strong—

Still nothing happened. And at last Shar had no choice but to admit defeat.

She sat back on her heels, a sob clogging in her throat. The amulet didn't even feel warm any more; it was just an inanimate object, and at this moment it didn't even matter to her that the ritual had succeeded and she had gained this precious treasure.

She was shivering with reaction now. The air in the Hall felt very cold, and the mists looked deeper and darker than they had done before. Suddenly Shar wanted to run to the sanctuary of her room, where Amber would be waiting and everything was safe and familiar. She picked up the crucible, steeling herself to cross the boundary of the circle again, and wrapped it and the amulet in the cloth. Then she turned and with slow, dragging steps walked away from the black mosaic, towards the door. On the threshold she looked back, one last spark of hope flickering. The Marble Hall was quiet, undisturbed, empty.

Fighting back tears, Shar closed the door and returned to the library. The vault felt bitterly cold, emphasising the smell of musty damp. She picked up the lantern she had left on a table and opened the door that led to the stairs.

The door creaked back, and a second glimmer of light showed in the stairwell.

Shar snapped out of her apathy, and reflex made her shrink away from the door, swinging her own lantern out of sight behind her. Tense, she listened. Was that faint sound a footstep? It came again, and this time there could be no doubt. Someone was coming down to the library vault.

Shar had no time for questions such as *who* and *why*. All she knew was that she was on the verge of being caught, and that she had no chance of talking her way out of the situation. She acted on pure instinct. Her hand clenched the amulet, and the image of her own bedroom flashed into her mind. It was desperate, it was haphazard, and if she had been able to think rationally she wouldn't even have tried it. But there was no time for think-ing.

The amulet pulsed in her hand, and the scene before her contorted. With a giddying lurch the library vanished. There was a hurtling rush of noise, colours, sensations – then ice-cold air snatched her breath away and she saw the chilly glitter of a clear, frosty night, and the castle walls black against a sky filled with stars.

The stack – she was on the stack, in the Maze itself – but nothing was real, nothing was solid—

The world lurched again. The stars and the castle's dark bulk shattered into fragments and whirled away. And Shar, her balance gone, staggered across a car-peted floor and collapsed on her own bed.

In the Marble Hall, a solitary figure gazed into the slowly moving mists, eyes and ears attuned as he searched for a sign that someone else was or had been there. Nothing disturbed the quiet, and after a minute or two Adept Gant pursed his lips and withdrew, closing the door carefully behind him.

There was a frown on his face as he walked back to the library. The divination he had performed a short time ago had warned him that something was awry in the Marble Hall, and, though the details had been vague, he was certain that Shar was involved. But it seemed he had arrived too late to catch her.

What had the wretched girl been doing? There was

no sign of any trouble or disturbance; the Hall was as quiet as usual. But Gant had a sure instinct for trouble, and it was working now. Something was in the wind. He was sure of it. And with patience – and possibly a little help from his cousin Fosker – he would find out what it was.

Seven vast, crystalline prisms rotated slowly in a sky the colour of blood. The light they cast hurled spears of brilliance in every direction, and created stunning rainbow reflections in the range of glass mountains far, far below. At the foot of the mountains, the landscape changed constantly: one moment it was a huge chequerboard of purple and blue; the next, a forest of black trees with silver leaves that clashed and sang in an eerie chorus; the next, a roaring, molten sea. In the heavens, bizarre creatures floated on ever-shifting winds, darting around and between the prisms as they played strange games of their own invention.

Here in the realm of Chaos, where no living mortal had ever set foot and survived, anything was possible. This world's wonders – and horrors – were limited only by the imaginations of its seven gods, and Yandros in particular loved variety and was easily bored. So greatly did his world change and shift and mutate with his changing moods that most of the changes went unnoticed by the Chaos lords.

So when a rift first appeared in one of the glass mountains, and a new river started to flow through the rift, Yandros and his brothers were not even aware of its presence. The river was not of water, and it flowed in mid-air rather than along the ground. Its colours were strange even by Chaos's standards, and there were voices in it, calling, singing, whispering. Soon, it attracted a horde of the tiny, mindless elementals that flitted freely between the supernatural worlds. These creatures were childishly curious about any novelty, and they flew and danced around it like brilliant fireflies, gathering in greater and greater numbers until they formed a second sparkling river beside the first.

If it hadn't been for the elementals, the river would not have attracted Tarod's attention. But he noticed the gathering, saw their eager agitation, and a tunnel of light opened through the mountains for him as he moved to investigate.

His cat-like green eyes studied the river, and his bony face in its frame of smoke-black hair grew tense as he realised that this had a connection with the Gate between the mortal world and the realms of the gods. No one had tried to open the Gate, at least not deliberately. But something was afoot. Unusual currents were stirring; currents that, if they were not controlled, could be too strong for humans to deal with. But who, or what, had disturbed them?

Tarod thought of speaking to Yandros, but decided against it as he saw that the river was starting to diminish. Its colours dimmed, the voices faded. The elementals were losing interest; some of them came flittering to him instead, and he brushed them gently away. The rift in the mountain was beginning to close now, indicating that the disturbance was over and the Gate returning to normal.

He smiled with faint irony. The Circle adepts were experimenting with some new and unfamiliar powers; they were sure to encounter a few problems before they learned proper control. The Chaos lords believed in letting mortals learn from their own mistakes; even if he did speak to Yandros, Yandros wouldn't intervene. *Ignore it,* Tarod told himself. It wasn't worth worrying about.

A lot of people in the castle had bad dreams that night.

If all the nightmares had been the same, the Circle would have suspected a supernatural cause. But everyone dreamed something different, so no more was thought of it. Physician Eln blamed the rheum – a lot of sufferers had reached the feverish stage, and nightmares were only to be expected. What he did not know, though, was that it wasn't only the castle's inhabitants whose sleep had been disturbed.

Fosker Sangen and Reyni Trevire had made good

time on their journey from Wester Reach. They had stopped for the night at an inn in one of the mountain villages, and if the dry weather held they should arrive at the Star Peninsula within a couple of days. They went to their beds early. Fosker was soon asleep, but shortly after second moonset he was woken by the sound of shouting from the next room.

Hastily pulling on a warm robe, he ran out on to the landing. The shouts were more muffled here, but there was no doubting it was Reyni's voice, and Fosker flung open the door and went in.

By the dim light from a lantern burning in the courtyard outside, he could see Reyni tossing and turning in his bed. He was still asleep, and Fosker hurried across the room to shake him by the shoulder.

'Reyni! Reyni, wake up!'

The young musician gasped, then, with a flailing of arms, he was suddenly awake.

'Fosker . . ?' He blinked blearily, then his body relaxed as he realised where he was. 'Oh, gods . . . I was dreaming. Such a *nightmare!*'

'You're free of it now, my son,' Fosker soothed. 'Do you want to tell me?'

Reyni swallowed. 'It was about my aunt.'

'Ah.' Fosker's expression darkened. 'Your Aunt Malia?'

Reyni nodded. 'I was a child again, in Prospect Province, and I was singing for her as I often used to do. Then suddenly she . . . changed.' He shuddered. 'It was *horrible* – like a dark tide creeping over her; over her face, over her mind, over her soul . . . I was terrified and I tried to run, but something held me fast. Then she reached out, and her hand was a tentacle, and her face—' He swallowed again. 'She was turning into a child, younger than me, as if time was slipping backwards. I was crying out, *stop it, stop it!* but it wouldn't stop. She became a baby, a hideous baby, twisted and evil, and a web grew from her hands and began to wrap itself around me, strangling me – and then you woke me.' He met Fosker's sombre gaze. 'Thank you.'

Fosker didn't say anything for a few moments. Reyni had told him about his Aunt Malia – Sister Malia as she had been – when he first came to the Keepers' mission house. No one knew how Malia became involved with Thel Starnor and his evil plans, but she had been one of Thel's closest accomplices, and the entities of the Sixth Plane had ensnared her as surely as the rest. She had repented at last, but the entities had taken their revenge, attacking her mind until she was driven insane. At the last she had fought them, but at the price of her own life. And Reyni, torn between grief at her death and bitter shame at her wrongdoing, had never been able to reconcile the two feelings.

Fosker wasn't a dream-interpreter, so he couldn't

say for certain what Reyni's nightmare meant. There was an obvious connection with their visit to the castle; but were Reyni's memories simply being stirred up, or was there some deeper link?

Well, he would find out more soon enough. For now, it was best just to reassure Reyni and let it rest at that.

He smiled kindly and said, 'It must have been very upsetting. But there's no need to worry. Our Lord Aeoris protects you now, and you have nothing to fear.'

Reyni returned the smile, though pallidly. 'I know, sir, and I take strength from that. The dream was just so malevolent . . . and so real.'

'I understand.' Fosker stood up. 'Let's give thanks that all that is in the past. Try to sleep now, and be fresh for the morning. Goodnight.'

'Goodnight, sir.'

Fosker went out, and Reyni lay back. He still felt shaken, but Fosker was right. A dream couldn't harm him. There was nothing to be frightened of, not any more.

He pulled the blankets up under his chin, recited a short prayer of reverence to the gods of Order, then closed his eyes and hoped that he would sleep.

10

Despite her efforts to stay awake and think, sheer exhaustion finally got the better of Shar two hours before dawn. She fell asleep fully dressed on her bed, and didn't stir until mid-morning. If she dreamed at all, she didn't recall the dreams; her only discomfort was a head aching from the combined effects of catarrh and tiredness. But though her skull hurt, her mind was crystal clear.

The shock of last night's experience in the Marble Hall had passed, and in its place was new excitement. Horrifying though it had been to see the scene of her father's murder, it was powerful evidence for her theory about the Maze. Now, with an amulet of her own, she could put the theory to the test and prove or disprove it once and for all.

She decided to proceed cautiously. Small forays would be safest until she was thoroughly accustomed to using the Maze, and for a while she wouldn't try to experiment with time. The near-disaster of almost being discovered in the library had proved again that she could reach the Maze from a distance, so there was no need to wait for an opportunity to sneak out to the stack. She was excused from study classes for the time being, had an excuse to isolate herself – it was the perfect chance.

The first experiment was a great success. Shar visited Wester Reach again; not the mission house this time but the heart of the town, where there was so much bustle that strangers went unnoticed. She saw the Bronze Bell tavern, where she had met Reyni and entrusted him with her message to Hestor, then she walked along the riverside quays, watching the unloading of newly arrived ships. There were no anomalies, no timeslips, and the return to the castle was easy. So far, so good.

Her second foray was to the Matriarch's cot in Southern Chaun. She didn't approach it directly but kept her distance on the road outside, looking at the rectangle of neat, white buildings with the contemplation tower a little farther off. Nothing had changed; it was just as she remembered.

The third experiment was a test of her nerve. The island known as the Brig, where Thel Starnor had been imprisoned and had later died at the hands of the Sixth-Plane entities, lay off the West High Land coast. Despite her frightening memories of the island, it still held fascination for Shar and she was morbidly curious to see it again. The temptation was too strong to resist;

so, steeling herself for whatever she might find, she visualised the island and willed herself there.

There was a brief and unusual blurring of her senses as the Maze carried her away. Something seemed to intrude for a few moments; the colours around her bleached to a peculiar silver-grey, and she heard a sound like distant laughter. But the phenomenon didn't last, and seconds later she reached her destination.

Like the Southern Chaun cot, the Brig looked just as she remembered it. There were the same forbidding cliffs, the same bleak inland heights frowning down on the rough and neglected harbour, and, in the distance, the grim granite walls of the ancient prison fortress. It held no prisoners now, but was visited only by the gulls that wheeled and shrieked on a biting north-westerly wind.

Shivering in the wrong choice of clothes, Shar gazed around at the empty desolation. The scene was familiar. *Too* familiar. She didn't want to stay. She closed her eyes, visualising her bedroom in the castle and preparing to transport herself back once more. Moments later the air around her shimmered, then her figure faded and vanished.

She thought that nothing on the island had changed. But in her hurry to return whence she came, she had looked only at the harbour and the fortress. If she had turned her gaze the other way, she would have realised that something was wrong. For the past century or so there had been a lighthouse on a promontory at the island's south-eastern tip. The lighthouse keeper was the Brig's only inhabitant now, and on her first visit, as a stowaway aboard the supply ship *Margravine*, Shar had seen the beacon glaring eerily and powerfully into the night sky. It was daylight, and she hadn't thought to look for it. If she had, she would have had a shock.

The lighthouse wasn't there.

Three expeditions, Shar decided, were enough for the first day. By her reckoning she had spent a total of four hours away from the castle; much more and she was likely to be missed. In addition, she was feeling the effects of the Maze. Her headache had returned and she had had several brief but powerful flashes of disorientation, accompanied by bouts of double vision. It was an obvious warning not to overdo things, so reluctantly she hid the amulet under her mattress, had a light meal in the dining hall and went to bed.

Shar slept, with Amber beside her. The fire had died to embers, and before long the only illumination was the glow from the two moons. Then suddenly the fire burned up again, brightly and strongly, lighting the room with warm red-gold.

And Amber was no longer there.

There was a click as though the door had opened; though the door did not move at all. Someone moved across the room; the figure of a young man in clothes that had gone out of fashion a hundred years ago. The contours of the walls were visible through him and, distantly echoing, the sound of his whistling was just audible. Walking to the far side of the room, where Shar had no furniture, he went through the motions of opening a cupboard and rummaging for something. Then his form wavered, and a moment later he was gone. As he vanished, the fire dimmed to embers again and Amber was back on his place on the bed.

There was a faint smell of sulphur in the room now. Shar and the ginger cat both slept on, unaware of it, though Amber's whiskers twitched once or twice. Outside on the stack, around the bright rectangle of grass that marked the Maze, the air shimmered momentarily.

And in the corridor outside Shar's room, a white cat sat on one of the window ledges and stared out at the courtyard with restless and uneasy eyes.

Shar woke early. She felt tired, but she had no intention of wasting any time. Physician Eln wouldn't exempt her from studies for much longer, and she still had a great deal to do.

She managed to have breakfast without seeing anyone she knew, then hurried back to her room.

Today, she intended to try to travel in time as well as in space, and she had worked out a plan that should allow her to do it safely. She would go to her childhood home on Summer Isle, in the far south. It was the one place in the world that she knew better than any other, and her memories of it were very strong. There was one particular occasion that she recalled with crystal clarity – a summer Quarter-Day six years ago, when a troupe of acrobats from the Great Eastern Flatlands had come to entertain the crowds at the great fair outside the High Margrave's palace. They had put on a spectacular show, and every detail of the event was fixed indelibly in Shar's memory. To return to that day would be an ideal first experiment with time manipulation.

As she was dressing in summer clothes, a new and intriguing idea struck her. If she bought something on Summer Isle – nothing elaborate, just a small trinket – could she bring it back to the castle or would it vanish when she returned through the Maze? It was surely worth trying. If it worked, the possibilities were very exciting indeed.

Quickly, Shar rummaged in her purse for some money, then eagerly took up the amulet and focused her mind on Summer Isle. The image of the Quarter-Day fair came quickly and easily. She closed her eyes; her fingers tightened on the metallic spiral . . .

The lurch of displacement was far stronger than she

had ever known it before. As always she glimpsed the castle, briefly, from the point of view of the Maze, and her pulse quickened as she saw that the sun was far higher than it should be at this time of year. Then a strange, high singing note sounded in her ears – the world collapsed into a mad whirl of silver and black and she was spinning away and away, faster and further, as the shrill note rose until it seemed to pierce her skull—

Colour slammed against her senses, and with a massive jolt Shar was standing on firm ground again. The singing sound was eclipsed by a medley of more natural noises, and as her vision cleared she saw a sea of people, banners, tents, booths, and the noises resolved into the cheerful din of a fair in full swing. The sun blazed crimson in a cloudless sky, and high summer heat washed over her, relieved by a breeze that carried mingled and delectable aromas of food.

She had done it! Overwhelmed by her success, Shar stood for several minutes simply taking in the sights and sounds and smells around her. She had arrived, as she had wanted to do, at one corner of the broad, sweeping meadows where the Quarter-Day fairs were always held, and the performers' arena was just a short distance away. The acrobats' brightly coloured and pennanted pavilion was not where she remembered it, but Shar wasn't worried. She could hardly expect to recall *every* detail perfectly;

doubtless she would find the pavilion on the far side.

She started to make her way around the edge of the arena. It was slow going, for there were so many things to distract her. Craftsmen, musicians, fortune-tellers, sellers of wine or sweets or pastries or spiced meats . . . Shar had almost forgotten how different Summer Isle food was to the plainer fare of the castle, and she craved to taste it again. Well, why not? She had money. People could see and hear her, and no one suspected anything; only a moment ago someone had jostled her, smiled and apologised before moving on. She was simply one of the crowd.

She turned to where a sweet-maker was selling her wares, and chose some fruit-and-honey comfits. The price was an eighth of a gravine, which seemed cheap for so many. Shar gave the stallholder a half-gravine and waited for her change. But the woman was studying the coin, and a frown appeared on her face.

'What's this?' she demanded.

It was Shar's turn to frown. 'A half-gravine. If you want something smaller—'

She didn't get the chance to finish. 'A half-gravine? Don't try that trick on me, girl!' Abruptly she snatched the sweets from Shar's hand and thrust the coin at her. 'Here, take it back, and don't let me catch you around my stall again! Brazen little swindler – by Aeoris, it isn't even a *good* fake!'

Shar was so astonished and confused that she didn't even try to argue, but backed away and fled. Reaching a quieter spot, she examined her coin. There was nothing wrong with it; on one face it bore the star-and-lightning-flash sigil, and on the other the mark of its value. So why had the woman caller her a swindler?

Uneasily, she looked at her other coins. They, too, seemed genuine, but she began to wonder if something had happened to them during the transfer through the Maze; something that she was unaware of but others could see plainly. The only way to find out was to try again, so she approached another booth where a thin man was selling small wooden carvings. One – of a cat – took her fancy, so she picked it up and held out a whole gravine.

'Is this enough?'

The thin man looked at the coin, and his eyebrows lifted. 'Enough for what, lass?' There was amusement in his voice. 'To make a pretty pendant out of, maybe. But for *buying* something . . .' He returned the coin, took the cat from her and placed it carefully back on the stall. 'If you want to spend make-believe money, you'd better find someone selling make-believe goods!'

'But it's real,' Shar said. 'A real gravine. I'm *sure* it is!'

'And my name's Ilyaya Kimi!' the man retorted.

She stared at him blankly. 'Who?'

His expression changed from amused-annoyed to downright astonished. 'Who?' he repeated. 'Great gods, girl, what backwood are you from, if you don't even know the name of our lady Matriarch?'

A hard, icy little knot seemed to form in Shar's stomach. The Matriarch's name was Ulmara Trin . . .

Then suddenly she saw the man with new eyes, as though a veil had been lifted. She hadn't even noticed it before, but his clothes were wrong. And so were the clothes of the crowds milling around her. And the styles of their hair. And the fact that the acrobats' pavilion wasn't where she remembered it . . . The acrobats weren't here at all, and nor was anyone else whom she had ever known. She had come back in time, yes. But not to the time she had intended.

What year was this?

She swallowed, struggling to find her voice. 'I – I'm sorry,' she said. 'You see, I—' But she couldn't explain to him; it was far too dangerous. 'Please,' she said. 'I know it sounds foolish, but . . . could you show me a real coin? I won't try to steal it, truly I won't.'

He clearly thought she was mad, but he took pity on her and put a hand into his pocket. 'Oh, very well. Here. A *proper* gravine, look.'

On the side that showed its value, the gravine was very much like Shar's own. But the other face showed a plain circle, with the lightning-flash sigil of Order cutting diagonally across it.

Shar knew that symbol from her history lessons. It had gone out of use when Equilibrium began.

'Best go along now, eh?' the stallholder said more kindly. 'Go and find your parents, or whoever looks after you. They shouldn't let a poor, simple creature like you roam around; you might come to harm. Go on, now, that's the way.'

Shar went. With her heart pounding and the icy knot making her feel sick now, she found a deserted space behind one of the performers' tents, took out her amulet and pictured her room in the castle. Praying to Yandros that the return journey wouldn't go wrong as the outward one had, she willed the Maze to open.

The lurching disorientation snatched her out of the bright world of two hundred years ago, and moments later she was hurled back into the safe, familiar surroundings of her bedroom.

Shar sat on the bed, stunned and shaking. How had that *happened?* She had visualised the scene so carefully, certain that she was in complete control. What had gone wrong? Was it her fault, was there some flaw in her amulet, or had the Maze itself caused the anomaly? Raking her memory, she tried to recall every detail of the transfer. The lurch *had* been unusually strong, and there had been that shrill singing sound, and a moment when the whirl of colours had changed to black and silver. But if any of those things were significant she didn't know how or why.

A lot of people – even experienced Circle adepts – would have been daunted by this newest experience. Shar, though, was not. Hestor would have called her cussed, she thought with dour amusement. Well, perhaps she was, for she certainly had no intention of giving up; in fact her resolve to fathom the Maze was strengthened by what had just taken place. The Maze always brought her back safely to the castle and to her own time, so there wasn't really anything to be afraid of. She would persevere, and she would solve this problem. An hour's rest would refresh her. Then she would try again.

A few minutes before Shar's return from Summer Isle, Physician Eln was in his infirmary when someone knocked at the door. Annoyed by the interruption – he was distilling a new batch of fever herbs and the process was at a critical stage – Eln called testily, 'Yes, yes, I'm here!'

He heard the door open but kept his eyes on his bubbling bottles and tubes and condensers. Then at the edge of his vision he saw a long skirt, and for politeness's sake he looked up. 'Yes? Can I h—'

The words froze in his mouth as his eyes and brain took in the figure of the woman before him. She was about thirty-five, with grey eyes and chestnut-brown hair pulled back into a practical knot. She had a medical bag in one hand, and a blue apron, its large pockets bulging with oddments, was tied over her dress.

Eln had never met her, but he recognised her face immediately. Any senior adept would have done so, for her portrait hung, along with those of all her forerunners and successors, in the council chamber.

He was face to face with Physician-Adept Karuth Piadar Voss. High Initiate of the Circle. And Neryon's great-grandmother.

Eln's mouth worked jerkily, but he couldn't say or even think anything that made any sense. The ghost (Ghost? But she looked as real as he did!) stared straight through him, focusing on a point behind his back. She smiled and said something, but no sound was audible. Then she put her bag down on an invisible surface, turned and walked out again.

As the door swung to behind her, Eln's frozen mind unlocked. He stumbled across the room, almost upsetting his equipment in his haste, and ran out into the corridor.

He could hear light, quick footsteps moving away in the direction of the main staircase. But the corridor was empty.

'Great gods . . .' Perspiration had broken out on the physician's face despite the cold day. Logic told him that he must have been hallucinating, but he knew he hadn't been. That figure had not been a fever-dream!

Suddenly he remembered the medical bag. He whirled round, looked at the place where she had put it down.

There was nothing there. The bag, like its owner, had vanished.

Eln was still staring at the empty air when he heard someone hurrying towards the infirmary. For a moment he thought the 'ghost' was returning, but as he turned eagerly, Pellis, who was recently up and about again after the rheum, appeared in the doorway.

'Eln!' Pellis was pale and flustered. 'I've just seen someone — on the main stairs — gods, I don't know where to begin! I thought it must be a return of the fever; I don't *feel* ill now, but—'

Eln interrupted quietly. 'Was it Karuth Piadar Voss?'

She froze, then realisation dawned. '*You* saw her, too?'

'She walked into my infirmary not two minutes ago.'

'Great Yandros!' Pellis sat down rather suddenly. 'Then I wasn't hallucinating.'

'It would seem not.' Eln described his own experience, and when he had finished, Pellis's expression was very sombre.

'Something's awry, Eln. I've never known, or even read about, anything like this happening before.' She looked up at him. 'Neryon ought to be told.'

'I agree. But he's still feverish, and until that passes there's not a lot of point in trying to talk to him. Especially as the vision was of his own ancestor.'

Pellis shivered. 'Why has she appeared to us? What does she want?'

'We're assuming that it really was High Initiate Karuth, and not some unhuman entity,' Eln pointed out. 'Even if it was an elemental or a demon, though, there must be a reason why it took her form.'

'A message, possibly. Or a warning.'

'I agree. But what's the link with Karuth? For the life of me, I can't see one!'

Pellis stood up again. 'I think we should call a council meeting,' she said. 'And we should also find out whether anyone else saw what we did.'

Eln, however, shook his head. 'I'd advise against that, Pellis. If the council convenes without Neryon, Gant, as his deputy, will take charge. And I have a strong feeling that Gant will use this incident as a weapon in his campaign against the Maze.'

Pellis stared at him. 'You think there may be a connection?'

'I don't know. But I believe it's possible – don't you?'

Pellis was thoughtfully silent for a few moments. Then: 'Yes,' she said slowly. 'Yes. I do.'

'So I suggest we do nothing for the time being. If anyone else saw the same vision, then as the castle physician I'm the most likely to find out about it. I'll keep my ears open, and as soon as Neryon has recovered, we'll talk to him.'

She nodded agreement and turned to leave. At the door she paused.

'Oh, one more thing,' she said. 'It's only trivial, but have you noticed anything odd about the castle cats in the last day or two?'

'No,' said Eln, 'I can't say I have.'

'Mmm. It's just that they seem very restless. I can't pick up any sensible images from them, but I'm sure they're agitated about something.' She paused. 'Ah well; it's probably unimportant. I'll see you later, Eln. Keep me informed – goodbye.'

11

Though she had planned to rest only for an hour, Shar fell sound asleep, and by the time she woke it was well after sunset.

She was furious. Time spent sleeping was time wasted, and she couldn't afford that. But there was nothing to be done. Her best choice, she decided, was to have something to eat – her stomach was gnawing with hunger – and resume her experiments when everyone else had gone to bed.

Luckily she had woken in time for the evening meal, and she found Hestor and Kitto in the dining hall. They were both out of sorts and grumbling; Kitto because of overwork, Hestor because an elemental conjuration he had had to perform for his tutor had gone awry and landed him in trouble.

'I've done that conjuration a dozen times before and I've never got it wrong,' he told them sourly. 'It was the elementals; they just wouldn't obey. They kept causing trouble – almost set the lecture-room curtains on fire at one point. And of course it *had* to happen in front of Adept Paon, of all people – he's so sarcastic, and it's not as if it was *my* fault!'

Neither of his companions really listened. Kitto had sunk into self-pitying gloom, while Shar's mind was on the Maze and her own schemes. But as Hestor's complaint continued, something he said abruptly caught her attention.

'. . . all grey and silver, not a speck of colour anywhere, and it was supposed to be a fire conjuration, so don't ask *me* where it came from! Then when everything distorted and there was that laugh—'

'Laugh?' Shar interrupted him sharply. 'What laugh? And what do you mean about the grey and silver?'

Hestor stared back at her, aggrieved. 'You haven't been listening, have you? I *told* you – I was in the middle of this blasted conjuration, or thought I was anyway, when suddenly all the colour in the room completely vanished. Then there was a noise, like something laughing dementedly, and Paon accused me of doing it.' He snorted. 'Some chance! I didn't even know what it *was* until he started ranting at me for "playing with powers that a junior of your low skill isn't fit to handle"!' His expression skewed as he savagely mimicked Adept Paon's tones. 'I ask you; would *anyone* who wanted to play up a tutor be stupid enough to choose him? He's nearly as bad as Gant!'

Shar's thought were moving like a rapid river. 'What powers did he mean?' she asked. 'What *did* you call up?'

'I didn't call anything except the fire elementals! But they decided to cause mischief by bringing something else with them.' Hestor scowled. 'According to Paon, it was from a higher elemental plane. But *I* don't know how it broke through. It certainly wasn't anything to do with me!'

So that was what she had glimpsed, before, in the Maze, Shar thought. The draining of colour, the strange, disembodied laughter – it was just as Hestor had described.

'Which plane was it?' she demanded.

Hestor didn't notice the new eagerness in her voice. 'I don't know. Paon wouldn't tell me; he just went on and on about arrogance and irresponsibility. All I know is, it wasn't the plane I was trying to reach.'

Shar was disappointed by his answer, but not surprised. Junior initiates were only allowed to work with the four elemental worlds of earth, water, air and fire. The higher dimensions were considered too dangerous until they had reached a certain level of magical skill, and most tutors thought it better not to reveal too much about those dimensions to their students. However, Shar knew now that one of the higher planes was directly concerned with Time. Grey and silver, and a disembodied voice laughing. It was the key. It *must* be.

Kitto joined in the conversation then, airing his own grievances about horses, head grooms and lack of sleep. Shar looked down at her plate. She had eaten enough. She wanted to get away, back to her room to begin work again, and abruptly she got to her feet.

'I must go,' she said, more sharply than she had intended.

Kitto stopped talking and both boys looked up in surprise. 'You haven't finished your food.' Hestor pointed at it.

'I know. I'm — not very hungry. I've got to do some studying; Physician Eln says I'll be fit for classes tomorrow, so I'd better try to catch up.' She gave them both a smile, but it was only a movement of her mouth; her mind was somewhere else entirely. 'Sorry. I'll see you tomorrow, I expect.'

'Well!' Hestor said indignantly as she walked away towards the doors. 'Much sympathy we've had from her!'

'If you ask me,' Kitto commented, 'she's up to something.'

'Oh, nonsense. She's just being moody; probably hasn't really recovered from the rheum yet.' Hestor shrugged. 'Ignore it, I would. She'll be her old self again in a day or two.'

Kitto didn't argue. But his eyes, as he watched Shar's departing back, were uneasy.

Shar made four more forays through the Maze that night.

The tale of Hestor's disastrous conjuration had given her an all-important clue, and she was determined to put it to the test. She would travel to Summer Isle again, to re-visit another event that she remembered with perfect clarity – the day of the High Margrave's wedding. Shar had been ten at the time, and was among the forty-nine girl attendants (forty-nine was seven times seven, and thus a very auspicious number) in the bridal procession. As the procession moved slowly back towards the palace after a gods-blessing at the harbour, a colossal Warp storm had come sweeping in from the sea, bringing with it a downpour of glittering blue rain. The glorious panoply had broken up in an undignified mass rush for shelter, and the rest of the celebrations took place in the palace ballroom, crammed almost to the rafters with upwards of five thousand guests. The festivities were riotous, for the Warp was the biggest to strike the island in living memory, and that combined with the rain – a great rarity in such a storm – was widely agreed to be a sign that the gods had given their emphatic blessing to the occasion.

Shar wanted to return to the celebration just before

the moment when the first, distant scream of the approaching Warp became audible. She visualised herself among the crowds lining the harbour road, far enough back from the procession to ensure that she wouldn't see – or be seen by – her own younger self (for who knew what anomalies that might cause?), clasped the amulet and willed herself through the Maze.

For all her efforts, the timing went completely awry. She had no way of knowing the date or even the year when she arrived on Summer Isle, but there was no crowd, no procession, no sign of a festival of any kind. The road was deserted, the harbour below tranquil and sleepy under the noon heat. And there was certainly no trace of an impending Warp.

Shar returned to her room. So far, so good; she had expected to fail this first time. Her second attempt, though, would be a little different. As the Maze opened, she had again experienced a brief draining of colour from her surroundings, and again heard the peculiar sound that might or might not have been laughter. This time, she wanted to snare that fleeting glimpse into another dimension and hold on to it, bend it to her will and use it. If she was right, it was the key to time's manipulation. Once she had mastered it, she would have cracked the Maze's secret.

Shar readied herself, picturing her destination once

more. There came the familiar lurch, the sense of spinning—

– Grey and silver –

Her mind snatched the image, stilled it. A sound swelled in her ears, more of a shriek than a laugh. It sounded angry but she wasn't daunted; there was silver light all around her now, flowing like water and shot through with black threads. Something murmured in a deep tone, rising and falling, a one-sided conversation in a language no human had ever heard or could ever speak, and prickles of heat and cold skittered over her face and arms. *Will it to happen! The year, the day, the event – will it, and this time it shall be right!*

Sight, sound and physical feeling came back in one huge rush, and Shar was on Summer Isle again.

The crowd was so big, and so busy jostling for a view, that no one noticed her sudden appearance. She was just one more anonymous figure in the press of hot bodies, craning necks, waving hands, and the noise of cheering swelled and beat against her ears like a sea-tide. Between the myriad bobbing heads in front of her she could just see the approaching palanquin with its cloth-of-gold curtains blowing in the hot breeze, and behind it the blaze of colour that was the procession; boy and girl attendants crowned with flower garlands and wearing twenty different shades of silk or velvet; militia in full ceremonial dress, polished steel and bronze glittering in the sunlight; the Matriarch and more than fifty Sisters, their white robes and silver veils so bright that they hurt the eyes . . .

An enormous surge of elation overtook Shar and she yelled out as loudly as anyone in the crowd; not for the High Margrave and his new bride but for the sheer exuberance of her triumph. It had worked, it had *worked!* She had harnessed the Maze's power, tamed it and controlled it, and returned to the exact time that she had wanted to visit!

The palanquin carrying the newly married couple was passing her section of the throng now, and behind it came the attendants. Suddenly Shar had an overwhelming urge to see herself, see what she had looked like all those years ago. She stood on tiptoe, straining every muscle – there was that tall, fair girl; Molline, was it? Or Missak? Anyway, she had been two ranks ahead of Shar in the procession, so if—

She felt the alert in her psyche then, and it wiped out all thoughts of her younger self. A stirring, a tingling, a thrill that seemed to start in the tips of her fingers and toes and run swiftly through her. An instant later, knifing through the shouts and cheers like the whine of an aggressive insect, she heard the first, faraway shriek of the supernatural storm.

She was the first to know, of course, because she alone had expected it, but within moments others started to realise what was afoot. Faces looked up, and everyone saw the sky changing and darkening as bands of deep, ominous colours started to wheel slowly across the heavens. Stunning crimson and orange lightning splintered over the sea, and the high, singing wail was growing louder. Then the blue rain began.

Shar didn't join the rush for the palace, but instead stood her ground as people raced past her, and laughed until tears streamed down her face and mingled with the pelting, glittering onslaught. She was soaked through but she didn't care; this was *exactly* as she remembered, *exactly* the way it had happened, and the hilarious, wonderful mayhem of it all only made her laugh the more. Bending, she picked a small wild flower from the grass and held it up to the rain. No one paid her any heed; they were all too intent on reaching shelter to spare time for any fool who didn't look after herself. Away they went, dignity abandoned, and as the last stragglers pounded up the hill Shar clasped her amulet and, hiccupping with the struggle to control her mirth, willed herself back to the castle.

She arrived with a jolt that landed her on her bedroom floor in an ungraceful heap. She was still laughing, still soaked through, and only when calm and sense finally returned did she change her wet clothes and stir up the fire and sit down to savour her success.

She had no doubts now. With Hestor's unwitting help, she had found the answer she was seeking, and the Maze was hers to command. Shar couldn't suppress a feeling of great satisfaction at the thought of just how far ahead of the Circle she had progressed. She had even brought the flower back with her, and it lay now on her bedside table, its sodden petals drying in the room's warmth. If the senior adepts only knew . . . But they didn't know and, though it was deeply frustrating not to be able to tell anyone, the secret must be kept for a while yet. One south breeze didn't make a summer, as the saying went: until she was sure that her method was foolproof, she must continue to work alone.

Sobered now, she considered the next step. A second test was the obvious choice; repeat exactly the same experiment and check that it still worked. If it did, she might try going back in time within the walls of the castle. It would be fascinating to see historical events as they had actually happened.

Her second expedition to Summer Isle proved as successful as the first. The scene was the same; the crowds, the procession, the sudden first herald of the unexpected storm – this time Shar did not stay to be caught in the downpour but transported herself back to her own time as the first bands of colour began to darken the sky. From her window she saw that the first moon was high and the second just rising.

About an hour must have passed since she began her experiments, which appeared to fit with the time she had spent away. That was reassuring, and made it easier to plan her absences to ensure that no one would miss her.

So, then: a foray in the castle itself . . . Mentally rummaging through the possibilities, Shar recalled a painting that hung in the gallery above the dining hall, among the portraits of past High Initiates, Matriarchs and Margraves. It depicted the banquet marking the inauguration of Neryon's father, Tirand, some thirty years ago, and the artist who painted it had been renowned for accuracy and detail, making visualisation much easier.

Taking up her amulet, she pictured the painting and focused her mind. The shift came startlingly easily, and with it the sense of the black-and-silver current, flowing faster and more strongly this time. Shar latched on to it, exerted her will – and moments later found herself in the great hall.

She almost lost her balance as the transfer was completed, and stumbled against a man sitting on a stool immediately in front of her.

'Excuse me!' she said as he turned in surprise.

'Think nothing of it.' The man smiled. 'I'm rather in the way here, I'm afraid.' He was holding a graphite stick in one hand, she saw, and in front of him was a large sheet of fine paper on an easel. Of course –

the painting showed the scene from the artist's point of view, so Shar's visualisation had placed her in the very spot where he had sat to begin his commission. Again, she had succeeded.

With an answering smile and a further apology, Shar backed away. Again it seemed that no one had seen her appear, so she found herself a vantage point by the nearest wall and scanned the scene. It was all very splendid. The new High Initiate sat at the head of a table on a raised dais. On his right was the Matriarch of the time, and on his left a pretty woman who, Shar guessed, was his wife. Beyond her sat three children, two girls and a boy. The boy was only about five years old, but he was very conscious of the occasion and was doing his best to behave with adult dignity. Shar's mouth quirked with amusement as she realised who the little boy must be. She would never be able to think of High Initiate Neryon in quite the same way from now on . . .

The hall was full of guests, eating and drinking and talking, while in the gallery above the hearth a group of musicians played quietly. In truth there wasn't a great deal to watch, so after a few minutes Shar worked her way round to the exit and slipped out. It was spring, and still light, so she headed towards the main doors, intending to go outside and look at the decorations in the courtyard. Only high-ranking guests were attending the banquet – the dining hall couldn't accommodate everyone without an uncomfortable crush – so there were plenty of people about in the corridors and the entrance hall. The doors stood open to the warm evening and the courtyard, too, was quite crowded. Shar emerged on to the steps and walked to the central fountain, where she sat down on the low circling wall to enjoy the sunlight and the festive atmosphere. Looking at some of the adepts in their different coloured cloaks – the formal marks of their rank – she wondered if she could recognise younger versions of anyone she knew. The red-haired girl giggling with her friends by the library door looked very much like one of the senior philosophy tutors. And that tall, thin young man – apart from the fact that he was smiling, he bore a startling resemblance to Adept Gant. Shar grinned to herself at the thought that Adept Gant had ever been able or willing to smile, and gazed around for more recognisable faces.

Then a burst of noise nearby made her turn her head. A group of first- and second-rank adepts, mostly boys of about Hestor's age, had gathered on the other side of the fountain. One of them had obviously just told a joke, and the rest were laughing. The joke-teller had dark brown hair and very intent eyes; something about him looked vaguely familiar, and Shar was trying to think who he might be when another of the group said loudly, 'Well, if you've got any more tales like that, Thel, you'd better not tell them in the new High Initiate's hearing!'

Shar froze. *Thel. It couldn't be . . . surely, it couldn't . . .*

The boy called Thel was grinning. 'Don't worry; I value my skin too much!' he said.

Oh, Shar knew that voice. It was younger, much younger, but . . .

'My cup's empty,' another boy complained. 'Let's go and get some more wine!'

'Excellent idea.' Thel glanced around him. 'Where's that brother of mine? Solas – oh, there you are. Come on; we'll use our charm on the servants, and see if we can get a flagon or two to ourselves!'

A younger, slighter boy moved from the group to join him, and the pair walked away together. Shar stared after them, unable to move. She had seen the second boy only for a few moments, but that had been enough. She knew him. She knew them both. Her dead father, and her murdering uncle . . .

A surge of sickness hit her then, as though she had swallowed foul water. For an awful moment she thought she would actually *be* sick, but she managed somehow to control it, and to force her limbs into motion. Lurching up from the wall she ran across the courtyard, in the opposite direction to Thel and Solas. She didn't care who saw her or what they might think;

she was overcome with a desperate need to escape and not see any more.

In a shadowed spot under the covered walk that led to the library, she snatched out her amulet and closed her hands tightly around it. *Home, I want to be home, in my own time, in my own room* — The Maze opened and she flung herself into its vortex with all the energy she could summon. She cried out at the giddying rush of it, and as the Maze whirled her away it seemed that something else echoed her cry in shrieking mockery. Colours flared blindingly; a net of silver lightning blazed across her vision, then with a huge shock she was plunged into blackness.

The world came back, and Shar was sprawling on the rug in front of her own bedchamber hearth, with Amber mewing anxiously in her face. She hugged the cat to her until Amber took exception and wriggled out of her arms. His fur was wet, and she realised that she was crying, the tears streaming down her face and splashing on the floor.

'Idiot, idiot, *idiot!*' Furiously Shar railed at herself, dragging her emotions under control and trying to calm down. How could she have been so stupid? She should have anticipated that this might happen; she should have thought of it and been ready, instead of letting herself be caught unawares! But to see her father and uncle together like that . . . it had *hurt*.

And the shock of being unprepared had made it all the worse.

The tears were stopping. Shar wiped her face on her sleeve, sniffed twice, then got to her feet. She still felt nauseous, though thankfully it was fading, but her legs were unsteady and she needed to lie down. She sagged on to her bed, letting out her breath in a long, shaky sigh. Her head was aching now, adding to her discomfort, and she told herself that there was no point in dwelling on what had just happened. She had made a foolish and thoughtless mistake, and if the result had upset her, it was entirely her own fault. The wisest thing to do was try to sleep, and forget about it until morning.

Shar slid under the bedcovers and closed her eyes. But sleep wouldn't come, for however hard she tried she could not banish the thirty-year-old picture of her father and uncle from her mind. Her headache was getting worse, too, so at last she got up and mixed herself an infusion to cure it. She had no hope of sleeping. Better to find some activity to distract her. A bath, that would help. It would soothe her body even if it didn't clear her mind.

Shar waited until the herbal infusion began to work, then took a towel and a dressing robe and went down to the bathing-rooms. These lay in the castle foundations; a network of small, artificial pools surrounded by a broad ledge and rows of privacy-cubicles. The pools were filled with water pumped up through the stack from the sea, and some were heated by pipes leading from a small furnace. With several hours still to go before dawn the baths were deserted, and Shar slid into the warmest pool she could find, immersing herself to her shoulders. The water was pleasant and comforting; within minutes the last traces of the headache faded away and she felt much better.

And able, at last, to think clearly.

The shock of seeing her father tonight had been less dramatic than the earlier, horrifying experience in the Marble Hall when she had created her amulet. But all the bitterness and grief locked in her had been stirred up afresh – and now, in the wake of it, a wild and fantastic idea was beginning to take form in her mind.

Tonight she had proved beyond all possible doubt that she had the power and the skill to manipulate the Maze as she chose. So why should she not use it for something more than exploration or pleasure? The scheme was more audacious than anything she had ever done, or even imagined, before, but she believed it was possible.

When she was still a baby, Thel Starnor had murdered her parents. Twice now Shar had looked back in time and seen her father; but on both occasions she had been merely a bystander, unable – or, tonight, unwilling – to play any part in the scene unfolding before her.

What, then, if that were to change?

She swam slowly across the pool, her face taut and her eyes very intense. She had proved that she could return to the past and become a part of it. So it would surely take only a small step to actually *alter* the past. Her mother and father had never suspected Thel of any treachery. But Shar knew the truth about him. What would it mean for her, here, now, in the present, if she went back to the time before her parents died, and stopped the murders from happening?

The answer was clear and simple. If she did that, then her parents would *not* die. They would still be alive today . . .

Shar stopped swimming and trod water as a shiver ran from the nape of her neck to her toes. The concept was mad; possibly the maddest thing that anyone had ever tried to do in the whole of history. Maybe it couldn't even *be* done. Maybe there were laws of time and space that would doom the attempt to complete failure. But until and unless she tried, she would never know.

Did she have the courage? That was the crucial question. Calmed by peaceful solitude and lulled by the sensation of floating in warm water, she felt strength coming back and doubt receding. Her mother and father alive. History undone. It would be the fulfilment of her dearest wish. And she knew how she would achieve it. That was the simplest thing of all.

She would go back in time, and kill Thel Starnor.

'Uncle Thel . . . She whispered his name with a venomous hatred that made her nerve-ends tingle. 'You're beyond my reach now. I can't pay you out in the present. But in the past . . .'

A second shiver went through her, and she welcomed it, revelled in it. She launched herself across the pool again and reached the far side. Gripping the edge she looked over it, but she did not see the neat cubicles, or her own towel and robe laid ready for her on a rack. Instead, she stared into another world, another time. Thel had been the cause of all her unhappiness. He had also tried to destroy her, and had almost succeeded. This would be the sweetest possible revenge. And, more even than revenge, it would be *justice*.

12

The High Initiate was on the mend by morning. His fever had gone, and Physician Eln pronounced that he would soon be fit to take charge again. Adept Gant in particular was very relieved by the news. Being in temporary charge of the Circle was all very well, but with more and more visitors arriving every day he'd barely had a moment to himself since Neryon fell ill. He would be extremely glad to return to his normal routine.

Gant's mood was further cheered later in the afternoon by the arrival of his cousin Fosker. Fosker and Reyni had made good time on the mountain road, and Gant was delighted to see them. He was favourably impressed by Reyni. The young musician seemed quiet, modest, unassuming – a great contrast to Hestor Ennas or that uncouth little ruffian Kitto, with whom Shar Tillmer was so friendly. Reyni would be a useful influence on Shar, Gant told himself with satisfaction. Which, if his latest suspicions were true, was just as well.

Although he had had no time to maintain his watch on Shar, Gant was convinced that something untoward was still going on. Rumours had reached his ears of some peculiar incidents in the castle; small oddities, but ones that couldn't be explained away. There was no obvious connection with Shar's activities, but it *was* coincidental – and Gant didn't believe in coincidence. As soon as the visitors had been shown to their rooms and had unpacked their luggage, he suggested that it would be a good idea for Reyni to make himself known to Shar straight away. The evening meal was about to be served; Gant and Fosker would eat in Gant's apartments, but if Reyni went to the dining hall, he was likely to meet Shar there.

'Not a word about our real purpose here, mind,' Gant warned. 'Let Shar think that you have simply accompanied your leader on his visit to the High Initiate.'

'Better still, let her believe that you *asked* to come because you wanted to see her again,' Fosker added, and smiled. 'She'll be flattered. Girls of her age are very responsive to flattery.'

Reyni returned the smile, though a little uncertainly. 'Of course, sir; I'll do as you say.' He made a small bow in Gant's direction. 'Adept.'

Gant nodded. 'Report to us later.'

It felt very strange to Reyni to be walking the castle

corridors again. His last visit had been as a player, hired to perform at the autumn Quarter-Day revels, when he had carried the letter that had started the whole terrifying course of his adventures with Shar, Hestor and Kitto. His life had changed so much since then, yet the castle was exactly as he remembered it; the same passages and rooms, the same smells, the same atmosphere. He could almost believe that no time had passed and nothing had happened.

But that was not true, and as he entered the dining hall Reyni reminded himself soberly of his mission. His first meeting with Shar wouldn't be easy. He wasn't sure how best to approach her, and in particular how to bring up the subject of the incident in Wester Reach. When he had encountered her at the mission house Shar was obviously horrified at being discovered, and had fled without giving him a chance even to speak to her. Now, seeing him in the castle, her suspicions were sure to be aroused. Fosker thought differently; but Fosker didn't know Shar. If she was playing with dangerous forces, she would be doubly on her guard, and Reyni knew that his chances of persuading her to tell him about it were slim. Still, he had to try. He owed it to Shar. She *must* be saved from herself.

He found an empty table, ordered his meal and started to think hard about his strategy. Then, breaking his concentration, a voice behind him said, 'Reyni?'

Kitto was standing a few paces away and gazing at him in astonishment. 'It *is* you!' The astonishment gave way to a broad grin, and Kitto came forward to thump Reyni squarely in the chest with the flat of his hand. 'Yandros and Aeoris, what are you doing here?' Then, before Reyni could even begin to think of an answer, Kitto pointed to his clothes. 'And whatever are you doing wearing *those?*'

So Shar hadn't told Kitto about her adventure. Reyni smiled gently. 'I joined the Keepers of Light a few months ago,' he replied.

Kitto stared. 'Great gods!' he said. 'Why?'

'It's a long story.'

'I'll bet it is!' Kitto slid on to the opposite bench. 'I mean, I know they're good people and all that, but you're just about the last person in the world I'd have expected to become one of them!' He paused, his eyes narrowing. 'Especially after what Lord Tarod did for us all.'

The comment was a direct challenge, and Reyni knew it. He looked down at the table and said quietly, 'And Lord Ailind of Order, Kitto. Don't forget that.'

Kitto hadn't forgotten. But he also remembered that the god of Order had tried at first to stop Tarod of Chaos from helping Shar. To him, Shar was 'irrelevant', and only when Tarod had pointed out that the danger she was in could spill over, and threaten them all, did he agree, reluctantly, to co-operate. But it seemed Reyni had overlooked that. Or had chosen to ignore it.

Reyni was telling him now about the mission house in Wester Reach, the people there and the work they did. Kitto had the distinct impression that he was deliberately changing the subject, and he also found something disturbing in the way the musician talked. The name of Lord Aeoris cropped up a little too often, and there was a zealous note underlying everything Reyni said. He was beginning to sound like a fanatic.

Then suddenly Reyni changed the subject. 'Well,' he said. 'How's Shar?'

Aha, Kitto thought. *So that's at the heart of it.* 'She's fine,' he said, keeping his voice casual. 'She caught the rheum that's been going round the castle, but she's over it now.'

'I'm glad to hear that. Is her training going well?'

Kitto shrugged. 'I wouldn't know; I can't make head or tail of that kind of thing. You'll have to ask her for yourself.'

'I'd like to.' Reyni smiled. 'In fact, I'd better confess something to you, Kitto. Shar's the main reason I'm here.'

Kitto's hackles went up. 'Oh?' he said warily.

'When our new leader said he was going to visit

the castle to pay his respects to the High Initiate, I . . . well, to tell you the truth, I asked if I could come too. I wanted to see Shar again.' He met Kitto's eyes and grinned sheepishly. 'I've missed her.'

'I see.' Hestor was going to love that, Kitto thought – if it *was* the truth and not a cover for something else. 'Well,' he added aloud, 'I'm sure she'll be pleased to see you. You'll have a lot to talk about.' *And I'd like to know what you want to say to her. Wouldn't I just.*

Reyni looked around the hall. 'She isn't here,' he said. 'Am I too early, or too late?'

'Can't say. She could be along at any time, or—' Kitto broke off suddenly as he saw a familiar figure entering. 'There's Hestor. He might know.'

Hestor had seen Kitto and was coming over. It would be interesting, Kitto thought, to see how he and Reyni reacted to each other. Hestor had got over his initial jealousy of Reyni, but there was a good chance that the musician's reappearance would stir things up again. That could be very useful, for it might reveal what Reyni was *really* doing here.

'Hey, Kitto!' Hestor reached the table. 'I was just—' Then he stopped, looking at Reyni and recognising him for the first time. 'Good gods . . .'

He asked the same questions that Kitto had asked, and Reyni gave the same answers, not rising to the bait when Hestor teased him about his new allegiance. Kitto, watching and listening carefully, knew that

Hestor was ruffled, and when Reyni asked again whether Shar was likely to come to the hall, he got a curt reply.

'She doesn't always come, you know. She's very busy with her studies these days. We both are.'

'Of course, I understand.' There was a pause, then Reyni stood up. 'Well, I'd better go back to my room and finish unpacking. If you see Shar, please tell her I'm here. And give her my love.'

Hestor didn't answer, and it was left to Kitto to say a polite goodbye. They both watched as Reyni left the hall, then when he had disappeared through the doors Hestor made a noise halfway between a snort and a snarl.

'Yandros and Aeoris! The *nerve* of it!'

Kitto raised an eyebrow. 'You don't believe that rigmarole, do you?'

'What do you mean? Of course I believe it, it's howlingly obvious! He's come back here, thinking he can charm Shar and twist her round his little finger!'

'I think there's more to it than that,' said Kitto.

'Isn't that enough? He probably even wants to convert her to that stupid cult!'

'He knows Shar better than that. I reckon he isn't telling the truth, Hestor. He *says* he only came to see her, but his leader's here, too. And Shar went through the Maze to Wester Reach. That's a very big coincidence, if you ask me.'

Kitto tried to describe his suspicion that Reyni's personal interest in Shar was only a small part of the story, but he soon realised that he wasn't getting through. Hestor saw Reyni as a rival, and he wasn't interested in any other speculations. Everything Kitto said was swept aside on the tide of his indignation, and eventually Kitto gave up. He couldn't explain properly anyway; his theory was still too vague and even if it wasn't, he didn't have the right words to put it across. Their food had been served, so with a sigh he concentrated on eating while Hestor picked at the contents of his own plate and continued to mutter darkly.

After a while Kitto said, 'Where is Shar, anyway? She's usually here by now.'

Hestor looked up briefly. 'Probably studying. She said she had a lot of catching up to do.'

'Oh. Right.' Silence fell again, but there was a nagging at the back of Kitto's mind. It had been there for a while, and though he had tried to ignore it, it wouldn't leave him alone. Various threads were tangling themselves together in his thoughts: Shar and the Maze, Adept Gant, now Reyni . . . He didn't like this. He didn't like it at all.

He said uneasily, 'She isn't usually this late, is she?'

Hestor shrugged. 'She'll turn up when she's hungry. But if Reyni Trevire thinks I'm going to give her his message, he can . . .'. His words trailed off and he stopped still with his fork in mid-air. *'Yandros!'*

Kitto looked alarmed. 'What's the matter? What are you—'

'I'll kill him!' Hestor scrambled to his feet, shoving his plate back so hard that it nearly skidded off the far edge of the table. 'I swear it, I'll *kill* him!'

'Hestor!' Kitto shouted. 'What are you talking about?'

Hestor rounded on him. 'He's gone looking for her, hasn't he? Anyone could have told him where her room is!'

'Hestor, where are you going?'

'To Shar's room, of course, where else? If he's up there—'

Kitto lost his temper. 'So what if he is? Don't be such an idiot! Shar's got a perfect right to see Reyni if she wants to, and if you go barging in and start a quarrel, what good will that do? It'll just turn Shar against you, and make things worse!'

Hestor subsided as he saw the sense of that, but he was still angry. 'I don't trust him,' he said darkly.

'Neither do I, if you want to know.' Kitto's reasons were different, though there was no point saying so to Hestor at the moment.

'Look,' Kitto said firmly. 'If you want to check up on Shar, then do. But you'd better calm down first, or you'll make a mess of everything. Sit down and let's finish eating. If she hasn't turned up by then, we'll go and look for her together.'

Hestor sighed. 'All right.' He sank back on to the bench. 'Sorry, Kitto, I shouldn't have erupted like that. It was just the way he talked, as if . . . I don't know . . . as if he thought he was superior and had all the answers. I felt he was patronising me.'

'You didn't hear the half of it. Before you came, he was going on and on about the Keepers and the Lords of Order. Gave me the crawls.' And Kitto's uneasy feeling was getting stronger . . .

'Come on,' he said. 'Eat. Then we'll go and find out what's what.'

Shar knew she should have waited until much later, when the coast would be clear, but the temptation had been too hard to resist. She had been tense and excited all day, and quite unable to concentrate on mundane work. Luckily, her tutors assumed that her absent-mindedness was simply a result of the rheum and so she hadn't run into any real trouble. But by the time the day's studies were over, she felt as if she were about to explode. She couldn't contain her impatience any longer – she *had* to start work on her plan.

The first step would be traumatic, but it had to be done. She would go back in time to the Marble Hall, and see exactly what had happened on the night her father was killed. She wouldn't make any attempt to intervene this time; all she wanted was to find out how Thel and his accomplices had carried out the murder. So, putting Amber out of her room – she didn't want even him to witness what she was doing – she took out her amulet, mustered all her mental strength, and willed herself to her destination.

The jolt as she materialised in the Marble Hall was much more severe than usual, bringing dizziness and nausea and an acute ringing in her ears. The mists looked different, too; they seemed to have lost a lot of their colour and hung, still and heavy in the Hall, like grey shrouds. The air felt cold and Shar shivered, rubbing her arms, before making her way towards the seven statues of the gods. She was uneasy at the thought of using the statues for cover, but there was no other choice. Hiding places in the Hall were few and far between, and from here she should be close enough to the adepts, when they arrived, to see and hear everything that took place.

She moved behind the statue of Tarod and Ailind, and settled down. She had planned to arrive a few minutes before the adepts came in to begin their ritual. If all had gone according to plan she would not have long to wait.

Time passed. Shar counted seven minutes, then another seven, but nothing happened and no one came. Had she miscalculated? She had worked every- thing out so carefully that it was hard to believe she could have made a mistake. At last she rose, stretched cramped and chilled muscles, then stepped out from behind the statue and moved cautiously towards the metallic door that was the Hall's only entrance and exit. No sound, no sign of movement. Something had gone awry.

Turning, she looked back. The statues seemed vague and slightly distorted, and if she let her imagination loose it would be easy to see movement in them; an arm lifting slightly here, a head turning fractionally there. She shivered again, then glanced to her left. The black mosaic circle wasn't visible, but if she took a sight line from the statues she should be able to find it easily enough.

Slowly Shar crossed the floor, until she could see the circle ahead of her. Three paces from its edge she stopped and stared at it, but her half-formed hope that it would provide a clue to her conundrum was dashed. It was only a pattern in the floor.

She sighed and reached for the amulet, which hung now on a thong around her neck. There was no point staying any longer – she had made a mistake, and the only thing to do was return to her own time and try again from the beginning.

Her fingers touched the amulet. And from the black circle came a soft, ominous hiss.

Shar's head came up sharply, and her pulse raced

with shock. Light was streaming out of the mosaic, flowing ceilingwards in a rushing, shimmering tide. Her mind flashed back to the night when she had created her amulet – this was the same phenomenon! The Gate was stirring again!

Fear overcame shock and she stumbled backwards, her hand clenching tightly on the amulet. The streaming light brightened, moving faster so that the view beyond it became a blur. Then, in the middle of the circle, and hovering above it, something began to take form.

It was a mouth. Not a face but just a mouth, grey and fleshy and weirdly exaggerated, like a shape drawn by a small child. It hung suspended, unmoving, and as its outline became more solid Shar realised that the Hall was suddenly unnaturally quiet. It was what Pellis called a screaming silence; so intense that it felt as if nothing had ever broken it, or ever could. From the racing of a few moments ago her pulse was slowing down to a crawl, and when she tried to breathe it was a terrible effort, as if all the air around her had been sucked away.

For a dreadful interval – she had no idea how long it lasted – she continued to stare at the disembodied mouth. Then it moved. Knowingly, horribly, it smiled.

Shar said, '*Ah*—' and her gasp was picked up and thrown around the Hall in myriad echoes,

AHAHAHAHAH. It sounded like a kind of false, unnatural laughter.

The mouth moved again. It shaped a word, and Shar heard the word spoken in a deep, ugly tone, as though something invisible had pressed close to her ear.

'WHERE?'

The voice was mocking, as though whoever – whatever – spoke was taunting her. Shar's teeth had begun to chatter; she clamped them hard together, swallowed an awful constriction in her throat and hissed, 'What are you?'

YOUYOUYOUYOUYOU. Echoes skittered around her, and the mouth laughed.

'KNOW OR GUESS. WHERE ARE YOU?'

Panic made her aggressive. 'I know where I am! The Marble Hall is—'

'NOT,' the entity interrupted. *'ASK AGAIN. WHERE ARE YOU? WHEREWHEREWHERE?'*

With each *WHERE*, the voice rose higher, until the ugly rasp became a high, shrill twittering. *'WHEREWHEREWHERE? NOT HERE. NOT THERE. WHERE ARE YOU? LOOK BEHIND YOU.'*

Shar's heart lurched and she jerked round. A mere few paces away, hovering at the level of her own head, was a huge, disembodied eye. As she recoiled in horror the eye blinked at her, and the voice said,

'I SEE YOU. WHAT DO YOU SEE? KNOW OR GUESS.'

With an enormous effort Shar dragged air into her lungs. 'Who sent you?' she demanded. 'Where did you come from, and what do you want with me?'

An extraordinary, hiccupping laugh sounded somewhere down by her feet. *'YOU CAME. YOU WANT. EARTH AND WATER AND AIR AND FIRE AND ME! I KNOW WHAT YOU WANT. I KNOW WHERE YOU ARE.'*

'Then tell me!' Shar shouted, and the echoes nearly deafened her: *TELLMETELLMETELLMETELLME!*

The eye closed, very slowly. *'EARTH,'* said the voice. Suddenly Shar's entire body seemed to be made of lead. Her feet grew roots that thrust down through the marble floor. She couldn't move; her own weight was dragging her down, crushing her—

'WATER.'

The crushing sensation jolted away and Shar was falling forward, plunging into ice-cold darkness, feeling it flow over her. Water was in her nose, her ears, her eyes, her mouth; she heard it surging and she was choking, drowning, with no breath to scream—

'AIR.'

Breath came back with an enormous impact and she was whisked around, hair and skirt flying, blown on a howling wind that tore her feet from the ground and whirled her up, up—

'FIRE.'

This time she had the breath to scream, and her shriek of terror exploded through the Marble Hall as an agonising blaze of flame engulfed her. She heard the crackling roar, felt the all-consuming heat, smelled the stench of smoke and charring—

'AND ME!'

Shar found herself sprawled, face down, on the floor of the Hall, in sudden and total silence. Everything was gone; the pain, the fear, the noise; even the terror she had felt a moment ago had vanished. A finger's length from her nose she saw the pattern of the marble mosaic, but it had no colour; it was all black and silver now, and the mist beyond it was grey.

In her ear, the voice whispered again: 'AND ME.'

Shar raised her head. She felt dizzy and sick, and her eyes weren't focusing properly. Something was shimmering before her, like an after-effect of looking at the sun; she shook her head in an effort to clear it, and the voice, behind her and above her now, said softly, 'WHAT IS TIME? KNOW OR GUESS.'

A shadow fell across her and the floating eye drifted into view. It gazed down at her, then, very slowly, blinked.

'HERE IS THE FUTURE.' The shimmering grew stronger, and suddenly Shar's blurred sight cleared and she saw what looked like a network of ropes, made of silver light, radiating outwards from the spot where she was lying. They hung suspended above the floor, like ship's hawsers, and they vibrated faintly as though some unnameable energy was flowing through them.

'BUT WHICH FUTURE?' whispered the voice. 'CHOOSE. KNOW OR GUESS. CHOOSE.'

Shar felt a tugging sensation that seemed to start in the pit of her stomach and drag at her muscles until she felt she was being pulled apart. Then came a sense of something snapping – and suddenly the silver ropes were not ropes at all but paths, each one stretching away into the distance.

And on each path, a different scene was unfolding.

She saw herself as a baby, being taken by Thel to live on Summer Isle after the murder of her parents. She saw Thel's crime discovered and punished, and herself growing up in the castle. She saw the murder attempt fail, and she and her parents living on happily together. And she saw what might have become of her if she had not suspected the truth about her uncle until it was far, far too late.

'WHICH FUTURE?' said the voice softly, enticingly. 'WHICH REALITY? KNOW OR GUESS. TO GUESS IS TO WONDER. BUT TO KNOW IS TO BANISH ALL DOUBT.'

Close by, a patch of the mist swirled and solidified, forming the shape of a thin, grey hand. The hand reached towards Shar; it was holding something long and pointed, that gleamed dully in the dim light. As it laid the object down before her she heard the faint sound of metal on stone.

A knife. The hilt was black and the blade was half the length of her forearm, honed to a lethal edge.

'KNOW, AND BE CERTAIN,' the voice whispered. 'OR GUESS, AND WONDER.'

A strange, red glare was fogging Shar's vision, and her mind burned dark and hot. She reached for the knife, and her hand closed round the hilt and gripped hard. It felt comfortable. It felt *right*.

Behind her, in the black mosaic circle, the mouth that had no face laughed a thin, hooting laugh. Ignoring it, hardly hearing it, Shar turned slowly towards one of the gleaming paths. The tableau to which it led was clear. She saw her uncle, her father, her mother, and all the adepts who had been present at the ritual when the 'accident' occurred. They had gathered in a circle, hands linked, and their chant was just beginning.

Shar smiled with a strange, ugly twisting of her mouth. She got to her feet. She raised the knife. Slowly, steadily, she began to walk towards the distant, unsuspecting figure of Thel Starnor . . .

13

Hestor's suspicion was right. As soon as he left the dining hall Reyni asked a passing servant where Shar Tillmer's room was, and within another minute he was making his way up the stairs.

The first thing he saw as he turned into the passage was the two cats. Amber was sitting in front of Shar's door, staring fixedly at it as though willing it to open. The other cat, a pure white one, crouched on a nearby window ledge. It, too, was gazing at the door, and now and then its tail lashed against the stonework. As Reyni approached, both animals looked up, and Amber mewed loudly.

'What's the matter, little friend? Have you been shut out?' Stepping carefully over Amber, Reyni knocked on the door. No answer came; he tried again, then pressed his ear to the wood, but could hear no sound from inside.

Gently he tried the door and found that it was not locked. Under normal circumstances he wouldn't have dreamed of entering anyone's private room uninvited, but these circumstances weren't normal. If he must break the rules to help Shar, his conscience would have to take second place.

He eased the door open. Amber darted in, and Reyni glanced back to the window ledge, wondering if the white cat would follow. But it had disappeared, and there was no sign of it anywhere in the corridor. It must have slipped away silently and swiftly while he was deciding what to do, Reyni thought. He just hoped that it wouldn't find Shar and alert her.

He entered the room, closed the door behind him, and began to look around.

It was obvious that Shar had not tidied up for some time. The bed was strewn with clothes, and several pairs of shoes had been kicked off and discarded on the floor. Some of the shoes were muddy or grass-stained, and one pair had grains of sand stuck to the leather. It seemed highly unlikely, thought Reyni, that Shar would climb down through the stack to the beach at this time of year, so this could well be significant.

Reyni turned next to Shar's work-table, and was surprised to find it neat and empty, in contrast to the rest of the clutter. The table had a drawer but it was locked, and there were no papers anywhere else in the room. A pile of books lay on the window ledge; just student books, so nothing important there. In fact, apart from the shoes and the suspiciously tidy work-table, there was nothing to give him any clues at all.

It wouldn't be wise to stay for longer than a few minutes, so Reyni took a last look around. Had he missed anything? It seemed not. Except . . . he paused as he realised that there was no fire in Shar's grate. That *was* odd. In this northern climate people kept their fires burning day and night when the weather was cold. And if Shar had been suffering from the rheum, she would need more warmth rather than less.

He crossed to the hearth and crouched down to feel the ashes. They were stone cold, so the fire must have been out for hours. It suggested that Shar had not been spending much time in here lately. So where had she been?

At his back, something giggled.

'*Ah!*' Reyni jumped as if he'd been shot, and swung round. There was no one there; but suddenly he had an awful, crawling sense of being watched. Sweat broke out on his face, and in an unsteady voice he whispered, 'Who is it? Where are you? Shar . . ?'

Silence. Outside, daylight had turned to dusk and the light was fading fast. In the gloom the room looked unreal; colours had drained to silvery grey; nothing seemed quite tangible. Reyni felt frightened. There were supernatural forces at work here – not the benign powers of Order that he had learned to put his trust in, but something uncontrolled and dangerous. *Chaotic*. He was out of his depth and didn't want to stay any longer – he would return to Fosker and Gant and give them his report.

He hurried to the door, checked that no one was about, and slipped out into the passage. But, as he turned to shut the door behind him, a flicker like pale lightning shivered across his view. Reyni blinked, recoiling – then stared dumbstruck at the vision that had appeared from nowhere in the room behind him.

Two figures were crossing the floor, grey as ghosts and utterly silent. Reyni recognised them both instantly. One was Shar; the other was Thel Starnor. And Shar had a knife in her hand.

'*Shar!*' Forgetting all thoughts of secrecy, Reyni shouted her name in horrified panic. It didn't occur to him that Thel was already dead and this could only be an illusion; in that one terrible moment he truly believed that the scene was real and Shar was about to commit murder. Her uncle had his back to her, unaware of her presence, and now she was raising the knife—

'Shar, *no!*' Reyni plunged back into the room, reaching out instinctively to grab hold of Shar and drag her away from her quarry. His grasping fingers closed on nothing – and the two figures vanished.

Reyni made a choking noise and stumbled backwards until his back slammed against the wall. Slowly, his reeling mind accepted the fact that there was nothing and no one here. No Shar, no Thel, no knife. It had been a mirage, a hallucination. It hadn't *happened*.

Reyni's pulse was roaring in his ears, and through it he could hear the ragged sound of his own breathing. Mustering all his willpower, he silently repeated a prayer to Aeoris, and after a minute it calmed him enough to loosen the paralysis that held him. On shaking legs he pushed himself away from the wall and left the room. The door shut behind him, and Reyni stumbled away along the corridor to find Fosker and Gant.

Hestor didn't bother to knock on Shar's door but simply opened it and marched straight in. Kitto shut his eyes and winced, expecting to hear the first explosion of a full-blown quarrel. However, it didn't come, and when after a few seconds he opened his eyes again and peered round the door, he saw Hestor standing, hands on hips, in a gloomy, empty room.

'She's not here,' Hestor said.

'So I see.' Kitto came in. 'Then where *is* she?'

'The gods alone know. But I'm going to find her. And when I do, I'm going to make her tell me what she's up to.'

'I think it's something to do with the Maze,' Kitto stated.

'Maybe; maybe not. We'll soon see, won't we?' Hestor turned back towards the door. 'Come on.'

He went out and away down the corridor, but Kitto didn't follow immediately; instead, he lit a candle and gazed carefully round the room. As usual, Hestor had taken one glance at the obvious, jumped to a conclusion and acted on it. Kitto wasn't sure that this was the wisest thing to do. Too many apparently unrelated threads seemed to be tangling together, and he wanted to see where they led before making any decisions. Reyni was involved, he was certain – he simply didn't believe all that folderol about coming here just to see Shar. The whole business with the Keepers of Light was fishy, too.

But there was no point in trying to explain to Hestor. Aside of anything else, Hestor's jealousy of Reyni would get in the way of common sense and make matters far too complicated. Better to wait a while, Kitto thought, stay alert and see what developed.

He turned to go—

'*No!*' The voice came out of nowhere, and it stopped Kitto in his tracks. '*No, I can't! I'm trying, but I can't!*'

It was Shar's voice! Kitto spun round, looking wildly in all directions, but there was nothing to be seen.

'Shar?' he called. 'Shar?'

'Uhh *it won't, I can't do it, it's too*—' The words snapped off into silence.

'Shar! Where are you?' Kitto cried. 'What's happening?'

He was answered by a sudden yell from the courtyard, and the stamp of running feet. There was a yellow glow outside that hadn't been there moments before, and as it brightened Kitto heard a man's voice bellow a single word.

'Fire!'

Kitto darted to the window, and his jaw dropped. Flames were rising on the far side of the courtyard. They hadn't yet got a strong hold – but that would change fast. For the fire was coming from the hay and feed store attached to the stable block.

And the stable was full of horses . . .

More voices shouted now, and people were converging on the stable carrying buckets, urns, anything that would hold water. The terrified scream of a horse echoed from one of the stalls, and Kitto forgot Shar, forgot everything except this new and horrifying emergency. Jack-knifing around, he pelted from the room and away towards the nearest stairs.

'WHAT IS THE FUTURE? KNOW OR GUESS . . .'

Shar crouched, panting like a wild animal, on the floor of the Marble Hall, as the voice from the disembodied mouth rang in her ears. She *did* know, now, where one of those thrumming silver threads, those magical paths, would lead her. And she knew, too, what manner of being had come to her in the Hall, and was speaking to her and guiding her.

Tonight, she had once again travelled far beyond the low elemental worlds, into a dimension more powerful than anything she had ever tried to reach before. Tonight, she had encountered an oracle of the Fifth Plane. And the oracle had opened the door of Time to her.

A prickling shudder penetrated through from her skin to her marrow as she remembered how she had felt in the moment when she'd plunged the knife into Thel Starnor's back. It had not been real, of course; it was an act, a theatre, to show her what might have been. But she had heard him gasp, and watched him fall, and then she had looked onwards down the silver path to a new future, in which her parents lived and there was no grief and no horror to taint her life. And she knew now that what could be done in the world of *might have been* could also be done in reality.

Very slowly, she rose to her feet. *Know or guess.* Oh, she knew now, and the knowledge had banished the last of her doubts. She *could* kill Thel.

'I'll go back.' She spoke half to herself and half to the entity that hovered behind her. 'I'll go back, and I'll choose the right time, and then I'll prepare . . .'

She flexed her hands, but the knife was no longer there; it had dissolved along with the silver paths and the tableaux, and now there was only the empty Hall and the mists.

The oracle didn't reply, but she sensed the eye staring at her as she groped for her amulet on its thong. Gathering her concentration, Shar willed herself back to her bedroom in the castle—

And screamed in shock as she was plunged suddenly and shockingly into a dizzying confusion of light and colour and noise. *This wasn't the Maze!* Shar fell helplessly, twisting and turning, and all around her there were flames and lightning and tidal waves and avalanches and hurricanes. She screamed again, though her cry was lost in the roaring elemental din. Then suddenly a new force snatched hold of her and spun her out of the mayhem, and she found herself in the Marble Hall once more, with the sound of the oracle's laughter ringing like a cold bell in her mind.

'*IT IS NOT SO EASY, DAUGHTER OF STORMS,*' the disembodied mouth said. '*YOU HAVE COME TOO FAR NOW. YOU MUST PASS THROUGH THE LOWER PLANES, OR TAKE ANOTHER WAY HOME. AND THERE IS ONLY ONE OTHER WAY.*'

Understanding struggled through to Shar's battered senses. She had found her way to this dimension through the elemental worlds, and now they lay between her and her own, physical dimension. She didn't think she had the strength to fight and control the storm of energies rampaging on the planes of fire, air, water and earth. She had come through them once, and survived, but then the oracle had helped her, and she dared not count on its help a second time. Yet a stubbornly ferocious streak made her rise to the challenge. She could at least *try!*

What happened in the next few minutes was painful and terrifying. Though she didn't know it, Shar did come close to succeeding – the fact that Kitto had heard her as she struggled to break through was proof of that – but at last, drained and exhausted, she was forced to admit defeat.

'I can't do it!' She was on hands and knees, anger and frustration raging like a physical pain in her. 'I've tried, but I *can't!* Not yet – I haven't learned, I haven't got the power!' Through the disordered strands of her hair she looked up at the eye floating above her. 'What is the other way? Tell me!'

The eye blinked, and in the black mosaic circle the mouth smiled a secretive, knowing smile. '*INTO THE GATE,*' it said. '*THROUGH THE GATE. WHERE CAN IT LEAD? CHOOSE, AND DISCOVER.*'

A way between dimensions, a door that could lead from any one realm to any other . . . Shar remembered Adept Farial's lesson. She stood up. Her legs didn't want to support her, but she forced her muscles to obey and unsteadily moved to the black circle. A moment's hesitation, then she stepped over the border and stood in the circle's centre.

'*CHOOSE, AND DISCOVER.*' The oracle's voice was softer, and the grey mouth seemed to be outside the circle now. Everything out there looked blurred and murky, as though a veil was materialising between herself and the rest of the Marble Hall. Shar remembered the river of light streaming up from the mosaic, and suddenly she wanted to get away. She focused her mind—

And an instant later she burst through the barrier between worlds, to crash like a thrown doll on to her bed.

The flailing, jarring thump of her fall knocked away what little breath there was in her lungs. Lights flashed and flared under her eyelids and there was a giddy banging in her skull. For more than a minute she could only lie gasping, like a stranded fish, among the disordered bedclothes.

At last the worst of it passed and she was able to move under her own volition. With an effort she shifted to a more comfortable position. Outside, the sun was setting, and the only light was a fading crimson glare that filled the sky and cast gloomy shadows in her room; but she didn't want the effort of finding and lighting candles. All she wanted – *needed* – was sleep.

The castle seemed very quiet. She heard footsteps pass by in the passage outside, and a murmur of voices reached her. Two people talking . . . one of them was Pellis, and the other . . . Shar thought vaguely that it sounded like Hestor, but it was too deep; an older voice. Not that it mattered. They were going away now, fading into blissful silence and leaving her in peace.

Like water soaking into dry ground, the last reserves of her strength ran out. She was so *tired;* far too tired to think clearly, or to take in anything around her in a way that made any sense.

Shar nestled more snugly into her pillows and pulled the bedcovers up around herself. Her eyelids drooped, then closed, and her body relaxed as her mind slid away into sleep.

14

'Bring him over here, Kitto! Gentle with him, that's the way!'

Through the slowly clearing smoke and steam Kitto saw the head ostler beckoning, and he turned the tall, iron-grey gelding away from the stables and towards a quieter part of the courtyard.

'Hey now, hey now, there's my boy, there's my beauty!' He talked to the animal in a soft, steady tone, reinforcing it with reassuring mental pictures as he might talk to a cat. Horses weren't telepathic, but it seemed to help anyway; the grey was calming down now, and followed him trustingly.

'Good lad, Kitto!' The ostler took the halter-rope from him, and Kitto reached up to remove his jerkin from the gelding's head. The jerkin had done good service tonight; he had tied it over the eyes of each horse he had led to safety, so that they could not see the smoke and fire and were less likely to panic. The garment was soaked and blackened now, but that couldn't be helped. What mattered was that the fire was out, and there were no casualties.

The ostler was running his hands over the gelding's flanks and legs, checking for injury.

'He's fine.' The ostler straightened up, and waved away something small and fast and noisy that flittered at him out of the darkness. The gelding snorted, jerking back, and Kitto laid a soothing hand on its shoulder.

'Quiet, now, quiet!' He looked at the ostler. 'I think they're more frightened of the elementals than they were of the fire!'

'Probably are, and I don't blame them. Still, we'd have been hard pressed to stop this without the elementals' help. I for one give thanks to them!'

Kitto nodded sombre agreement. They had been fighting a losing battle until several senior adepts, including Gant, Pellis and the High Initiate, had arrived on the scene. Rather than join the chain of people toiling to put water on the fire, they had summoned a horde of small water-elementals. Excited by the tumult, the elementals had been over-enthusiastic, drenching everything in sight with fountains and cataracts and miniature rainstorms. But at least now the fire was out; saturated clothes and ruined feed was a small price to pay.

More people were converging on the courtyard now, among them many of the visiting dignitaries, anxiously enquiring about their horses. Their arrival was more of a hindrance than a help, and the ostler sighed as one group headed in their direction.

'Put the grey in the lines with the others while I deal with this,' he said. 'I'll try and keep them back – don't want the horses getting upset all over again.'

As Kitto led the gelding away he heard the ostler's voice rising loudly and confidently. 'Yes, sirs, all's well and there's no cause for concern! Now, if you'll just gather over here . . .'

Kitto breathed a sigh of relief. Then someone else loomed out of the evening and said, 'You, boy. Kitto, isn't it?'

Kitto looked up and found Adept Gant confronting him. The grey gelding snorted and jinked; Gant laid a hand on its nose and – rather to Kitto's surprise – it quietened.

'I saw you bringing this horse out just now,' Gant said. 'Is it hurt?'

'No, sir,' Kitto said. 'The head ostler checked him just now. He's come to no harm.'

'Good. My cousin will be relieved.' Gant actually *smiled* at him. 'He's very fond of the animal. Well done, Kitto.'

Kitto blinked in astonishment and was still groping for a reply as Gant walked away.

The ostler came back, having reassured the other

enquirers, to find him still staring after Gant's departing back. 'Close your mouth; there aren't any flies to catch,' he said. 'What are you gawping at, anyway?'

Kitto told him, and he shrugged. 'Oh, so he's Adept Gant's cousin, is he? I wondered when I heard his family name.'

'Whose family name?' Kitto asked.

'Fosker Sangen. That cult leader who arrived this afternoon with his acolyte. You know; the ones who wear the peculiar clothes and don't like Lord Yandros.' The ostler made a religious sign to show that he meant no irreverence.

In a single instant, several of Kitto's apparently unrelated threads tied themselves into a firm knot, and he stared. 'He's Adept Gant's *cousin?* Are you sure?'

'I took the horse from him myself, so I ought to be. Anyway, what's it to you?'

'It's nothing to me,' said Kitto quietly. 'Nothing at all.'

The ostler laughed. 'Just the shock of getting a compliment from that dry old stick, eh? Ah, well. I doubt it'll ever happen again, so enjoy the glory while you can. Come on, now. There's no time to stand around like a fencepost; we've got work to do!'

Kitto said, 'Yes, sir,' but he wasn't really listening. As the ostler walked away he stared across the courtyard, ignoring the restless horses. Gant's cousin, Reyni

Trevire and the Maze . . . they were all connected. Kitto didn't know *how* they were connected, but he was as certain of it as he had been of anything in his life. And in the middle, pulling all the threads together, was Shar.

Kitto recalled, with a shiver, the eerie incident in Shar's room just before the fire broke out. Her voice, calling as though from another world . . . Where had she been at that moment? And far, far more importantly, where was she now? Kitto knew that he wouldn't have a moment's peace of mind until he found out.

He stood, dithering, as a sense of duty warred with an urge to search for Shar. If Hestor were here . . . But Hestor wasn't here, and to track him down now would waste time. It wouldn't take more than a couple of minutes to go to Shar's room, see if she was back. If she wasn't, then he would find Hestor, and after that—

Kitto didn't pause to think what would happen after that. He had made his decision, and he called to one of the stable-boys who was tending the line of tethered horses.

'Hey, Amit, take this animal for me!' He thrust the grey gelding's reins into the surprised boy's hand. 'Put him with the rest, and if the head ostler asks, tell him I've had to do something for someone!'

Before Amit could reply, Kitto was sprinting away

across the courtyard and up the steps to the main doors.

From where he stood in the lee of the castle wall, Adept Gant watched Kitto's small figure race into the castle, then turned to Fosker at his side.

'Excellent.' There was quiet satisfaction in his voice. 'Kitto is a very intelligent boy. He's already made the connection we wanted him to make, and I don't doubt that he's gone in search of Shar. It's time for another word with Reyni.'

Reyni had joined in the rescue and they found him by the hay store, helping to mop up. Gant explained, briefly, the bait that had been laid for Kitto, then told the musician what they wanted him to do. It was important that Shar's whereabouts should be discovered as soon as possible; Gant believed that Kitto knew where she was, and Reyni was to follow him and keep a discreet watch.

Reyni was thankful that Gant wasn't asking more. He had had a bad fright in Shar's room, and he wasn't keen to repeat the experience or anything else like it. Relating the event to Gant and Fosker had brought it back with horrible clarity – and their reaction had unnerved him even further. They wouldn't tell him what they were thinking, but they were obviously alarmed, and when Reyni had asked bluntly whether Shar was in danger, Gant's mouth had clamped shut, while Fosker would only say that they must pray and hope. Reyni had wanted to ask more questions, but then the fire had broken out in the courtyard and there had been no time for anything but the emergency. Now though, the emergency was over and they could concentrate on Shar again.

And as he set off on his assignment, Reyni remembered Fosker's words and murmured a private, fervent prayer.

Like Hestor earlier, Kitto didn't bother to knock on Shar's door but flung it open and went in. He was praying that he would find Shar there, but his hopes crashed as, by the light of the candles he hadn't finished extinguishing, he saw that the room was empty.

'Oh, Shar . . .' His voice came out as a croak. 'Where *are* you?'

He shivered, wondering if Shar's voice would speak out of thin air as it had done before. But nothing answered him. Even Amber wasn't here, so he couldn't try to learn anything from his telepathic mind. There was just Shar's rumpled bed, her discarded clothes, and the guttering candles. Nothing else.

Advancing cautiously into the room, Kitto took a look around. He noticed the stained shoes, which he hadn't seen before, and frowned. Grass, earth, sand

. . . yet as far as he knew, Shar hadn't been outside the castle gates since before she had caught the rheum. There were some coins on her bedside table, and a withered flower. A *flower*, at *this* time of year? It was a mystery.

But a mystery wasn't a clue, and Kitto's worry started to turn into dread. On impulse he snatched up the withered flower and put it in his jerkin pocket, then he made for the door.

'All right,' Hestor said, spreading his fingers to count on them. 'Let's go over it one last time. Shar isn't in her room, she isn't in the courtyard, and no one's seen her in the dining hall. She left the study-rooms when her last lesson finished two hours before sunset, and you've told me her pony is with all the other horses, so she can't have gone riding.'

Kitto snorted. 'At night? And in this weather?'

'I know, but never mind; we've got to consider everything.' Hestor looked round the dining hall, where one or two latecomers were still eating their meals. 'Amber isn't about, either, and that's very peculiar. If anything was wrong, he'd surely have alerted us.'

'Maybe he's gone with her.'

'That's what I'm thinking. But where *are* they?'

Kitto shivered. 'We haven't even moved from square one, have we? We just don't know where to start looking.' He paused, then: 'I'm scared for her, Hestor. After what I heard in her room—'

'I know. But we could comb the castle from the spires to the cellars and still not find a trace of her.' Hestor hesitated. 'I'm not very good at scrying. But it might be our only hope.'

Despite his mistrust of sorcery, Kitto nodded. 'I'll try anything.'

'Right. Then we'll go to Shar's room later tonight, and I'll see what I can do. We'll round up some of the cats, too; they might give us a clue about Amber.' Hestor stood up. 'I'd better go and get some things, books and so forth; I'll probably need them.' He paused. 'Don't worry. We'll find her.'

'Yes,' said Kitto, wishing he felt as confident as Hestor sounded. 'We'll find her.'

When Shar woke, she thought at first that it was dawn. Her room wasn't exactly light, but it wasn't exactly dark either; a reddish glow, deeper than the sun, was coming in at her window, and long, early-morning shadows stretched out across the floor.

She sat up. Her mind was still hazy, but as it slowly cleared, the previous night's events came back in greater and greater detail. With them came a mingling of excitement and dread. What she had done, what she had achieved . . . she had dared more, and travelled farther, than she could have dreamed of doing even two days ago. Now, she believed she was only a short step from her ultimate goal.

She got out of bed and went to the window. The courtyard outside was deserted, but the sun had obviously risen, for the entire sky was suffused with blood-red light. There wasn't a cloud to be seen; the temperature was spring-like, and Shar yawned and stretched, enjoying the warmth. She felt hungry – little wonder, as she hadn't eaten anything since yesterday morning – and decided to go down to the dining hall for an early breakfast.

When she looked around for the clothes she had discarded, they weren't there. She must have put them away, she thought, though she couldn't remember doing it. Just as well; if anyone had come in and found them, awkward questions might have been asked. It didn't seem worth rummaging through her linen-chest for a fresh change, so she smoothed down the crumpled dress she was wearing, ran the comb from her reticule through her hair, and left the room.

The corridor was as deserted as the courtyard, and as she walked towards the main stairs something nagged at Shar's mind. For a minute or two she couldn't focus it, but then it came. By now, the crimson dawn light should be brightening and growing paler as the sun started to climb . . . but it wasn't. Since she woke, it had not changed at all.

Shar stopped in the middle of the passage, attuning her senses to the castle around her. Everything was so *quiet*. There were no sounds of footsteps, no distant voices, nothing. However early it might be, *someone* was always up and about by sunrise. And where were the cats? Normally, she only had to step out of her room and at least one or two would emerge from nowhere to greet her. But this morning, even Amber wasn't anywhere to be seen. Where was he?

Where was everyone . . ?

She could see the staircase ahead of her, and abruptly she ran towards it, halting again at the top and peering over the balustrade to the entrance hall below. It was empty. And still the silence continued.

Slowly, Shar started down the stairs. She was acutely aware of the noise her feet made; each step seemed to echo from one end of the castle to the other. Reaching the ground floor, she turned towards the dining hall. The double doors were open, but even before she reached them she could see that there was no one inside. No fire burned in the huge hearth, and the long tables, which should have been set last night in readiness for breakfast, were bare.

Shar's heart now thumped excruciatingly as she ventured into the hall, and her mouth was so dry that at first she couldn't find her voice. When she did, her tentative call wavered with fear.

'Hello? Is anyone here . . ?'

No answer. *Where were they all?* Near panic now, she groped for a mental link with one of the cats – any cat, it didn't matter – but there was no response.

Whirling round, Shar ran back to the entrance hall and down another passage that led to Neryon Voss's study.

'High Initiate!' She knocked hard on the study door. 'High Initiate, are you there?'

The door wasn't latched properly and suddenly it burst open, catapulting Shar into the room beyond. She tripped on the edge of a rug, stumbled, regained her balance . . . and froze.

There was no one in the room. But, above the desk by the study window, a disembodied eye hung in mid-air.

And a voice behind her said, *'WHERE ARE YOU NOW? ANYWHERE. TIME IS WHAT YOU WILL IT. CHOOSE.'*

Chilly, silvery laughter echoed from far away in the depths of the castle, and Shar turned to see the grey mouth of the Fifth-Plane oracle smiling at her. Slowly but certainly, understanding dawned. This was not the castle. Or if it was, it was not the castle of stone and mortar, but a mirage, a reflection. She had not returned to the physical world. Instead, she had broken through another barrier, into a dimension where time and space were not fixed, but everything existed in potential.

Everything . . .

'*TIME IS WHAT YOU WILL*,' the entity said again, more softly.

Tentatively, her heart palpitating, Shar closed one hand round the amulet at her neck, and focused her mind. *The High Initiate is at work in his study, but he is not Neryon. This is two hundred years ago . . .*

She felt a flick of mental energy, though whether it came from within her or from some outside source, she did not know.

Then the eye and the mouth vanished, and a fair-haired man looked up from where he sat in the chair behind the desk. Shar recognised him immediately from the old portraits; though he looked a little older and there were lines of strain around his hazel eyes.

Keridil Toln smiled a polite query at her and said, 'Yes? Can I help you?'

Shar's wit came to her rescue and she made a quick bow. 'I – I'm sorry, sir; I must have taken a wrong turning. Please excuse me—'

She fled from the study, closed the door behind her and leaned against the cold stone of the wall while a measure of calm returned. *Two hundred years.* And she had stepped into that ancient time as easily as stepping through the door of her own bedroom.

She became aware of noises then. Footsteps, voices, busy sounds from the direction of the dining hall. The castle was no longer deserted but had become a hive of activity, as the past she had conjured stirred fully to life. Someone in extraordinarily old-fashioned clothes passed by at the end of the corridor, and with a jolt Shar realised that anyone who took more than a casual glance at her would realise instantly that something was awry.

She said, aloud and urgently, *'Stop!'*

The sounds faded, ceased. The steady crimson light glowed outside the windows once more. And, again, the eye and mouth of the oracle hung before her.

'*WHAT YOU WILL . . .*' the mouth whispered. Then a hand like faint smoke appeared, holding something in its grasp. A knife, the blade glimmering blood-red in the eerie light . . . Shar felt a rising sickness of excitement and, almost without her conscious knowledge, she reached out to grasp the knife's hilt.

Twenty years would be enough; that was what she had decided at the start. Before she was born; possibly even before Thel Starnor had begun making his evil plans. This time, though, it would not be a pretence or a rehearsal. This time, his death would be *real*.

The ghostly hand released the knife, and Shar slipped it into her belt, hiding it behind a carefully tucked fold of her skirt. She touched the amulet; focused her will. And as the oracle winked out, sound and life began to return to the castle . . .

15

This time, Tarod did alert Yandros.

The disturbance had been much more powerful, and the Chaos lord had a strong suspicion that the Circle adepts were in danger of running into trouble. Yandros came in answer to his call, and stood watching the streaming river of light, which now was following an impossible spiral path through the ever-changing walls of a cliff made from liquid fire. The colours in the river were changing, too – becoming darker and less clearly defined – and after studying the flow for some time Yandros nodded.

'You're right; there is potential trouble here,' he said. 'But I'm not going to intervene. The Gate hasn't actually been opened yet, and just because someone is tampering with it, that's not reason enough for us to take any action.'

Tarod looked sidelong at him. 'You surprise me.'

'Do I? Good.' Yandros smiled his humorous, dangerous smile. 'No, seriously, I'd take a guess that this is pure accident and the adepts don't even know that it's happening. They've probably made a mistake in the ritual for creating the Maze amulets, and that's set up a ripple in the Gate. It'll settle down in its own good time.'

'So we do nothing?'

'Correct.' Yandros yawned. 'For one thing, any move on our part would bring the wrath of our old friend and cousin Aeoris down on our heads, and I *really* don't want the tedium of having to argue with him again. Let it be, Tarod. Let the mortals make their own mistakes and put them right. They'll harm only themselves, and the lesson will be good for them.' He started to turn away, then paused. 'If you want to speak to your counterpart, Ailind of Order, that's up to you. But I wouldn't go to the bother.'

A faint, high singing note, a little like the first sound of a Warp storm, rang through the air as Yandros stepped into another dimension of the Chaos realm and vanished. Tarod, left alone, stared at the river of light again. He didn't feel completely reassured – but he also took Yandros's point about stirring up trouble with the lords of Order. The two sides had been less hostile to each other since the battle with the Sixth-Plane entity a few months ago, but it probably wouldn't be wise to test the truce too far.

Although, if this anomaly happened again, he might indeed speak to Ailind. Just as a precaution.

★　　★　　★

'I can see the pictures clearly enough.' Hestor sat back on his heels, gazing glumly at the scrying glass on the floor before him. 'But the trouble is, I don't know what they're trying to tell me.'

Kitto, kneeling nearby, craned forward to look at the glass for himself, but all he could see was the unsteady reflection of the one candle they had lit.

He wished they had been able to find Amber; or any of the castle cats, for that matter. They all seemed to have taken themselves off somewhere, and he had an unpleasant feeling that that was significant. If Hestor was getting nowhere, as seemed to be the case, then the cats were about the only hope they had left.

'What *are* you seeing?' he asked. It was a slim chance that he would be able to interpret the images, but it was worth a try.

Hestor sighed. 'There's an eye,' he said. 'Just an eye. It keeps appearing, but only for a moment. It looks straight at me, then it vanishes again.'

Hope flared. 'Is it Shar?'

'I don't think so. I don't think it's even human.'

'Does it look . . . friendly?'

'Not exactly friendly . . . but not hostile, either.'

That didn't help. 'What else?'

'Something like – like a silver cobweb.' Hestor pushed hair out of his eyes. 'And before you ask, no, I don't know what that means any more than you do. But I get a strong feeling that it *leads* somewhere.'

'Can you see where?'

'I've been trying, but it blurs and fades whenever I start following any of the threads.'

Kitto chewed his lower lip. 'Then maybe,' he said after a few moments' thought, 'you haven't picked the right thread to follow?' Hestor looked at him keenly, and he added, 'It's just a thought. Probably way off the mark—'

'No,' Hestor interrupted. 'I don't believe it is. I should have thought of it myself.' He looked into the glass again. 'Trouble is, there are so many to choose from. We could be here all night before I find the right one.'

'I can't see any other choice. Can you?'

A pause, then: 'No. No, I can't.'

Silence fell once more as Hestor returned his mind to the task. Several minutes passed. Kitto wanted to cough and was battling the urge for fear of breaking Hestor's concentration, when suddenly Hestor hissed, 'I've found it! I'm following it; the picture's changing—'

His words cut off, and even in the dim light Kitto could see that the colour had drained from his face.

'Hestor, what is it?' Kitto's heart thudded with dread.

Hestor moved slowly, carefully back from the glass, as though retreating from something deadly. 'A knife,' he said in a low voice. 'A bloodstained knife. It cut through the strand I was following. And then it—'

He got no further, for at that moment, and without any warning, the door of the room was flung open from outside. Both boys jumped violently, Kitto swearing in shock – then they froze as they looked at the doorway.

There was no one there.

'How . . ? The question died, unfinished, on Kitto's tongue.

'I bolted it,' Hestor whispered.

'I know. I saw you. What in the name of—'

This time it was Kitto who was interrupted, for from somewhere behind them a man's voice said, quite clearly, 'Damn!'

They whipped round.

Nothing. No intruder, no apparition, nothing but the still, quiet room.

Until a shadow, that moments ago had not existed, moved.

'*Look!*' Kitto grabbed Hestor's arm in a ferocious grip, his other hand pointing to the window. Hestor saw the dim, human shape that reflected momentarily in the glass, as though a ghost had passed by. For one moment its face showed clearly; then came an echoing footstep, like something heard in a dream, and the door slammed shut.

At Kitto's side, Hestor made an inarticulate noise.

Kitto turned. Hestor was sitting on the floor, legs sprawled as if he had lost his balance and fallen. He had knocked the scrying glass aside, but he was oblivious to it; his face was blank with shock.

'Hestor . . ?' Kitto quavered.

Hestor's mouth worked convulsively. 'It was Sanquar,' he said. 'Adept Sanquar.'

'That—' Kitto waved a helpless hand at the windows. 'That *figure?*'

'Yes.'

'Who's Adept Sanquar?'

'A f-friend of my family.' Hestor's body was shaking, as well as his voice. 'He . . .'

'He *what?*'

'He – died when I was ten.' Suddenly a flush of high colour flared back into Hestor's cheeks, and perspiration broke out on his forehead, though the room was cold. 'Oh, great Yandros, what has Shar *done?*'

'What do you mean?' Kitto didn't understand. 'How can this have anything to do with Shar?'

'It has,' Hestor said hollowly. 'Believe me, it has.' He was recovering from the shock, and pulled himself up until he was kneeling on the floor. He picked up the scrying glass and examined it, but its surface was blank now.

'Just before the door flew open,' he continued, 'I was about to tell you something.'

'The knife – you said it cut through the strand you were following, and then . . . Then what?'

'The strand divided into a lot of smaller strands,' Hestor said. 'Like the end of a cord fraying. And the knife turned into a pendulum; it swung across the picture, and then it – it broke.'

'Does that mean something?'

'Yes.' Hestor looked at him. 'Haven't you ever seen the timepiece in the High Initiate's study? It's got a mechanism that marks the hours; the mechanism's worked by a pendulum. *Time*, Kitto! That's what the glass was showing me; that's what it means. Shar isn't just experimenting with the Maze – she's meddling with Time itself!'

Kitto was aghast. 'How can she? Time isn't a – a *thing!*'

'I know; and I don't pretend to understand. But I'm sure that's what the glass was trying to tell us.' Hestor scrambled to his feet and looked around the room. 'Light some more candles, Kitto. We won't learn anything more from scrying – it's time for more ordinary methods.'

Kitto did as he was asked, and as the room brightened, Hestor started to explore.

'We must have missed a clue,' he said. 'No one can cover their tracks perfectly; there has to be *something* here to lead us in the right direction!'

Kitto recalled the puzzles they had already unearthed,

but none of them added up to a sensible picture. However, there was one thing they had not investigated.

'Her work-table . . .' he said.

Hestor paused. 'What about it?'

'It's too tidy. The rest of the room's a complete mess, but there's nothing at all on the table. That isn't like Shar, is it?'

He was right, Hestor realised. Shar *never* put her study papers away; if he had a gravine for every time she had been late for a tutorial because she couldn't find her notes among the clutter, he would be rich by now. Yet here was the table, cleared and empty.

'She's hidden something.' An eager note crept into his voice. 'I'd take any wager on it! And where's the most obvious place?'

'The table drawer!' Kitto tried it. 'It's locked.'

That, to Hestor, was confirmation enough. 'Have you got any tools on you?' he asked.

'Yes, but—'

'Give me something to force the lock with.'

No ostler was ever without something useful in his pockets, but Kitto was dubious. 'We can't go prying into Shar's private things!' he protested.

'We've got to! If I'm wrong, then I'll apologise to Shar later and take the blame, but we can't worry about her privacy now. Come on, Kitto, just give it to me. Hurry *up!*'

Defeated, Kitto handed over a folding clasp with

a short blade, a hook and a spike on it. Hestor tried the spike, and after a few moments' prising they both heard the drawer lock snap.

The drawer was full of notes. Some were in Shar's handwriting, others were not. Pulling them all out, Hestor spread them on the floor and began to riffle through them quickly, while Kitto hovered uncertainly behind him. Kitto could make out some of what Shar had written, but the other hand defeated him; his reading simply wasn't up to it.

Hestor picked up one of the pages to examine it more closely. The rustling of paper stopped, and in the silence that followed, Kitto thought he heard a foot shuffle outside the door. He tensed – then intuition struck him sharply, and in three strides he was across the room and wrenching the door open. Even as Hestor looked up and said, 'What—', Kitto lunged out into the corridor.

And came face to face with Reyni.

For an instant the two of them stared at each other. Then with a quick movement Kitto pulled the door shut behind him.

'You!' he said aggressively. '*What* a surprise. What do you want – as if I didn't know?'

Reyni had done exactly what Fosker and Gant had warned him to avoid at all costs, and he cursed himself for a careless fool. Following Kitto and Hestor to Shar's room he had positioned himself outside the door, hoping to learn something useful. There had been a long period of silence followed by the murmur of voices, but Reyni couldn't overhear what was being said. Then had come the sound of something breaking, and a lot of rustling; intrigued, Reyni had pressed closer to the door, and that was when Kitto had caught him out.

Now, he could only try to make the best of it. In what he hoped was a genuinely casual way, he said, 'I'm looking for Shar. Is she in her room?'

He tried to move past to the door, but Kitto blocked his way. 'Who says this is Shar's room?' he demanded.

Reyni smiled. 'Someone told me.'

'Oh, *did* they? Well, for your information—'

Kitto didn't get any further, for the door opened behind him and Hestor appeared. Hestor looked at Reyni, and his eyes became ferocious.

'Well, well. A little late for social visiting, isn't it?'

'I might say the same to you,' Reyni replied levelly. 'Do I assume that Shar isn't back yet?'

Kitto didn't see the significance of the question – but Hestor did. '*Back?*' he repeated. 'Ah, I see. How, may I ask, did *you* know she's been away?'

It was Reyni's second mistake. Hestor's appearance had raised his hackles, and he hadn't paused to think before speaking. But if he had let something slip, so had Hestor, and it gave Reyni the evidence he needed.

He made a decision. Fosker wouldn't like it, Gant even less so. But it was an unlooked-for chance, and it might not come again. If he could convince Hestor and Kitto that he was sincere, he would learn more in the next few minutes than in a month of subterfuge.

'All right.' He let his breath out, and made his shoulders relax. 'I *did* come earlier, to see her. She wasn't here. But something else was.'

Hestor stiffened. 'What do you mean?'

Reyni hesitated. 'Look, can I come in? I know Shar isn't in the room, so it's just the three of us. And under the circumstances I don't think it's wise to stand talking in the corridor, do you?'

Hestor began aggressively, 'If you think I'm going to—' but Kitto interrupted him.

'Wait a minute, Hestor. Reyni's right; we don't want to be seen or heard. Besides, if he knows anything we don't, it might be helpful.' He glanced uncertainly at Hestor. 'We *need* help. And he was Shar's friend.'

But Hestor shook his head mulishly. 'He doesn't know anything! He's just trying to pry, worming his way in here and—'

Reyni cut across him. 'She's gone into the Maze, hasn't she?' he said.

His words silenced Hestor as though he had been struck dumb. Softly, hollowly, Kitto said, 'Oh, gods, Hestor. There's no point pretending . . .' And before Hestor could stop him, he looked Reyni squarely in the eye and added, 'Yes, she has. And we think it might be a lot worse than that.'

This time, when Reyni moved to push the door open, neither of them tried to stop him. They all went into the room; Reyni saw the papers strewn on the floor and Hestor quickly made to gather them up and out of his reach, but Reyni held up both hands as though for peace.

'Please, Hestor. I know you don't trust me—'

'You're right. I don't.'

'Very well; and I think I know why. But because of that, I also think you believe that I care about Shar. So, in that sense at least, we're on the same side.'

Hestor relented slightly. 'Go on.'

Reyni took a deep breath. 'If I tell you what I know, and what I've seen, will you do the same? Because if Shar *is* in trouble, the only thing that matters is to help her, and we've got a better chance of doing that together than separately.'

'It makes sense, Hestor,' Kitto said.

Hestor shot him a filthy look. 'You're changing your tune fast enough! What's happened to all your dark mutterings of a few hours ago?'

'Dark mutterings?' Reyni queried gently.

'Oh, yes.' Hestor swung back to face him. 'Such as the fact that your precious leader is Adept Gant's cousin. *What* a coincidence – especially as we all know Adept Gant's views about the Maze!'

'I'm sorry,' said Reyni, 'but I *don't* know. I'm not involved in Circle politics – how could I be? I came here with Fosker to—'

'To spy on Shar!'

'No, Hestor. *Because* of Shar, yes; but not to spy on her.' He sighed. 'Look, I hardly even know what the Maze is; all I've been told is that it's very powerful and potentially very dangerous. When I saw Shar at the mission house, and Fosker told me later that she must have used the Maze to get there—'

'Wait a moment,' Kitto said quickly. 'You *saw* her there? She said she wasn't seen by anyone.' His eyes narrowed. 'That was the part I couldn't understand; how your people got involved in all this.' He looked at Hestor. 'I think Reyni's telling the truth, and it's Shar who's been lying to us.'

Hestor's anger had abated now and he was listening, considering. 'All right,' he said after a few moments. 'I accept that. It makes sense. But that still leaves Gant to be reckoned with, and if Reyni tries to tell me that he hasn't been spying for him, that's something I *won't* believe!' He stared challengingly at Reyni. 'Well?'

Caution – and his instructions – told Reyni to deny it, but if he did, he knew he would lose all the ground he had gained. He was honest by nature, and from the start he had not felt comfortable with all the stealth and secrecy that Gant and Fosker insisted on. It was almost as if they had another motive that they were hiding from him; and that thought didn't sit easily with Reyni. They were using him. Loyalty was one thing; blind obedience was quite another.

'I'm not going to deny it,' he said. 'Yes, I've been acting on instructions from Fosker and Adept Gant. I *do* believe they have Shar's well-being at heart. Why shouldn't they? They're not evil men like her uncle. But whatever their motives are, they're not *personally* involved.'

'And you are?'

'Yes, I am.' Reyni smiled, a little sheepishly. 'You may not like me saying this, but I'm going to say it anyway. I care about Shar. I'm very, very fond of her. And when it comes to loyalty, she's got a stronger and older claim on mine than the Keepers of Light.'

For several seconds Hestor gazed penetratingly at the musician's face, while Kitto held his breath. Then, at last, Hestor ran his tongue over his own lower lip, and spoke.

'If you really are that loyal to Shar,' he said, 'you can prove it by telling us everything you know.'

Reyni did tell them everything; from Shar's appearance in the Wester Reach mission house to the vision he had seen in this room, of Shar stalking Thel Starnor with a knife in her hand and murder on her mind. As he shakily reached the end of the tale, he realised that both Hestor and Kitto were very still.

'What is it?' A cold sensation clutched at his heart.

'Thel's already dead. Shar didn't kill him – I was there, remember; I saw what happened!'

'A silver cobweb and a bloodstained knife,' Kitto whispered. 'Don't tell me it's a coincidence . . .'

'It isn't.' Hestor's voice was grim. Abruptly, he returned to where the papers lay and started to rummage through the pile.

'What are they?' Reyni asked.

'Shar's own notes,' Kitto told him. 'We'd just started to look at them when you turned up.'

Reyni leaned over. 'Can I help?' He reached out to take a page; Hestor would have snatched it away, but Kitto said wearily, 'Let him, Hestor. It's gone too far now.'

Reluctantly, Hestor allowed Reyni to carry on. No one spoke for a while – then suddenly, and sharply, Reyni said, 'I've got something here. Instructions for making—' He looked up uneasily. 'An amulet . . . ?'

'*What?*' Hestor pounced, and scanned the page rapidly. 'Great gods, this must be the ritual the High Initiate used to create the key to the Maze! *How did Shar get hold of it?*'

'The elementals,' Kitto whispered.

'Then she's created her own key, and she's using it! *Yandros!*'

'But the knife,' Kitto said. 'Reyni's vision of Shar killing Thel – what could that possibly have to do with the Maze?'

'I don't know. But there *is* a connection.' Hestor glanced at Reyni. 'We've got to keep searching.'

They found it a few minutes later. A page of hastily scribbled notes, in Shar's writing, with some odd little drawings doodled in places, where she had obviously paused to think. The notes were cryptic, though time was mentioned in several places. But the drawings gave the truth away. One was simply a picture of a plain black circle. Another looked like a diagram of the preparations for a ritual, with marks showing where each adept should stand. Hestor and Shar had both learned to construct such diagrams as exercises in their studies, but this one was different. Beside one of the position marks was a letter T, so heavily filled in that the stylus had dug through the paper in places, as though Shar had been burning with anger as she drew. And above the letter, rapidly sketched but unmistakable, was the outline of a knife.

T for Thel . . . Hestor's hand was unsteady as he held the paper. He knew what the diagram could only be. A plan of the last ritual Thel Starnor had ever performed as a Circle adept. The ritual in which he had murdered Shar's father.

'She's going to try to go back, isn't she?' Kitto's face was grey with shock, and his voice didn't sound like his own. 'She's going to try to kill him. And if she does . . . oh, gods!'

All three of them stared at the drawings Shar had

made. They didn't know what to say; there was nothing they *could* say that was of any use whatever. Rifts in time. Anomalies in history. They thought of the strange things that had already happened: disembodied voices, visions of people long dead . . . Shar was playing with a force far greater, far more perilous, than anything she had ever touched before. And the results of her tampering were already starting to take effect.

Suddenly, startling them and breaking the inertia that had frozen them, a loud and agitated miaow sounded outside the door.

'Amber!' Hestor was at the door in three strides, and he pulled it open expecting to see the ginger cat outside.

It was a cat – but not Amber. The white cat looked up at Hestor, and its vivid emerald gaze snared him. Hestor gasped as a single clear image snapped into his mind, and with it an urging, not in words or in any form he could have explained, but so commanding that he had to obey.

Hestor swung round to face Kitto and Reyni. 'We've got to stop her!'

'How?' Kitto asked helplessly.

In Hestor's vision a second picture formed. He swallowed, and the white cat meowed again.

'There's only one way,' Hestor said. 'And the cat's telling me how to do it. I've – we've – got to go into the Maze after her!'

16

Kitto flatly refused to go, and nothing Hestor said or did could persuade him. It wasn't that he was afraid, Kitto insisted defensively. It simply made basic sense for someone to stay behind, in case anything should go wrong and they were forced to turn to the Circle for help. Hestor argued that in that case Reyni should stay, but Reyni would not hear of it, and at last, in the face of the others' determination, Hestor was forced to give in.

The second moon was setting as he and Reyni made their way quietly along the corridor that led to the Marble Hall. The white cat trotted ahead of them, pausing every now and again to look back and send an impatient mental message to *hurry*, *hurry*. Hestor knew from past experience that the cat wasn't an ordinary animal but had a strong link with the powers of Chaos. Above all, it was a friend to Shar. He could only trust it, and hope his trust was justified.

Around his neck, on a leather thong, hung the amulet that he had taken from Neryon Voss's study.

Getting it had been extraordinarily easy. The magical guard had gone, the study was unlocked, and the cat had led him straight to a cupboard in the corner, where he found the amulet in less than a minute. There was something uncanny about that, Hestor thought, but he was too grateful to question his good fortune. He only hoped that the luck would hold until this was over.

Reyni had never entered the Marble Hall before, and Hestor felt a secret, smug pleasure at his awed reaction. There was no time to savour it, though; the cat was urging them on, leading them across the floor to the black mosaic circle. Hestor still wasn't sure of the circle's significance; Shar's notes had said something about 'The Gate', and the cat's behaviour suggested that it had a vital part to play in this, but beyond that he knew very little. He had seen the circle many times but never thought anything of it. Tonight, though, as he stood on its edge and looked down, it seemed different. Darker; denser – alive, somehow. As if it had been waiting for them . . .

For the first time Hestor's nerve wavered, and he thought he must be mad. This was so far out of his sphere that he shouldn't, by any sane standards, be attempting it. He should stop, right here and right now; go back into the castle, go to the High Initiate, tell him everything and let the Circle deal with the problem. The high adepts were *trained* for such things; he was just a junior, inexperienced, unprepared—

Beside him, Reyni cleared his throat gently and said, 'Hestor? The cat's getting impatient.'

Hestor's head came up sharply. Reyni was looking at him, his expression faintly quizzical, and something in the look made Hestor feel patronised. In an instant his doubts fled and he was on his mettle. Maybe he *was* inexperienced – but in this, at least, he was far ahead of Reyni. *I'll show him*, he thought. *And I'll make Shar realise that I'm worth ten of him any day!*

He stepped into the circle. He was a little surprised that nothing untoward happened as he crossed the perimeter, but the momentary unease faded. After a gratifying pause, Reyni followed – but the white cat did not. Instead, it sat down just outside the circle's boundary, silent now, and fixing Hestor with its green stare.

Reyni looked at the cat. 'What does it want us to do?' he asked.

'I know what it wants me to do.' Hestor's tone was curt. 'You'd better just keep still and quiet.' He flung a short glance over his shoulder and couldn't resist adding, 'Or pray to Lord Aeoris, if you think it'll help.'

To his chagrin, Reyni clasped his hands and closed his eyes, and his lips began to move silently. Hoping that the gods of Chaos wouldn't take exception – the cat was their creature, after all – Hestor closed both his hands around the amulet. Will the Maze to open; that was the principle. He didn't know how to make it carry them through time as well as space, but the message the cat had put into his mind told him that didn't matter. The black circle would give him the link he needed.

He pictured a scene. Night; summer; with both moons full in the sky. In the castle someone was celebrating their birth-aniversary, and a party was in full swing in the great dining hall. *Twenty years ago*. Shar had not yet been born. But she was there.

Find her, Hestor's will said. *Wherever she is, find her!*

An inarticulate grunt broke involuntarily from his throat, and his fingers clenched so hard on the amulet that its spiral edge cut his palm. And with a shattering flare of black and silver, and a noise like a yelling laugh, the world fell away into nothing.

Two rooms from where Kitto sat huddled on Shar's floor, Pellis woke with a start, to see her grandfather standing at the end of her bed.

'*Ganda?*' Her childhood name for him came so easily to her tongue that she didn't even realise she had said it until, rather belatedly, the shock hit her.

At the same moment, her grandfather vanished.

Pellis sat up, groping for flint and tinder to light a candle. Had she been dreaming? She didn't think so; or if she had, the dream had no connection with this. Her memory flicked back to the peculiar incident a few days ago, when both she and Physician Eln had seen, impossibly, High Initiate Karuth Piadar Voss,

Neryon's great-grandmother. *Ancestors*, Pellis thought. Why *ancestors?* What did this *mean?*

Going back to sleep was out of the question and it was nearly dawn anyway, so she rose, washed and dressed, then went out into the corridor. Listening briefly at the door of Hestor's room she heard no sound. Nothing had appeared to him, then; he must still be sleeping. Glad of that, Pellis headed for the main stairs.

At the top of the staircase she met a servant, who bowed to her before standing back to allow her to go first. Pellis had descended three steps when the entrance hall below changed. For one moment it wasn't empty and unlit, but ablaze with torchlight, and packed with milling human figures.

Pellis stopped sharply, and behind her the servant gave a cry of shock. She blinked. Everything was normal again. Then the servant said: 'Madam—'

He was clinging to the banisters, white-faced and trembling, and his eyes met hers with a look of desperate appeal. 'I– I'm sorry, madam. For a moment I saw – I thought—'

'That the hall was full of people.' Pellis spoke gently. 'Yes. I saw it, too.'

'What does it . . . ?' He couldn't finish, and she smiled sympathetically.

'I don't think it's anything to be afraid of.' *Pray that that's true*, she added silently to herself. 'I'll find the

High Initiate and speak to him. Don't worry. But if you see any more anomalies like that, please report them at once to a senior adept.'

Luckily, castle servants were used to strange happenings and the man was already recovering his composure. Pellis hurried on. She didn't like to wake Neryon at such an early hour, but this was too urgent to wait, so she went to his private rooms.

Neryon, though, was not there. Instead, Pellis found him in his study, and Physician Eln was with him.

Neryon raised his head quickly as she came in. For an instant he looked alarmed, then relief took its place. 'Pellis! Thank the gods; for a moment I thought you were another apparition!'

'Another?' said Pellis. 'Then you've been seeing them, too?'

'Half the castle's been seeing them since first moonset,' Eln told her tersely. 'I've had a queue of people at my infirmary thinking that they're losing their minds! But if they are, so am I. Not an hour ago I came face to face with someone – the gods alone know who he was – in a style of clothes that hasn't been worn for four hundred years. And before that I saw a couple in the passage outside my rooms. The woman had silver skin and was taller than this door, and the man had seven fingers on each hand.'

Pellis sat down rather quickly. 'What's going *on?*'

'We don't know,' Neryon replied. 'But a lot of the reports we've heard have one thing in common. People are seeing apparitions from the past; dead friends or relatives; even ancestors whom they never met but recognise from portraits.'

'Like High Initiate Karuth,' Eln added.

'And my grandfather,' said Pellis.

'Ah. Then you've seen another?'

'Yes. A few minutes ago, in my bedroom. He died when I was four.'

Neryon spread his hands on the table. 'There's little point in our sitting here relating tales to each other. I'm calling an immediate meeting of the Council of Adepts, and I want a list of all the incidents that have been reported so far. In addition, I'll put out word to everyone in the castle that—'

He stopped as someone knocked on the study door.

'Another?' Eln raised his eyebrows.

'Visions don't usually trouble to knock.' Neryon raised his voice. 'Enter.'

To everyone's surprise, Adept Gant came in.

'I'm sorry to disturb you, High Initiate, but this matter is—' Then he saw the others and drew back in surprise. 'Pellis – Eln—'

'Come in, Gant,' said Neryon. 'I have a feeling I know why you're here.'

'With respect, Neryon, I rather doubt it,' Gant told him.

Neryon smiled sourly. 'Visions? Apparitions of people long dead? Changes in the castle, that appear and vanish?'

Gant was taken aback. 'You know about them?'

'We've all been experiencing them. I was about to call a meeting of the Council, to investigate.'

'I'm thankful to hear it,' Gant said. 'But there may be more to this than any of us knows. Someone has disappeared.'

'Disappeared?' Neryon tensed. 'Who?'

'Reyni Trevire.'

'*Reyni?* I didn't even know he was here!'

'He arrived yesterday, with my cousin Fosker Sangen.' Briefly, Gant explained about Reyni and the Keepers of Light – saying nothing, of course, about his own and Fosker's plan – and continued, 'The Keepers always rise before dawn to make their early devotions. But when my cousin went to rouse Reyni this morning, he wasn't in his room. Reyni is punctilious about his prayers to Aeoris; he wouldn't neglect his duty, so Fosker searched for him. It seems he has vanished.'

Pellis felt queasy. Apparitions were one thing; but if people were starting to disappear, the situation was far more serious than they had thought.

'Is he the only one?' she asked.

'I don't know,' said Gant. 'Until we can check among the castle inhabitants—'

'That must be done immediately,' Neryon interrupted, getting to his feet. As he pulled the bell-rope that would summon his steward, an awful thought struck Pellis. Reyni Trevire had been closely involved with Hestor and Shar and Kitto. Could there be a connection with this new mystery? Where was Hestor now?

'Neryon—' She stood up. 'Please, will you forgive me if I . . . that is, I think I should make sure Hestor's safe . . .'

Gant looked at her keenly. 'I'll come with you, Pellis.'

She was surprised. Did he suspect something, which he hadn't yet voiced? Did he *know* something?

'Yes,' she said. 'Thank you, Gant – Neryon, I won't be long.'

She almost ran from the room, with Gant at her heels.

'Hestor!' Reyni was crawling across the mosaic floor towards him. 'Hestor, are you all right?'

Hestor raised himself dizzily on his hands, hoping against hope that he wasn't going to be sick. The jolt had been huge – greater even than his first experience with Tarod.

'I'm – all right.' The nausea and the disorientation were fading at last, though lights still flashed at the edge of his vision. Beyond them, he could make out the contours of the Marble Hall. It didn't seem to have changed, but he had an instinctive feeling that *something* had. The air felt different; it seemed to have no life to it. And there wasn't any colour anywhere. Everything – even his own skin and clothes when he looked down at them – was a shade of grey.

Reyni said softly, 'Where are we?'

Hestor opened his mouth to reply, 'The Marble Hall, of course,' then hesitated. *Was* this truly the Marble Hall, or was it only a reflection of reality; some kind of halfway house between the present and the past? The thought was unpleasant, and suddenly he wanted to get out of the Hall and take a look at the rest of their surroundings.

'Come on.' He climbed to his feet, wincing as muscles twinged. 'We've got to find Shar.'

'If she's here,' said Reyni.

They hurried to the metallic door, which looked reassuringly normal, and on along the passage to the library. No lights burned in the library vault, and they climbed the stairs to emerge into the courtyard.

The night was still and stifling, and both moons were full, glaring down on the courtyard and making the scene dream-like and strange. There wasn't so much as a breath of a breeze, and when Hestor listened for the distant, ever-present sound of the sea, he heard nothing.

There was no sign of the celebration that should

have been going on; in fact there was no sign of anyone or anything. The courtyard was deserted, the castle unlit. Reyni said quietly, uneasily, 'Something's gone wrong.'

Hestor didn't answer. A theory was nagging at him but he couldn't quite formulate it. He thought about the Circle's first experiments with the Maze; tried to remember—

Reyni gripped his arm, making him jump.

'There! I saw—' He stopped. 'It's gone!'

'What has?' Hestor demanded sharply.

Reyni shivered. 'Just for a moment I saw lights in the dining hall, but they vanished again. And I thought I heard music.'

Hestor turned to look at the hall windows. They were dark, but he had a peculiar intuition that what he was seeing was not what was truly there. As if his eyes, and his mind, weren't fully open.

Then, fleetingly, his ears caught the sound of the sea. And for a single second the air turned wintrily cold.

'Come on,' he said. 'Let's go inside.'

They ran up the steps to the main doors. They were – or appeared to be – closed, and what Hestor did then didn't even register on his brain until it had happened. But suddenly he found himself in the castle's entrance hall, with the doors, still closed, between him and Reyni.

In the same moment the faint sound of music and laughter skimmed past his ears and was gone.

Shock set Hestor's heart crashing against his ribs. From the other side of the door Reyni's muffled, bewildered voice called out to him.

Hestor swallowed. 'Wh . . . what happened? What did I do?'

'You ran straight through them. As if they weren't there.'

Hestor shut his eyes; opened them again. The doors looked as solid as before. Tentatively, he reached out for the latch ring.

His hand went through it and closed on nothing.

He stared. As he tried to touch the ring, the doors' outline had seemed to waver and distort, and he had the disorientating impression that they were, in fact, standing wide open. It only lasted for a moment – but the moment was enough. Hestor began to understand.

'Reyni,' he said. 'Try to walk through, the same way as I did.'

'I can't!'

'I think you can. Pretend that the doors are open. Picture them open, in your mind.'

He stepped back, watching carefully. There was a pause – then Reyni stepped through into the entrance hall.

'Aeoris!' Reyni stumbled, righted himself and turned

to stare at the doors. 'For an instant I thought they really *were* open, and I just—'

'Walked in, as if everything was perfectly normal. I know.' Hestor, too, had seen the momentary change, as if one reality was overlaid on another. Which was, he suspected, very close to the truth.

'I think I know what's going on,' he continued. 'We've come to where we wanted to be all right, but we haven't completely broken through the barrier. Something like this happened when the Circle first experimented with the Maze – the adepts couldn't materialise properly; they got stuck between one location and another. In our case, though, the problem's with time rather than space. Part of us is in the past, but another part's still in our own reality.'

'In our reality it's winter, so the doors would be closed . . .'

'Right. And there's no celebration going on; everyone's in bed.'

Reyni frowned. 'What about Shar? Is she only half here, too?'

'Shar has special abilities, remember. Chances are that she's been able to break through completely, and merge into this time. In which case, she's going to be perfectly capable of doing what she came here to do.'

Reyni paled. 'How can we stop her, if we can't attune ourselves? We can't even see or hear her!'

'I know. But we've got to try.' Hestor's fingers

closed round the amulet. 'Willpower; that's the key. Take the doors. They *look* shut, but we both walked through them as if they were open. Which, in this time, they are. And it's summer, and there's a party in the dining hall, and . . .'

His words tailed off as they both heard the music again. Reyni's eyes lit eagerly; Hestor tried to grasp hold of the sound, focus on it.

The entrance hall shimmered as though it was a reflection in water, and suddenly there were people around them. They were only dimly visible, like ghosts, but they were *there,* walking and talking. And warm air wafted in where the doors stood open to the night.

'It's working!' There was exultation in Hestor's voice. They couldn't hear the people around them, and it was clear that no one could see or hear them. The music, too, kept fading and returning, as though it was drifting from a great distance. But the barrier was weakening.

'Come on,' Hestor said. 'Let's look for Shar.'

The party gave Shar perfect cover. The great hall was so crowded that no one took the least notice of a stranger in their midst. Twice she had even been asked to dance, though she had politely turned down the invitations.

Now, with a glass of wine in her hand (which tasted as real as any wine in her own time), she stood to one side of the hall, away from the press of activity. She had seen a number of disconcertingly familiar faces – even Neryon, in his teens – but she was only interested in one.

It had taken her some while to find Thel Starnor, but once she did, she had shadowed him persistently, determined not to let him out of her sight for a moment. He had joined in a few of the dances but now he was over by the food tables, talking to some people whom Shar didn't recognise. Occasionally he glanced in her direction, and though she took care to look the other way, she wondered uneasily if he suspected she was watching.

But what if he did? He didn't know her. In this time, she didn't exist.

Making a play of smoothing her skirt, she felt for the knife hidden in the fold. It hadn't once occurred to her that she would baulk at using it; her hatred for Thel was so powerful that it blotted out everything else, and her only concern was with when and where the chance would come. The celebration was winding down now, and a number of guests had left. Thel had started yawning. He, too, would leave soon; and then she only had to follow him to his room and wait until he was asleep . . .

A few minutes later Thel decided that he had had enough. He took a while to leave, stopping to exchange a few words with people who crossed his path, while

Shar sipped her drink and continued to watch him. At last, he went out through the double doors.

Shar set down her glass. She smoothed her skirt again, feeling the hard contours of the metal blade. Then, as sedately and unobtrusively as if she was going to the courtyard for a little fresh air, she walked from the hall in Thel's wake.

'It's no good.' Hestor covered his eyes with his hands, needing to blot out for a moment the riot of confusing images around him. 'She could be *anywhere*. And if we don't find her soon . . .'

There was no need to say the rest; he and Reyni both knew only too well what the consequences could be.

Reyni looked around the dining hall, trying to fight back the vertigo that assailed him. Keeping hold of the ground they had gained had not been easy. Though they were in the thick of the celebration, it was like a mirage overlaid on the more solid reality of the dark, deserted castle. Often the scene wavered and faded, and they could only regain their grip on it by ferocious concentration. When they had first ventured in here the effect had been horribly confusing; the music rose and fell feverishly, and there was something hollow and unreal in the light and colour and noise of the lively crowd. They had got used to it, up to a point, but every now and then the disorientation came back sharply.

And they had failed to find Shar.

Someone brushed past them, smiled an apology and walked on. Hestor shuddered, for he hadn't felt the contact. But the fact that they had been seen, and noticed, gave Reyni an idea.

'There's only one thing we can do now,' he said in an undertone. 'Stop looking for Shar, and find Thel instead.'

'How? He could have left already, for all we know.'

'Then we'll ask someone where his room is.' A thin smile touched Reyni's mouth. 'That's what I did when I wanted to see Shar, after all.'

Before Hestor could reply, he moved to where a group of people wearing gold adepts' badges stood talking a few paces away.

'Excuse me—'

They turned. For a moment it seemed to them as if there was no one there – then Reyni's figure snapped into focus.

'Please forgive the interruption,' Reyni said, 'but I have a message for Adept Thel Starnor. Can you tell me where I might find him?'

One of the women blinked and shook her head as though to clear it. The man beside her said, 'Thel? He left a while ago. Probably gone to bed.'

'Could you possibly direct me to his room? The message is urgent and I've been told it can't wait until morning,' said Reyni.

'Have you, now? Well, on your own head be it if you

wake him.' The adept gave some brief, clear directions, then added, 'Those are strange clothes you're wearing, young man. Aren't they the dress of that new cult in Wester Reach?'

'Yes, sir.'

'Hmm, well; we're not sure that we approve of some of these sects, are we?' He looked at his companions and raised an eyebrow. 'Favouring Order above Chaos – it doesn't sit well with the rules of—'

He had been turning back to face Reyni as he spoke, and stopped in mid-sentence. Reyni had vanished. There was simply no sign of him; it was as if he had never been there at all.

The adepts were silent for a few seconds. Then, without a word, one of them went to fetch another flask of wine.

Shar had been counting the minutes, and at last she knew that she couldn't wait any longer.

Thel's apartments were dark as she eased the door open and went in. She closed the door silently, then stood still until her eyes adjusted to the gloom. Two rooms. The outer was his study, the inner would be his bedroom. The bedroom door was ajar, and from beyond it came faint snoring.

She slipped off her shoes and tiptoed towards the sound. *Sleep well, Thel Starnor,* she thought savagely. *In a minute from now, you'll embark on a sleep that will never end – and my parents will live on in your place!* The knife was in her hand now and she relished the feel of the hilt, almost caressing it. At the bedroom door she paused. The bed was a darker rectangle in darkness, and she could just make out the shape of the sleeper lying there. *Don't hesitate*, her mind said. *Don't stop to savour this moment. Just strike!*

Four quick paces and she was at the side of the bed. Thel's head was on the pillow, and because of the hot night he had only a light covering. His shoulders were exposed. And his throat.

Shar poised the knife above his neck. She raised it—

'Shar, *NO!!*'

The frantic yell came from the direction of the door. Shar whirled. She saw two figures hurling themselves towards her, and incredibly, impossibly, she recognised Hestor and Reyni. *But they couldn't be here – it was impossible, it couldn't happen, they couldn't exist in this place—*

At that moment, Thel woke. From the corner of her eye Shar saw the flurry as he sat up with a violent start – and something triggered in her that she had no hope of stopping or controlling. Her voice rose in a shrill, animal shriek – and she plunged the knife-blade down, straight towards Thel's neck.

17

'Hestor!' Pellis hammered on her son's door. '*Hestor!*'

Still there was no reply, and suddenly Pellis couldn't stand it any longer. She thrust the door open, ran into the room, and stopped, staring miserably at Hestor's empty bed.

'It hasn't been slept in.' Her voice was small and frozen. 'Where *is* he?'

'I don't know,' said Gant. 'But if my suspicions are right, Shar Tillmer does.'

Shar, Hestor and Reyni . . . Pellis turned and ran towards Shar's room. This time she didn't knock but burst straight in.

'She isn't here—' Quickly, Pellis looked at Gant and saw his grim expression. 'You know something about this, don't you?' she challenged. 'There's a connection with Reyni and your cousin.'

Gant sighed. 'Come back with me to the High Initiate,' he replied sombrely. 'He, too, needs to hear what I have to say.'

He headed away back towards the stairs. Pellis stared after him for a few moments, then ran in his wake.

In Shar's room, Kitto looked up and frowned. He hadn't been asleep, he was sure of it; but he could have sworn just now that he had heard voices in the passage outside. One of them sounded like Adept Gant, and Kitto had tensed, half-expecting the door to open and Gant to walk in. But then the voices faded abruptly, as if he had imagined them, and everything was silent again.

Kitto shivered. He couldn't guess how long he had been sitting alone here, but it felt like a very long time. Long enough, in fact, for dawn to have begun breaking by now. Yet the sky outside was as dark as ever.

Suddenly he felt very uneasy. Something was *wrong* – he couldn't put a finger on it, but he knew it in his bones. Sliding off the bed, he went to the window. The courtyard was quiet, but the fountain was playing. Odd . . . they didn't usually start it until after the Spring Quarter-Day. And what was that light, over by the stables?

As Kitto peered harder, a voice in the distance yelled, '*Fire!*'

Kitto's jaw dropped as he saw flames leap skywards from the stable roof. Thoughts flashed in his mind – *Not again, it can't possibly be happening again* – and his muscles bunched to run for the nearest stairs—

Then froze.

There was no fire. The flames that moments ago had been roiling up from the stable block simply weren't there any more.

Kitto backed away from the window. As he did so, loud footfalls hurried past in the corridor.

'What—' Kitto ran to the door and opened it. The corridor was empty. But he could still hear the footsteps.

'Oh, Yandros—' Kitto recalled what Hestor had said about Shar meddling with time. First a flashback to the stable fire, now noises made by invisible people . . . something was *horribly* out of kilter.

The footsteps were diminishing; in desperation Kitto called out, 'Hello! Who's there, who are you?'

The steps halted, and he had the awful sensation that unseen eyes had turned and were looking back at him. Then there was the sound of an irritable sigh, and the steps continued on.

Really frightened now, Kitto ran towards the main stairs. At the top he paused, looking down into the entrance hall. No one there. Or if there was, he couldn't see them.

He went down, and started to explore. The dining hall was empty and the tables bare. But the servants always laid the tables for breakfast the night before . . . Kitto ran through to the kitchens. Nothing. No preparations, no people. What had happened to them all?

Or, perhaps more to the point, what had happened to *him?*

Somewhere, far off, a cat yowled, and Kitto followed the direction of the sound. He thought it had come from the entrance hall, but when he reached it there was no sign of anything. Then he heard the cry again, this time from the courtyard.

'Cat?' Kitto ventured out on to the steps. The double doors were open – surely they had been closed a few minutes ago? 'Cat-cat! Come here, little one; come to Kitto!' He tried to open his thoughts to any telepathic probing, but felt no answer from the cat's mind. 'Come on, cat-cat! You know me!'

A small, four-legged shape moved near the fountain, and with relief Kitto hurried after it. He was halfway to his goal when a tingling sensation, like a charge of lightning, swept over him from behind. The short hairs of his neck stood on end; he spun round—

And was nearly sick with shock as, from the tops of the castle's four spires, four titanic bolts of energy speared skywards with a *crack* that shook the foundations.

Kitto found himself on his knees, covering his head with his hands, as the colossal noise died away. When he dared to look again, networks of spitting blue brilliance were dancing between the spire summits, and behind them the distorted, pockmarked shape of the first moon was rising into the sky at an unnatural, impossible speed.

From the castle came shouts of alarm, and several figures ran out on to the steps. Kitto's spinning mind registered the faces of Pellis and Gant, and with a cry he sprang to his feet and raced towards them.

Pellis saw him, said, 'Kitto—?'

And the entire group vanished.

Kitto skidded to a stop halfway up the steps, mouth gaping, eyes bulging. When he looked at the spires again, they were black and silent.

'No—' The word was a plea. 'Oh, no . . .'

He stumbled on, into the empty castle.

Gant took Pellis's arm to steady her and said tersely, 'We *must* speak to Neryon!'

Pellis let him hurry her away towards the study. She felt dizzy and bewildered, and the momentary illusion she had seen of Kitto running across the courtyard had frightened her, for if he was somehow mixed up in this, Hestor must be involved, too.

They reached Neryon's room, and Gant went in without knocking. 'Neryon, I have to—'

He stopped in mid-sentence. They both stared.

A total stranger was sitting behind Neryon's desk, and they could see the contours of the chair through him.

Pellis made a gargling sound, and Gant roared,

'Who are you? What in the name of Aeoris is going on?'

The man – or phantom – ignored them. He wasn't even aware of their presence, they realised. His lips were moving, but he was talking to someone else; someone completely invisible to them.

Suddenly Pellis turned, rushed from the room, and cannoned into Neryon, who was coming along the passage.

'*Neryon!*' She almost shrieked his name, and in the doorway Gant whirled round.

'That noise and light—' Neryon broke off as he saw her face. 'What? What's happened?'

Gant looked back into the study. 'He's gone . . .' he said unsteadily.

'Who's gone?' Neryon demanded. 'Gant, will you please explain!'

Gant faced him, his expression grim. 'I don't know how much I can explain, High Initiate,' he said. 'But I believe this is Shar Tillmer's doing. And I also believe that it is directly linked to the Maze!'

'*No, Shar!*' With a cry of sheer desperation, Reyni launched himself across the room. He charged at Shar and struck her at the run, buffeting her aside. She yelled with fury; Thel bellowed in astonished outrage. Then the scene was blotted out as a brilliant glare shuddered across Hestor's eyes. For an instant he felt as if he, or the rest of the world, had turned upside-down and inside out; he flailed, struggling to regain his balance — and found himself sprawling on the floor of a silent room.

Thel, the bed, the furnishings; all were gone. But in the middle of the floor Shar and Reyni stood facing each other, and Shar's face was filled with blind, miserable rage.

'You've wrecked it!' she wailed. 'We've been thrown out of his time, and my chance has gone!'

Reyni held out his hands towards her. 'Shar, listen to me—' he began.

'*No!*' She still had the knife and she brandished it savagely, making him flinch back. 'Get away from me! I'm not going to let you ruin what I've worked so hard to achieve!'

With her other hand she grasped her amulet. The room seemed to shudder again — and Shar vanished.

Reyni stood staring helplessly at the spot where she had been standing. 'She transported herself! Just like that; she—'

'Shar can do a lot of things,' Hestor said tersely. He got to his feet. 'But we've got an amulet, too. Help me. We've got to find her!'

'How? We don't even know where she's gone!'

'I think I do know.' Hestor started for the door. 'She said, "we've been thrown out of time". That means we're back in the nothing-time where we first arrived. Anything's possible from here, and Shar knows it. She's going to look for another chance to kill Thel, and the key to it is in the Marble Hall. Come on – and pray we can get there before she finds another time-thread!'

They ran through the dark, deserted corridors, down the main stairs and out into the courtyard. Hestor didn't know if he opened doors or simply raced through them; all he could think about was catching up with Shar. She, of course, had used her amulet to carry her directly to the Marble Hall, but Hestor and Reyni had no such skill. Their legs ached with exertion by the time they plunged down the steps to the library vault, but they forced themselves not to slacken and raced through the library and down the narrow passage that led to the Marble Hall. The metallic door stood open; with a last burst of speed they rushed through.

Shar was there, crouching in the black mosaic circle. From the circle's perimeter a river of black light was streaming upwards. Threads of silver lightning danced in its current; and Hestor recognised and finally understood the image that the scrying glass had shown him. *Time* – it was the cobweb, the network, each thread leading to a different possibility. Shar was chanting; they couldn't hear her words, for the sound was distorted and confused by strange echoes.

And one of the silver threads was growing brighter.

'Shar!' Hestor stopped six paces from the circle. The Hall's mists were swirling and agitating, and their pastel colours had darkened to threatening grey. Shar's chanting stopped. She raised her head and stared back, then her voice snapped out harshly. 'Don't come any closer, Hestor. Just *don't!*'

'Shar, listen to me,' Hestor said, trying to keep his voice calm and level. 'What you're trying to do – it's wrong, it's dangerous.'

'You don't know anything!' Shar fired back. 'Keep out of this. Just *go!*'

'You can't change history!' Hestor pleaded. 'Things are already going awry in our own time, and it'll get worse! *Think*, Shar! Think what might happen to you, to all of us, if you meddle like this!'

'*I have thought!*' Shar shouted. 'Go away, Hestor. Leave me alone. This is none of your business!'

In that moment, as she stared at him through the rushing shimmer of the light-river, Shar almost hated Hestor. A part of her still struggled to see reason and knew the hatred was an illusion; but that part was crushed by her burning desire to see the tragedy of the past put right. What did it matter if changes were made in her own time? They wouldn't be serious. And her parents would be *alive*.

'Times means nothing,' she said. 'I can change the past, and I will – the Gate can give me the power.' Through the streaming light her face looked strange and distorted. 'I'm going through, and this time you won't be able to follow me. No one will, because no one else knows how to!'

She shut her eyes, closing her hands tightly round her amulet. An eerie singing sound echoed from the heart of the circle, and high above Shar a roiling cloud took form, twisting like a whirlpool, sucking the mists into itself. Hestor felt power building; felt the floor beneath his feet quake. A pulse like a vast, slow heartbeat started to reverberate deep underground, and the silver web shivered and broke up into a rush of particles that began to flow faster and faster. Shar was still visible through the stream, and Hestor knew that it was far too late, now, for any words.

'Get her!' he shouted to Reyni. 'I don't care what it takes – get her out of that circle, *NOW!*'

He and Reyni lunged forward together, and threw themselves like divers into the rushing tower of light.

The Marble Hall shuddered from end to end as they crashed over the boundary of the Gate. Hestor had a momentary glimpse of Shar's shocked face; heard Reyni shout in pain or terror or both – then he was falling, spinning, over and over through a raging storm of power and energy that smashed through his body and mind like a tornado. A mad spectrum of colours shattered over and around him, an appalling din beat against his ears; he thought he was screaming—

It ended in one monstrous concussion, so vast that

it seemed to suck colour, noise, air, *everything* out of the world in one stunning instant.

And Hestor was crouched on hands and knees, in utter darkness.

'Reyni . . . ?' He croaked the musician's name.

'I'm here.' The reply was weak but close by; there came a faint scuffling and Hestor felt groping fingers connect with his arm. 'Wherever *here* is . . .'

Avoiding any answer to that, Hestor whispered, 'What about Shar?'

They both listened, but the only sounds were the hiss of their breathing and, for Hestor, the noise of his own pulse like a thudding hammer in his skull.

'Shar?' he called at last. 'Shar, where are you? Where is this? *Shar!*'

No reply. 'Shar,' Reyni called sharply, 'If you're here, for all the gods' sakes say something!'

Still no answer came. Hestor began to feel into the darkness around them, but his hands found nothing but emptiness. And he had a horrible feeling that the emptiness might well go on and on for ever.

'She isn't here,' he said. 'She's gone somewhere else. She must have broken through the Gate, and left us behind . . .'

'Can we get out?' Reyni's voice was distinctly unsteady now.

'I don't know. We could be anywhere – in the mortal world or another dimension, or . . .' Hestor didn't want to admit all the possibilities that his imagination was conjuring. He felt his own neck. 'I've still got Neryon's amulet. But whether it'll be of any use to us now—'

'Try it,' Reyni urged. 'Try *anything.*'

Licking dry lips, Hestor closed his eyes, grasped the amulet and attempted to visualise something; a scene, anything, it didn't matter. But his mind couldn't grasp and hold on to any image; all he saw was a confusion of black and silver patterns. Nothing would come, nothing would *form.*

Until—

'Ah!' Hestor started violently as a disembodied eye appeared. The patterns winked out. The eye blinked.

And Reyni drew in a sharp breath and hissed, *'Look!'*

The eye vanished, and Hestor's own eyes snapped open.

The silver web had appeared again, but this time Hestor and Reyni were at its heart. Myriad threads radiated out from where they stood, stretching away into a distance that lost all perspective and seemed to go on forever before them into the distance.

'What is it?' Reyni whispered.

'It's a link with Shar.' Hestor's voice was soft – and as he spoke the word *Shar*, one strand of the web vibrated like the plucked string of a musical instrument, and a strange, high note skimmed past their ears and was gone.

Hestor's heart had started to pound again. Or *was* it his heart? The slow beat seemed to be coming from outside him; he could feel it through the soles of his feet, as if something was moving rhythmically down beneath the floor.

He reached out and touched the thread. It had no substance and his hand passed through it – but as it did so, the whole web quivered.

'Shar . . .' Hestor said again. The quivering stopped, but for a single strand.

'The same one—' Hestor was beginning to understand. 'Reyni – take hold of me; get a grip and make sure we don't get separated.'

He felt rather than saw Reyni's uneasy glance as the musician asked, 'Why?'

'Because I'm going to use the amulet to follow this thread and find Shar.' He took a step forward. Reyni hesitated; then abruptly Hestor felt his fingers close and lock through the leather of his belt. His own hand closed on Neryon's amulet, but this time he didn't try to visualise a scene. His only thought, his only focus, was on the shining silver thread, which now spanned away from him in a perfect line.

'Ready?' he whispered.

Reyni swallowed. 'Yes.'

Hestor shut his eyes. And opened his mind.

18

The gods of Chaos and Order could not enter each other's realms, so Tarod and Ailind met in a place between dimensions, where time and space were irrelevant. Unlike their Chaotic cousins, the lords of Order all looked identical, and when he first saw Ailind's tall figure, silver-white hair and disturbing, pupilless golden eyes, Tarod wondered for a moment if Aeoris had decided to come in person. As he soon discovered, Aeoris didn't consider the situation to be that serious – but nonetheless, the lords of Order were troubled.

'We've been aware of the disturbances in the Gate for some while,' Ailind told him. 'Like you, we presumed they were a side effect of the Circle's experiments with the Maze.' His mouth pursed slightly. 'Which we, of course, would not have let them meddle with in the first place. However, it appears that the Circle don't even know about this.'

'I think they're beginning to find out,' Tarod said.

'Quite.' Ailind sighed with annoyance. 'You're sure it *is* Shar Tillmer's doing?'

'As sure as it's possible to be, without paying a visit to the mortal world.'

'Yes, well; I suppose it was inevitable that she'd run into trouble again before long. Now, though, I very much doubt if she has the least idea of what she could be unleashing. Manipulating time is beyond even the High Initiate's powers; if this gets out of hand, the Circle will have no hope of controlling it.'

'I suspect it already is getting out of hand,' Tarod said. 'If the Gate's showing signs of instability in our realms, then in the mortal world the effect must be magnified.'

Ailind nodded, then looked at him speculatively. 'Have you intervened in any way?'

'I've set – a watcher, you might call it.' The image of a small, white cat skimmed through Tarod's mind. 'But I've not made any direct move.'

Ailind wondered briefly if he was telling the truth, then decided that he probably was. 'Well, it's a refreshing change for Chaos to consult us *before* interfering.'

Tarod smiled thinly. 'Perhaps we all took the result of our last encounter to heart.'

'Yes . . . perhaps we did. So the question is, do we make a move? There's been no direct appeal from the High Initiate, though some members of the Keepers of Light have been praying to us for help. If we're to hold to the terms of Equilibrium . . .' He let the sentence trail off, and shrugged. 'I don't think Aeoris would approve of our taking any action.'

'Nor would Yandros. Nonetheless—'

'If we don't interfere but just observe, to find out how serious the problem is?' Ailind's strange eyes glowed darkly. 'I see no harm in that; in fact I think it would be a sensible precaution. After all, if the Gate's powers were to run out of control, it wouldn't just be the mortal world that was affected.'

Tarod was relieved. He had anticipated a long wrangle, but far from vetoing the idea of a visit to the castle, Ailind had actually suggested it himself.

'Very well,' he said. 'Then I suggest we don't delay.'

They turned their minds to the castle, intending to step between dimensions and manifest in the courtyard.

Nothing happened.

There was a moment's sharp stillness as they looked at each other, both thinking the same thing but neither wanting to voice it. Then, with unspoken agreement, they tried again. Still nothing happened. The way between worlds did not open.

Tarod said, very quietly, 'This *is* more serious than we thought.'

'We'll have to go through the Gate.' Ailind frowned. 'I don't like the idea; if it's already unstable, opening it from this side could make matters worse. But I don't see that we have much choice.'

Together, they focused their wills as they had done

before. The Gate had as many different forms as there were physical and magical dimensions; from here it should have appeared as a column of bright, steady blue light into which they could both step.

But it didn't. Instead there was a rush of wind, and a section of the air before them turned into a wildly fluctuating vortex of black and silver.

Tarod looked at his cousin of Order, and his eyes were like green fires. 'It's gone too far,' he said. 'The Gate's out of control – we can't get through!'

'Unless the mortals at the castle can find a way to stabilise it for long enough to establish a link with us—' Ailind's face was grim, and Tarod voiced what they both knew.

'Then there's nothing whatever we can do to help them!'

Every muscle felt as if it was on fire, but still Shar knew she had to run faster. Time and space were racing ahead of her – she had to catch up!

The corridor showed no sign of ending. It wasn't even properly a corridor now; the walls to either side of her were a blur of streaking lights and haphazard noises, and the floor seemed to be moving too, faster than she was and in the same direction, streaming ahead and away and leaving her behind. She wanted to call out to someone or something, but she had no breath to spare; all her energy had to be given to this terrible, bone-aching race, or everything she had tried to do would be lost!

Suddenly the passage twisted in on itself, and there was a door directly ahead of her where moments ago there had been nothing. Her voice came to her at last in a cry – or a gasp – of thankfulness, and with a final effort she flung herself towards the door. It flew open as she reached it; she stumbled through—

Silvery laughter rang in Shar's head, and she found herself crouched in the middle of a silver web, surrounded by nothingness.

'*No . . .*' Tears sprang to Shar's eyes as rage, frustration and fear warred in her mind. It had happened yet again! Another hope, another chance, another race to reach her goal, only to be thwarted at the last moment. Three times now she had been hurled back to the beginning, back to the web and its confusion of choices. It was like a huge, tangled puzzle, every thread a different possibility. In the Marble Hall it had seemed so easy, but now she was hopelessly lost.

She gripped the amulet, squeezing as though trying to crush it to shards. *Take me back!* she commanded silently. *Take me back to the castle!*

Nothing happened. The scene didn't change; the Maze didn't open. Until and unless she chose another thread, the amulet would not work for her. But which one to *choose?*

Suddenly, of all Shar's warring feelings, rage took the

upper hand. This was Hestor's fault! He had ruined her plans for the second time when he tried to drag her out of the black mosaic circle – because of his action something had gone terribly wrong, and she had lost the path she had worked so hard to gain. She didn't know what had happened to Hestor and Reyni, and at this moment she didn't care. All that mattered was to break this deadlock; find her way again.

She reached towards the shining, radiating skeins that surrounded her. Merely touching any of them set the whole web quivering, and each one she did touch gave off a different, coldly musical sound. This was a crossroads, but she had no signs to guide her. *Know or guess . . .*

'Bush or branch, apple or pear, nowhere to here, and here to there!' Shar spoke the rhyme from a half-forgotten children's blindfold-game. As she recited it, other, childish voices seemed to join in and echo a heartbeat behind hers, but she was too preoccupied to notice.

Clasping the amulet again, she shut her eyes and touched a thread at random . . .

'Kitto!' Neryon's voice rang through the entrance hall. 'If you're there, if you can hear me, then for all the gods' sakes show yourself!'

'Kitto, we're not angry with you!' Pellis called. 'But we need your help. Please, Kitto!'

Kitto didn't appear, and the High Initiate sighed. 'It's no use. We're having the entire castle searched for him, but there's no trace of him anywhere. I suspect your theory's right, Gant. Even if he hasn't gone through the Maze with Shar and the others, he's somehow got himself caught up in this confusion of times and we can't reach him.'

As he spoke, the dawn light in the entrance hall dimmed suddenly and the torches on the walls flared into life. A wave of noises – chattering, laughter – skimmed across the hall and faded, and Neryon thought he saw a tall, burly man surrounded by shadows loom and glide across his path.

Gant, who had also seen the apparition, suppressed a shudder. 'We must try magical means to find him, Neryon. It's our only hope now, I think.' He paused, glancing at Fosker who stood beside him. 'That, and prayer.'

Neryon gave both of them a sharp look. 'If you'd only spoken to me when you first suspected something, it might not have come to this.'

'I had no *proof*, High Initiate.' Gant's face stiffened. 'It would have been my word against Shar Tillmer's and, if you'll forgive my bluntness, I don't think that would have been enough to convince you. Especially as we have always held very different views about the Maze experiments.'

Neryon sighed. 'I take your point, but it doesn't

help us now. My amulet is missing, so Shar, Hestor and Reyni have presumably used it to disappear through the Maze.' His expression darkened. 'Damn the girl – it's obvious these illusions and phantoms are a result of her tampering, but *how?* What has she unlocked, that we don't even know about?'

'High Initiate!' A voice shouted suddenly and they turned to find a servant running towards them.

'I've seen him, sir!' the man panted. 'The boy, Kitto – just now in the dining hall; I was stoking the fire when a voice called out, and when I looked round—'

Neryon didn't wait to hear the rest but raced for the corridor with the others at his heels.

The dining hall was being prepared for breakfast. As he rushed in, it seemed to Neryon that two scenes momentarily overlapped; in one – the real one – servants were quietly busy at the tables, while in the other the entire vast room was packed with people all talking or shouting agitatedly. Confused, he shook his head; the illusion vanished and he snapped out a crisp order.

'Out, please, all of you! Leave the hall!'

Everyone in the castle knew better than to question that tone, and the servants all hastened away. As the last one departed, Neryon signed to Pellis, Gant and Fosker to be silent, and pivoted slowly on his heel, trying to see beyond the hall's contours to something else.

'Kitto.' His voice was level now. 'This is the dining hall. The sun's first rays are coming in at the window, the tables are set for breakfast and there are four people in the room with you. There are new logs on the fire. Concentrate on them; see them. Will yourself to come to us. Will yourself to be here.'

Something flickered at the far end of the hall and Pellis hissed, 'Neryon!'

'I see it. Pellis, Gant – link with me.' They clasped wrists and started to walk forward, in line, while Fosker watched uncertainly. Neryon began to speak the words of a summoning, a ritual that the Circle often used to calm and control troublesome powers. The flickering grew stronger and more urgent; then faintly they all heard a distorted voice:

'Uhh . . . 'm trying . . . oh, Yandros damn everything to the Seven Hells—'

A patch of emptiness seemed to lurch, and Kitto appeared. He swayed, hands flailing, and Pellis ran forward to catch him under his arms before he sagged to the floor.

'Thank you, oh, thank you, thank you!' Kitto mumbled, clinging to Pellis's arm. He sucked air into his lungs. 'I could hear people, and sometimes I could see them, but I couldn't get *through* – then when you came in—'

'Never mind that now,' Neryon cut in. 'We need answers, and fast! Where are Shar and Hestor and Reyni?'

Kitto looked up at him, focusing on his face with an

effort. 'Shar's in the Maze. Been there ages. We found out what she's done; Hestor and Reyni went after her to stop her . . .'

In a few garbled sentences it all came out. Neryon and the others listened with increasing astonishment and alarm, and when they had heard enough to guess at the rest, Neryon demanded, 'Where did Hestor and Reyni go, Kitto? After they took my amulet, how did they plan to find Shar?'

'Marble Hall . . .' Kitto was still feeling groggy. 'Shar's notes – there was something about a Gate, and Hestor said—'

'The *Gate?*' Neryon's expression froze. 'Great Yandros and Aeoris, how did she discover that?'

'It could explain everything,' Gant said grimly.

'It most certainly could! If Shar's using the Gate to try to change history, she could disrupt the entire fabric of time!' Neryon hauled Kitto unceremoniously to his feet. 'Come on, boy. You're coming with us to the Marble Hall, *now!*'

Hestor yelled: 'There she is!'

The figure ahead of them was no more than a phantom in the swirling confusion, but they both knew it *was* Shar. She was racing as though a hundred demons were on her heels, her hair and skirt flying behind her like streamers in a gale. Other, ghostly shapes rushed and tumbled around her; scenes and people of the past, constantly changing and warping as the currents of time ran riot. Nothing stayed the same for more than a few seconds; day became night, stone walls became open moors or churning sea or toppling mountains; joyous laughter clashed with screams of pain or terror; all about them, spectral figures were dancing, riding, fighting—

But the silver thread was still there, a path now, on which Hestor and Reyni ran in their frantic efforts to catch up with Shar. For a giddying moment they were caught up in a procession of men and women who all wore purple mourning clothes; then they vanished and a child who looked alarmingly like one of Hestor's elderly tutors toddled across their path, gleefully chasing something invisible. The child disappeared and suddenly they were in the middle of a party, with the walls of the dining hall rising dimly around them. But the celebrating crowd wore the fashions of hundred years ago . . .

'We're going – further back!' Reyni panted. 'We've got to catch her, Hestor!'

They both screamed Shar's name. Their cries were answered by a swelling chorus of voices, chanting a Circle ritual – but Shar heard them. She flung a glance over her shoulder; they saw her expression change to one of fury, and then she ran on again with renewed intensity.

'Shar, you're only making things worse!' Hestor cried desperately. 'Come *back!*'

'*Leave me alone!*' Shar's voice reached them like a strange bird-cry, and her pace didn't slacken. For a few seconds a man dressed in black and wearing a fearsome silver half-mask was galloping beside Hestor on a huge black horse; then he veered away and a blinding snowstorm swept over them. The flakes scorched like fire; yelling a warning to Reyni, Hestor flung his hands up to protect his face—

The blizzard vanished. The burning snow whirled away and suddenly they could see again. And what they saw brought them both flailing to a halt.

Shar had stopped. She had turned to face them, and she was standing in the centre of a new radiating web of silver strands. Her eyes met Hestor's across the distance that divided them, and a strange, fanatical light blazed in her look. In her hand she held the knife.

'Shar . . .' Hestor said softly. 'Shar, please listen to me.'

Shar didn't move. From somewhere in the distance came a sound like the first rumble of a mountain avalanche, and the web quivered.

'Shar, this isn't going to work.' Hestor felt as if he was dealing with a dangerous and unpredictable wild animal, and it made him very, very nervous. 'You won't find your way back to Thel's past. You won't find him at all.'

Shar glared back challengingly. 'I will!'

Hestor shook his head. 'No. You won't. It's gone

too far, and you've lost control. I know you have; otherwise you'd have got to him and killed him by now, wouldn't you? You *must* stop what you're doing, or you'll put everyone in danger!'

She continued to glare at him. 'I don't care! This is more important!'

'How *can* it be? You can't change the past, it isn't *right*! Shar – Shar, listen. *Try* to listen—'

'*No!*' Shar screamed. '*You're lying, Hestor Ennas, and I won't listen to you! This is what I want, and you're not going to stop me!*'

She raised the knife. Hestor and Reyni both realised what she was about to do, but they also knew that they wouldn't reach her in time to stop it. They flung themselves towards her. Her arm swung, the blade in her hand flashing as it sliced down, and with one savage stroke she slashed through the silver web.

As if in slow motion, Hestor and Reyni saw the strands of the web snap and recoil. Like the lash of a huge whip, the thread that linked them to Shar rebounded straight towards them, and through its blurring, oncoming shape Hestor saw Shar grasp hold of her amulet. With unthinking instinct his own hand closed around the amulet at his neck—

There was a pause that seemed to last forever but in reality was less than a second.

Then the whole web flew apart.

19

Things were going seriously awry in the castle. Emerging from the entrance doors, Neryon and his party ran straight into a downpour of rain, which in moments changed to snow and then, shockingly, to dazzling sunlight and midsummer heat. They tried to ignore it – but they could not ignore the sudden ghostly outbreak of a full-scale battle in the courtyard. Kitto heard men and horses screaming, saw swords and staves and clubs swinging wildly in a trampling, jostling mêlée of people; saw the castle's huge gates smashed and shuddering as reinforcements poured in. There were demonic creatures among the human fighters, some beautiful and some hideous, and from the courtyard steps bolts of energy hurtled into the struggling throng.

Neryon shouted, 'Don't look at it – just run!' and they pelted for the pillared walkway and the stairs to the library vault. As they reached the door, the mad scene vanished. Silence and darkness crashed down as day turned to night. Something huge was moving by the gates; glimpsing it on the edge of his vision Kitto turned his head, and saw a patch of darkness so complete that it seemed to devour the space it occupied. He faltered, but Neryon gripped his arm more tightly, hustling him on.

There were people in the library, but they wore clothes of a bygone age and they were oblivious to the newcomers. Kitto saw a woman walk straight through Gant; the adept's face turned pale but he said nothing. Then they were in the passage beyond and heading for the Marble Hall.

The metallic door stood wide open – and it was obvious at once that something was horribly wrong. The mists were agitating and swirling like wild sea currents, and vivid flashes of light shuddered through them from end to end of the Hall. Kitto didn't want to go in, but Neryon didn't hesitate; still hauling him along, he hurried inside with Pellis, Gant and Fosker on his heels.

The tower of black light stopped them in their tracks. The silver currents were streaming at a fantastic speed now, and from the mosaic circle a huge version of Hestor's silver cobweb reached out in every direction, turning and spinning and filling the Hall with its shimmering, ghostly filaments. Fosker gasped and made a protective religious sign; for a moment they all stood paralysed, staring in amazement – then the High Initiate started forward.

'Neryon, be careful!' Gant called. 'Don't go too close to the Gate!' He and Pellis ran after Neryon, catching up with him three paces from the circle. The black tower shuddered and distorted, and brilliance flared outwards from it, making them recoil as it overflowed the circle's border.

'Great gods!' Neryon sprang back, pushing the others with him. 'The power's running wild – we've got to stabilise it!'

As if something had heard him, there was a distant but awful noise like insane laughter. 'Quickly!' Neryon shouted. 'Take positions around the circle!'

Pellis and Gant hurried to join him, leaving Kitto standing weak-kneed and terrified with Fosker. The three adepts took up stances around the black mosaic, facing inwards but standing well back. Neryon raised his arms, and his voice rang through the Hall:

'Hear me, O you princes! Hear me, you creators and contenders, you lords of Life and Death, you lords of Air and Earth and Fire and Water and Time and Space—'

A howl erupted from the Gate, drowning the next words of the ritual, and a new and ferocious surge of energy exploded upwards. Buffeted by an invisible force the adepts staggered backwards, and Pellis cried, 'Neryon, it's no use! It's gone too far; we can't control it!'

Suddenly, from another part of the Hall, Kitto heard

a sharp, strange cry. He whirled round – and saw the white cat running towards him from the direction of the seven statues. Its eyes glowed emerald in the light glaring from the spinning silver threads; streaking past him it ran to the edge of the circle and uttered another yowl.

For one instant the black light seemed to rip apart – and in the circle, Kitto glimpsed two ghost-like shapes.

'High Initiate!' He shouted out before he even knew what he was doing. 'Look, look! It's Hestor!'

He tried to rush forward, but Fosker caught hold of him. 'No, boy, stay back! There's no one there!'

'There is!' Kitto struggled to get free. 'I saw him! Oh, Yandros—' He stamped down on Fosker's foot, and as Fosker yelped with pain he broke away and ran after the white cat, shouting, 'Hestor! *Hestor!*'

'Kitto!' Neryon dived to intercept him. They collided, and as they rebounded the Gate howled again, the noise rocking the Marble Hall from end to end. Neryon and Kitto were flung backwards, cannoning into Gant, who had tried to come to Neryon's aid. They all crashed to the floor, and as they fell, a gale roared out of the Gate's core. Kitto just had time to roll clear as the streaming particles erupted outwards, then a gargantuan flash lit the Marble Hall, slamming against his eyes and blotting out all vision as, in another time that was no time at all, Shar severed the strands of the web.

★   ★   ★

The shock of the web's breaking ricocheted through dimensions and hit Hestor and Reyni like a blow from a massive, invisible hand. For a horrifying moment all their senses shut down – sight, hearing, touch, everything – and Hestor truly thought his last moment had come. Then, shattering the suspension, a piercing shriek rang through his head.

'*Shar!*' Hestor cried. He could see her; she was falling from him, falling into nothingness, with the shreds of the ruined web whirling around her. Hestor made a desperate lunge for the thread that had linked them, but it snaked out of his reach. Its fragments scattered and dissolved; as it collapsed into nothing Hestor and Reyni felt a huge force take hold of them, wrenching them sideways through time and space. They had one last, horrifying glimpse of Shar's spinning figure, heard her cry out in terror, '*Oh, no, NO-O-O!*', and then the force flung them back into their own world.

In the Marble Hall, the white cat uttered a loud cry and Kitto, who had just begun to pick himself up from the floor, yelled, 'There they are!'

Two figures had materialised in the shuddering light-tower of the Gate. They were only dimly visible, but suddenly and momentarily the streaming darkness tore apart, and Hestor's face appeared.

'Hestor!' the High Initiate shouted. The face had vanished; then it reappeared as the darkness ripped a second time, and they saw that Reyni was there, too. Hestor was calling out, but what he shouted was eclipsed as a new burst of energy shook the Gate.

'Hestor – Reyni – you've got to break out!' Neryon bellowed. 'We can't control the Gate, and it could snatch you away again at any moment!' He beckoned wildly. *'Come on!'*

They understood, and hurled themselves at the rushing barrier. Kitto thought they would burst through, but instead they seemed to slam against a solid, invisible wall. They rebounded, then attacked it again, kicking, clawing, struggling to get through. But it was useless.

The Gate shuddered again, distorting. In the mosaic circle, Hestor was still beating at the barrier, but Reyni had raised his arms above his head, crossing his wrists and clenching both fists. They could see his mouth moving, and faintly, misshapenly, his voice reached them: 'Aeoris help us, lord Aeoris help us—'

'It's too late for prayers, boy!' Neryon shouted despairingly. 'Try again – *try!'*

'Wait, High Initiate!' Neryon whirled at the sound of Fosker's voice. The Keepers' leader was running to join him, and his eyes were alight. 'Prayer can succeed! Lord Aeoris can help us!' Drawing a deep breath he roared out, *'REYNI!'*

Through the storm of surging particles they saw Reyni's head come up sharply, and Fosker bellowed again. '*REYNI, SPEAK THE BINDING RITE! WITH ME, REYNI – SAY THE WORDS WITH ME!*'

Inside the circle Hestor heard the distorted echoes of Fosker's words. Reyni heard, too, and he grabbed Hestor's arms, pulling him back from the barrier. 'Hestor, it might work!' he gasped. 'Help me – speak the words as I do, call on our lord Aeoris!' And raising his voice, he cried, 'Aeoris of Order—'

'*Aeoris of Order!*' Fosker's voice echoed again as he chanted in unison.

'—Aeoris, lord of Light, Master of the day—'

'—*of the day*—'

'—and ruler of all its hours—'

'—*all its hours*—'

In another dimension, Ailind inhaled sharply as he felt the impact of the ritual's beginning, and Tarod, alerted, said, 'What's afoot?'

'A rite – one the Keepers of Light devised some years ago. It's a chance—'

'*Bind us, Aeoris, in the enduring brotherhood of Order, one to another and all to your will*—' Reyni's fingers dug savagely into Hestor's arm. 'Say it, *say* it!'

Floundering, Hestor tried to follow the words, adding his own frantic plea not just to Aeoris but to all fourteen of the gods of Chaos and Order alike.

Tarod hissed, 'The boy's giving it greater strength!'

'Hold to it!' Ailind urged. He moved tensely towards

the churning mayhem that the Gate had become. 'If they can only create the link—'

'*We forge the chain that will not be broken!*' Reyni was almost shrieking now. And in the quaking tower of light, a golden thread took form. It grew more solid and more stable, and a glow began to radiate out from it, cutting through the churning darkness, forcing it aside, driving it back.

Fosker cried, 'Yes, Reyni, yes!' And in the realm of the gods, Ailind shouted, '*NOW!!*'

A blindingly brilliant rent appeared in the portal before the two lords, and in the Marble Hall the black tower roared and split apart. Reyni and Hestor lunged together at the golden thread, their fingers clamping hold of it even as Fosker snatched at it from the far side.

And Ailind, with Tarod a step behind him, reached into the portal and smashed it open.

Hestor and Reyni were hurled from the circle, like leaves from a storm-tossed tree, as a howling gale swept out of the Gate. Neryon and Fosker were knocked flying by the force of it; Pellis and Gant, hair streaming as they leaned into the blast, ran to help, and only Kitto saw the other figures, tall and unhuman and shimmering, that took form in the havoc behind them. The white cat, which was crouching beside him with ears flattened and tail lashing, gave a high-pitched yowl of recognition, and Tarod and Ailind stepped out of the

Gate in Hestor's wake. Tarod turned on his heel, made a sharp downward gesture with one hand, and instantly the gale and the tumult stopped. Silence hit the Hall like a wall, stunning everyone. Kitto's ears rang; the adepts froze where they stood, staring at the two gods.

Then Fosker fell to his knees.

'*My lord!*' He bowed until his forehead touched the floor, shock and wonder choking his voice. Ailind looked down at him and smiled affectionately.

'You have done the gods a great service, my friend,' he said. 'Your prayer formed the link that enabled us to reach you. Without that,' his golden eyes turned to Hestor and burned an ominous colour, 'this reckless folly could have brought disaster on you all.'

Hestor stared back, too numb to react. Behind the two gods, the light of the Gate still streamed upwards, though silently now. Tarod looked at it. He raised one hand.

'My lord—' Hestor croaked.

Tarod paused. 'You have something to say to me, Hestor?'

Hestor swallowed, his chest heaving. 'The Gate—'

'Will be closed and sealed, to prevent any more meddling.'

'But Shar—'

Tarod's green eyes took on an extremely dangerous edge. 'What of her?'

'My lord, she's still in there! She's trapped — we

have to save her!' Hestor paused, then realised to his horror that Tarod was not reacting; the Chaos lord's expression hadn't changed an iota. '*Please*, Lord Tarod – please, there must be something you can do! Don't you understand? Shar's *trapped!*'

Tarod's lips narrowed into a thin, stern line. 'What I understand, Hestor,' he said, 'is that Shar brought this about through her own wilfulness and arrogance. She defied the Circle, presumed to think herself wiser than the gods, and did a stupid and selfish thing that could have wreaked havoc throughout the mortal world. When we helped her before, there was a good reason. There is not now – and my patience has run out.'

Hestor couldn't believe what he was hearing. He looked beseechingly at Ailind, but before he could speak Ailind said quietly, 'My cousin speaks for us both, Hestor. I'm sorry. Shar chose her way, and she must take responsibility for it. If that responsibility has proved too great for her, she must take the consequences.'

Hestor began to shake. 'She's dead, isn't she . . . ? When she cut the web . . . it killed her . . .'

'No,' Ailind told him. 'She isn't dead. But she is held in a single moment of time from which she can't break free. Nor can she find and kill Thel Starnor; the past can't be changed now. She's in limbo, and that's where she will stay.'

Kitto, listening, felt a sick sense of dread clutch at

him. 'Sir . . .' he quavered. 'Please . . . you *can't* mean to leave her there?'

The white cat mewed as though in agreement. Tarod looked at them both, and his eyes were cold.

'Your feelings are very noble, Kitto. But it's too late. As Ailind says, Shar made her choice.' He glanced in Ailind's direction. 'Let's get this over and done with.'

They turned towards the Gate again – and suddenly a new voice spoke up.

'My lord—' Fosker had risen to his feet and was standing, hands clasped deferentially but with determination in his eyes. 'May I speak?'

'Of course,' Ailind looked at him. 'We have no quarrel with you, Fosker. Speak.'

'Thank you, my lord. I . . . you said that I – and Reyni – have done you a service.'

'Indeed.'

'Then . . . if service deserves some small reward, I want to plead for Shar Tillmer.' Fosker glanced across to where Reyni still knelt on the floor. 'I believe I understand a little of what drove her to do what she did. Reyni has told me what it's like to lose a loved one to the powers of evil; it was the death of his aunt, Sister Malia, that made him turn to the Keepers of Light for comfort. We're all only human. And Shar is very young.'

'Old enough to have learned a little wisdom,' Tarod said softly.

'Yes, my lord. But she isn't beyond hope. Reyni and Hestor know that. They cared enough for her to risk their lives for her sake, and if anyone deserves reward, I believe they have earned it for that reason alone. They want her back. Please, my lords – can it not be done?'

There was silence for some time. Everyone watched the two gods, but for Kitto, who had shut his eyes and was hugging the white cat close to him as if it was a talisman. Ailind looked thoughtful; Tarod was gazing down at the floor and his long black hair obscured his face, so that no one saw his slight smile.

At last, Ailind nodded. 'Very well, Fosker. You speak eloquently in Shar's defence.' He glanced at Tarod. 'If my cousin of Chaos agrees, we will grant your request.'

Tarod raised his head; his smile broadened and now everyone could see it. He didn't answer Ailind directly; instead he beckoned to the white cat, which left Kitto's side and ran to him. Tarod picked it up, and murmured something in its ear. The little animal chirruped. Then, as Tarod set it down, it ran to the black circle. For a moment it stood in the middle of the mosaic, looking back at them all, then there was a quick disturbance in the rushing particles, and it vanished.

20

Shar crouched in darkness, hunched and huddled on a floor that she could not see. She knew she was alone, and she was fighting the knowledge with all her strength, for if she once accepted the truth, she knew she would lose her sanity.

She had lost everything. Her world, her friends, her hopes . . . they were all gone. And it was her fault. Now, there was . . . nothing. Just the dark, and the constant, mind-bending boom of the huge pulse that filled the air and filled her head and throbbed through her bones. Time. Only there *was* no time, not any more. Not for her. Not ever.

A whimper escaped from her throat, though she couldn't hear it above the noise in her head. Her lips formed a name: 'Hestor . . .' but Hestor wasn't in this world and couldn't hear her and wouldn't answer. No one would answer. No one would *ever* answer. And she could feel the start of the terror that would lead her down the long, treacherous slope into madness.

'*Forgive me* . . . She whispered the words like a

prayer. '*I'm sorry, I'm so sorry . . . Oh gods, oh Hestor, Kitto . . . forgive me!*'

A clear mew sounded nearby. And the booming pulse stopped.

Shar froze. Her head turned; her wild, terrified gaze ranging about but unable to penetrate the darkness.

Then one small patch of dark shivered and changed, and she saw a pale shape coming towards her.

Shar stared at the white cat, unable to believe that it could be here and almost convinced in that first moment that she truly had lost her mind. But the cat reached her and rubbed against her, so that she felt the soft tickle of its fur. It was real. It was *real . . .*

Slowly, hope leaping, she rose to her feet. She was trembling, but she made her legs move, and as the cat walked away she followed it. Five paces, six, seven—

The darkness turned inside out, and Shar emerged into the Marble Hall. Nine faces confronted her; seven human, the other two—

A huge surge of emotion rose in Shar, and she burst into tears.

Hestor, Kitto and Reyni ran in a concerted rush, reaching Shar together and all trying to throw their arms around her. As they hugged her, though, Tarod spoke a stern word of warning. They fell back, and the Chaos lord moved to stand between them and Shar.

'Your reunion can wait,' he said sternly. 'The High

Initiate will have a great deal to say to Shar – and before he does so, we intend to speak with her.' His glance swept over them all. 'Leave us, please. Go back into the castle. Shar will join you when we're done with her.' Then his look relented a little. 'And I think you can rest assured that there'll be no more phantoms from the past to plague you.'

They all filed out in silence. For a moment the white cat remained, and would have sat down at Shar's feet. Tarod glanced at it; a message passed from his mind to its, and with a flick of its tail it trotted away and disappeared in the mists.

Shar watched it go. She had stopped crying, though her cheeks were still wet, and now she felt sick, shamed, and horribly, vulnerably afraid; not the hideous fear she had known before the cat found her, but a far more immediate terror. Bizarrely, she was still clutching the knife she had conjured, so long ago it seemed now. Ailind touched it lightly and it dissolved, leaving a sharp, stinging pain in her hand. Then Tarod reached out and took hold of the amulet. He twisted it; the thong broke, and Tarod held the amulet in his palm. He closed his hand. Briefly Shar saw strength pulse through his fingers. Then a handful of dust fell to the floor of the Marble Hall, faded, and was gone.

'Shar.' The two lords looked down at her and Shar hung her head. She felt their gazes like fire on her face.

'What we have to say will not take long,' Tarod said.

'It will not be pleasant. But you will *listen*. And you will pay heed . . .'

As the Marble Hall's door closed behind Shar's departing figure, Ailind looked at Tarod and said, 'Well?'

Tarod smiled. 'She had long enough in limbo to contemplate her folly. It gave her a fright that she'll never forget, and we've now added an extra savour to her fear. I think we can safely say the lesson has been learned.'

Strange colours and patterns moved in the mists, as though the Hall acknowledged their presence in its own strange way. Ailind said, 'You had no intention of leaving her there, did you?'

Tarod shrugged. 'I hadn't decided. But Fosker's speech convinced me.' He paused, then added, 'What Yandros will have to say about it is another matter. He'll probably call me a sentimental fool who's too fond of mortals for anyone's good.'

Ailind thought privately that the great Chaos lord was more likely to enjoy the joke, once he had got over his annoyance at Tarod's interfering – again – in human matters. Aeoris, too, would be far from pleased at first. But even his anger wouldn't last for long. It had, after all, been nothing more than a favour granted to a faithful follower.

'I wonder how hard Neryon will be on her?' he mused.

'Very, if he has the sense I think he has. But she'll

be forgiven, in time. A sojourn at Wester Reach will do her good, and the Keepers' influence – for all their dislike of us – will be a steadying one.'

'She might even join their numbers,' Ailind suggested, with a hint of mischief.

'A Daughter of Storms and a Dark-Caller?' Tarod returned his gaze, and raised a dark eyebrow. 'I doubt it, my friend; I doubt it very much. Like or dislike it, Shar Tillmer is one of our kind, and I don't think anything can change her.'

'Which is, perhaps, why you agreed to relent.'

'Yes,' said Tarod. 'Perhaps it is.' He paused. 'We have a lot in common, Ailind. It's just that in the past we've all been too proud – or too stubborn – to admit it.'

Ailind's laughter rang softly through the Hall, and echoed back through the mists. The two gods moved towards the black mosaic circle. It was quiet now, the Gate closed and the tower of light gone. Shar's amulet was gone, too, and Neryon's restored to its rightful keeper. The Circle planned to continue their experiments with the Maze. But – though they might learn a lot from her experiences – Shar would not be part of those experiments. At least, not for a good while to come.

They stepped into the circle. Tarod took a last look at the Marble Hall, and as he did so, something small moved in the distance.

The white cat looked at Tarod. Tarod looked back. He smiled. The cat's mouth opened in a soundless mew, and just for a moment its eyes and the eyes of the Chaos god were identical.

Tarod stepped into the mosaic circle, where Ailind was waiting. There was a soft sound, almost like a sigh. Then the gods were gone from the mortal world.

All three of them were sitting in Hestor's room; Hestor, Kitto and Reyni, perched on chairs or, in Hestor's case, on the end of the bed itself. Shar was asleep in her own bed, with two cats keeping watch over her. Amber had been waiting in the castle. No one knew where he had been – Kitto had picked up some very strange pictures from his mind, but they were muddled and explained nothing – but, whatever effect the time-slip had had on him and the other castle cats, they all seemed untroubled by it now. And the white cat had been outside Shar's door when she returned from her interview with the High Initiate. It had played its part, and through he had said nothing to the others, Kitto believed it intended to stay. To keep watch. With Lord Tarod's eyes . . .

Shar had spent three hours in Neryon's study, with the door firmly shut. When she finally emerged, no one asked her what the High Initiate had said to her; and certainly they had not asked, and would never ask, about her interview with Tarod and Ailind. There would be some changes. Shar was to go away from the castle for a while, to stay at the Keepers' mission house in Wester Reach. She had not been expelled from the Circle; this was a recuperation and, as Neryon pointedly said to Hestor and Kitto, a chance for them all to think hard about their foolishness and be penitent.

None of the three had said anything for some minutes, but at last Kitto broke the silence.

'She'd been crying again,' he said.

'I saw.' Hestor sighed and looked sidelong, distrustfully, at Reyni. 'I wish she wasn't going away.'

Reyni caught the look and understood what it meant. 'She'll be back soon enough,' he said. 'And time with us isn't going to change her.' A faint, shaky grin appeared on his face. 'I'd like to think it would, and you know why – but I'm not a complete idiot, Hestor. I know where Shar's heart really is.'

'*I* think,' said Kitto, 'that it's about time you two stopped being so suspicious of each other and agreed to be proper friends. Because I'll tell you one thing – however Shar does or doesn't change in the future, she'll change in her own way and there's nothing any of us can do to influence her!'

Hestor opened his mouth to argue – then shut it again. Reyni was looking at him keenly, and abruptly they both laughed.

'You're right, Kitto,' Hestor said. 'You're absolutely right.' He faced Reyni directly. 'Friends?'

'Friends,' Reyni agreed. 'All of us, I hope. For a long time to come.'

Outside the door, Neryon and Pellis paused on their way to the main staircase. They couldn't hear any sound from Hestor's room, but they could both guess the gist of what was being said.

'Do you think they'll learn, this time?' Pellis asked.

Neryon smiled. 'Lord Tarod and Lord Ailind seem to think so, and that's got to be good enough for me.'

'It will take Shar a long time to recover.'

'I know. But she'll be stronger for it in the end.' Then Neryon laughed a soft, private laugh.

Pellis raised her eyebrows questioningly. 'What's amusing you, Neryon?'

'Oh . . . just an idle thought.'

'What is it?'

Neryon looked along the passage towards Shar's closed door, and his expression sobered to something more thoughtful.

'I don't really know if it's idle, or amusing, or downright crazed,' he said after a pause. 'But it has just occurred to me that one day, against all the odds, Shar might be one of the best High Initiates the Circle has ever had.'